HOW TO CONFUSE
A DRAGON

by

Jane Palmer

DODO BOOKS

First published in Great Britain
by Dodo Books 2014

This is a work of fiction and any
resemblance to persons living or dead is
purely coincidental.

ISBN 978 1 906442 32 3

CHAPTER 1

Darkle Deeps was very deep, and far beneath it was the home of the Hurglabat, an entity hideous enough to stop even an army of ogres dead in its tracks.

It had been lurking in the primeval slime beneath their realm for aeons, waiting for the opportunity to become corporeal and, at last having fleshed itself, the Hurglabat allowed no one but the ogres to be aware of its existence. There was always some bold adventurer or clever witch who saw it as their duty to rid time, space, and mythology of monstrous parasites.

And the Hurglabat could afford to wait. The vibrations from Lustreland, the neighbouring Province of Light, were growing more and more confused as the land's radiance started to dim.

Not knowing the entity's true nature, the ogres were willing to obey the mysterious, malevolent commands that issued from the bowels of the Great Underneath. Bribed with the occasional shower of precious stones spewed up from the lower depths, a wiser person wouldn't have questioned its instructions either. The Hurglabat could not control the ogres by insinuating its way into minds that didn't have enough room for a subconscious, so was reduced to using the highly nervous Kot Kut, the ogres' high priest, to communicate through. He was the only one of them insecure enough to visualise monsters from the bowels of their benighted realm.

Ever since the ogres had lost their right to be totally beastly curtailed by the Lustreland authorities, their frustration had spilled down the many holes that honeycombed Darkle Deeps, a place where the even hand of Nature had been rapped before she could infiltrate those dismal cracks.

The Hurglabat rolled in its ooze and rumbled contentedly. A few stones toppled from the ogres' fortress far above and the outlying orchards of Lustreland prematurely shed fruit. As the darkness slowly encroached, The Province of Light had no idea that its luscious domain would soon be crushed in the monster's voracious tentacles.

Like the malignant growth that expands without betraying its presence, the Hurglabat stretched its tentacles, and then lay dormant.

The female ogres took exception to the Hurglabat's parasitical presence, resenting that it only spoke to their mates, and occasionally hurled rocks down the nearest hole at the odd pulsating glow in its depths. Few things ever spoke to the males, even the females, and then it was in monosyllabic grunts. Now they felt like warriors as the Hurglabat burbled up orders for them to invade Lustreland. Best of all, the ogres wouldn't have to take the blame when that domain's witches and warlocks waved their wands in the direction of Darkle Deeps. All the ogre chief, Jobaloba, needed to do was point to the voice under the ground and let those smart, self-righteous egotists try casting a spell on their all powerful patron deity instead. For once, he would be on the winning side. All the curses, spells, and wand waving would count for nothing against a creature as powerful as the Hurglabat.

Unfortunately, the only one who had the ability to destroy the voracious, evil entity spent more time watching butterflies than casting spells.

CHAPTER 2

The blizzard of last week was now venting its rage in mid Atlantic, leaving a fierce bite behind in the freezing air.

Peter wanted to jog a few paces despite his doctor's advice against sudden exercise. Then thought again. Hypothermia was probably easier to treat than a cardiac arrest. Whatever the weather, few things short of stray shells from the military manoeuvres up the road could dissuade him from his morning walk. If there was one thing Peter had learnt from a long lifetime of experience it was to avoid heavy artillery; its recoil was invariably less fatal for the person firing it.

The neighbourhood resented the army waking it up at four in the morning, yet petitions were usually fobbed off with the justification that the enemy was bound to attack at this time. To Peter this only proved that as soon as people put on military uniforms they developed insomnia as well as allowing the Y-chromosome to override their common sense.

Peter, full name Peter Olan Martin, was a mountain amongst men. Over six and a half feet tall with a substantial girth, he awed yapping dogs and their tiresome owners. Despite this, he was a benign person with a large friendly, brown face and soft husky voice that never did more than rumble peevishly whatever the provocation.

He cursed himself for thinking about the army when they weren't even making a noise. To take his mind off them he watched surprised ducks slither about the ice after wedges of bread hurled by small children, only to recall the letter from his two wives relating the sad progress of their country. Irrational guilt gnawed at Peter for not being there. As the bright winter sun picked out doilies of frosted white snow this warm African landscape was a world away. In fact, it seemed so distant at that moment he might as well have been viewing the world from another planet. He began to wish that Indrina, his accountant, had never pointed out the sinister billions suddenly invested in that fertile country. A consortium of faceless people now owned its mines and agriculture, virtually controlling the economy.

Why did these conundrums keep pursuing Peter when he was trying to relax? Indrina couldn't be blamed for merely pointing out something she found financially intriguing. No, the manipulation of that country's economy was something he had always suspected, but dared not admit to himself. Though never in a position to do anything about it, he still fretted despite the condition of his heart.

Then, once more, the world started to spin.

Peter's heart began to race. The crunch of his own footsteps on the icy gravel could no longer be heard as reality was nudged to one side and his thoughts were once again invaded by that eerie, cracked voice. It was distant, as though it had travelled up through Pre Cambrian seams, elbowing aside carnivorous dinosaur fossils on the way. This time he could understand what it was saying, though at that moment would have much rather been patronised by a paramedic with a defibrillator.

'You're not the brightest of creatures are you? But then, giants never have been.'

Peter somehow managed to walk in a straight line past the duck feeders without keeling over.

The voice in his head was undeterred. 'You'll have to do, though. There is no other choice.'

Not only was he hearing voices, Peter's subconscious now seemed to be volunteering him for an unworldly experiment, probably involving life forms from the Magellanic Clouds and Jurassic DNA.

Damn those blood pressure tablets! He always knew they would reduce him to a gibbering idiot eventually - they certainly never did anything for his circulation.

As the curls in his grizzled, greying hair crackled with static he desperately craved a double brandy. He would have pulled out a cigar, but the last time he did that within four metres of a young mother he had been scolded as though he were a diesel guzzling pantechnicon. So he thought better of it and concentrated on controlling his heartbeat. Managing to reach a stand of mahonia, he steadied himself on a park seat donated by some corrupt councillor to expiate his civic sins.

Just as Peter thought he was back in control, something shot past him and crashed into the bushes. He lost his balance and tumbled onto the seat. It was probably only been a cat or large bird, but his imagination was now primed to expect something far more bizarre.

Then that unearthly voice snapped, 'What's wrong with you man! Don't bother to take out your glasses. You aren't able to see me. Pull yourself together. I'll come back this evening.'

Then the phantom in his head departed, leaving a void which he would have preferred to be filled with the tumultuous concerns of the real world.

What should he do? Humour this subconscious intruder in the hope it would go away, or ignore it and risk being institutionalised before he was 70? If Peter feared anything more than heart failure, it was dementia. The only way he could deal with that prospect was to prove to himself, one way or another, what was really going on in his head.

That afternoon was the longest in Peter's life as he agonised over some logical explanation for the voice in the park that had singled him out for his apparent status as a giant.

As he sat and sipped a brandy, watching the sun go down on the orchard outside his basement window, the air crackled with a faint whisper.

'Find a dish of frosted glass.'

Frosted glass? It was absurd, but the voice was unlikely to leave him alone if it was ignored. Was there any frosted glass in his bachelor's apartment? Only the hotel above had a use for ornaments, but there were tea chests filled with the unused tableware stored under the staircase, which he fortunately had a key to.

Peter rummaged through the polystyrene chips of an open box until he found a huge cut glass ashtray with a frosted centre too expensive to put outside, and just reflective enough to mirror his dark features. It was in store because it could no longer be used since the smoking ban. He took it to the dining table and propped it up on the folded towels he would have put in the bathroom if the voice in his head hadn't intervened.

Against his better judgement he gazed into the glass.

Shapes inside it seemed to be resolving themselves.

'Look deeper,' came the order.

No, this couldn't be real. Somebody was playing tricks, though he had no idea how. His mind was already plagued by monsters from his own subconscious; Peter wasn't up to dealing with ones created by anyone else.

'Concentrate! You've had long enough to get used to the idea,' the voice persisted.

Peter scratched his grizzled curls. 'What idea? Why all this performance with a saloon bar ashtray?' He had never spoken to the illusion in his head before and now felt ridiculous.

'Frost is my element. As the flowers and trees are to the sprites, as fire is to the dragon, as music is to the minstrel, as pomposity is to my Second Minister, I am cold logic, the cold logic you try to live without.'

To Peter, it was an absurd answer. 'Who are you?'

A face at last formed in the crystal. Its skin may have once been golden; now it had the patina of silver where the gilt had worn away to reveal a network of wrinkles resembling the road map of an inner city. A pair of ancient eyes twinkled with cunning below an unruly mop of white hair that had been gathered up and pinned with an ornate medallion.

Peter jumped back in surprise.

'There is no reason to be alarmed,' announced the apparition. 'I am merely your other self. You have always known I was here but refused to acknowledge the fact. Now we have mutual problems you must open your mind and let me in.'

Until then Peter thought the worst difficulty was with his heart. 'Problems?'

'You need my help to solve your world's greatest crime.'

'Crime? What crime?'

'And in return I need your permission.'

'Permission for what?'

'You ask too many questions.'

'Don't get inscrutable with me - this is all too bloody weird to take seriously! I want to die in the comfort of my own bedroom, not a padded cell.'

'Patience.'

'I have a heart condition which no longer permits that luxury.'

'That is something we will come to later.'

'So, who am I expected to sell my soul to? Beelzebub?'

The ancient face cracked a smile. 'Call me Rimonay.' Then she began to fade. 'I will be back when you are in a calmer frame of mind.'

Would he ever be in a calmer frame of mind? 'Why?'

'Oh the wonders you will learn...'

Without warning she was gone and the light infusing the crystal ashtray faded into the towels propping it up.

The experience was unnerving, but so real Peter was perversely persuaded that this couldn't have been dementia after all. The hallucination was too structured, and with a logic of its own - at least in the realms of magic: it certainly didn't hark back to any past experience. Perhaps it was akin to a religious revelation? Having been a disbeliever for so long his subconscious might have been priming him for a miracle, however unlikely a holy messenger this Rimonay was. Peter was pragmatic enough to take it into account with the absence of any other explanation. All he could do now was hear her out.

Over the following evenings his sinister alter ego returned to the frosted ashtray to weave such a wonderful account of the realm she inhabited Peter was eventually persuaded to believe.

Rimonay avoided naming her price for this "permission" she had previously mentioned by regaling him with descriptions of the parallel world of Lustreland, the Province of Light, in which he learnt everything about its geography, creatures, politics, deities - and the monster that was about to consume it all, ogres included.

But Peter was most intrigued by the twin beings of his friends. If he had believed them a trifle eccentric before, this new insight made him wonder why their Lustreland incarnations had not managed to burst through the walls of reality to belabour their earthbound counterparts. Fortunately the Province had boundaries which prevented its residents wandering too far afield. Only the rara avis, occasional giant and wandering minstrel possessed the magical stamina to blunder across them, to and from other exotic realms beyond the Province of Light. Giants didn't have the vocabulary to describe them, the rara avis seldom chatted to Lustrelanders, and it was inadvisable to believe anything a minstrel sang about. Even the Mystic Trine took the word of their librarian that those lands were better seen through the eyes of a soaring dragon or seeing glass. It was just as well. Lustrelanders were so self-satisfied they didn't see the point in travelling anywhere else only to be disappointed.

Although populated with sprites, gnomes, changelings, griffins, unicorns, harpies, goblins, as well as elfin creatures like Rimonay and her more substantial Second Minister, in time Lustreland became as real to Peter as his own dimension. He had no choice but to grow fond of it.

And only then did Rimonay dare name her price.

It was a steep one.

He struck the bargain all the same. It was not an unreasonable demand for saving a realm, even one as bizarre as Lustreland. If they had the equivalent of Satan there, Rimonay was about to sell her soul to him anyway.

CHAPTER 3

The Province of Light Rimonay had described to Peter was known as Lustreland because of the clarity with which an unseen star illuminated it. There was no night and the inhabitants believed that their perpetual day was bestowed by a celestial marvel called the Ligh Tofrea Sun. Some outlying regions lived in permanent twilight as its benevolent light became weaker beyond the domain's woodland boundaries. The Lustrelanders assumed that the griffins, dragons, and rocs living in the mountainous heights of Rara Avis Ridge did not need the Ligh Tofrea Sun's brightness; with so many peculiar powers, seeing in the dark was known to be one of them.

As well as the wonderful woods, hills, and quartz outcrops circling Lustreland, there were caves - many, many caves; caves studded with gems, caves gouged out by rivers, caves filled with stalactites and stalagmites resembling worms woven into organic tapestries, caves with bottomless pools that could drown the soul, and caves with deities so mysterious they even frightened the trolls.

The Province of Light's heartland lived contentedly inside this protective girdle; a gently undulating land of waterfalls and candyfloss mists haloing anything that rose above the height of a dragon's extended tail. It was believed that dragons extended their tails directly upwards as a sign of contempt, there being something peculiarly disconcerting about the anatomy revealed beneath them. Few had ever described the sight as one glimpse was enough to silence a person for weeks.

But dragons weren't the problem; it was the ogres preparing to invade the gleaming domain of

Lustreland. Repugnant as anything that had ever managed to clamber out of the pitch bogs in Darkle Deeps, the ugly nature of the ogres had been made even surlier by existing in this gloomy realm on a diet of marinaded dinosaur bones and pickled jellyfish, which their digestion required egg sized pebbles to break down. They once had a ravenous appetite for Lustrelanders before some ancient witches cast a spell from The Old Theolopolis Book of Humane Diets on them. That had been aeons ago. Since then the Old Theolopolis diet book had disappeared, probably bored with sitting on a dusty shelf with other crusty volumes on how to cure dragon diarrhoea and beard mildew, despite the darkest endeavours of the Mystic Trine's sinister librarian to magic it back. Now the ogres were about to invade Lustreland there was nothing to deter them from reverting to their original menu once within a hairy arm's reach of a few tasty Lustrelanders plump with well-stocked larders and complacency.

As with most things that involved exertion, mental or physical, Lustrelanders had no idea how to repel these odorous hordes. Only a pragmatic few were aware that their only hope perched in Rara Avis Ridge. This was large and gleaming red. The last dragon in the realm was so relaxed about life it took the occasional nap when on the wing, frequently waking up under some other domain's rainbow or colliding with a less agile roc, and it would take some persuading to come to their assistance.

Unfortunately there was one important dignitary who wouldn't have recognised pragmatism if it donned hobnailed boots and marched about inside his skull for a week. Bruno, the Second Minister, possessed a phobia about dragons that could only be explained away by one having devoured him in a previous incarnation. That being the case, some centuries old fabulous beast probably still had indigestion.

Minister Bruno exuded self-important pomposity as though it was lettered through his sturdy trunk like the rings of a tree and his strong, oval face was always tilted upwards as though mundane mortals were below the horizon of his worthwhile attention. His robe of office clung to his solid frame like silk over a barrel, and the sleeveless overgown dropped from wide shoulders without so much as a misplaced fold. It would have been impossible for a flock of sprites to lift his ornate staff, even with the aid of fairy dust, and his hefty chain of office required the neck muscles of a troll who wound the lift cage in a goblin mine. All this told anyone expecting reasoned discussion on the impending ogre invasion that the Second Minister was not open to negotiation. Frequently inconvenient, his intransigence had now become downright dangerous and threatened the very existence of Lustreland. And all because he hated dragons.

As Minister Bruno strode out through gleaming, cobbled streets towards the golden avenue leading up to the Halls of Government, a gaggle of sprites, elves and other generally unoccupied members of the population, streamed after him like the uncoordinated tail of a large embarrassed dog as though anticipating gladiatorial entertainment. Far behind them scurried a wizard, the breeze catching his robe and beard in an attempt propel him in the opposite direction. Being tall and very thin, Qulio resembled the mast of a racing merchant ship with flapping sails battling the elements. Despite this, the wizard dare not be late. No one else was willing to throw themselves under the wheels of the juggernaut that was Bruno to prevent him mowing down the last opportunity for Lustreland's survival.

Resembling a colossus that had stepped from the sculptor's plinth before any more could be roughed from its girth, the Second Minister strode across the Government lawn and passed under the ceremonial arch into the member's only courtyard. Like a tail suddenly severed from its body, the phalanx of followers skidded to a halt on the polished chalcedony pavement. Qulio picked his way through the felled elves and sprites in pursuit of Bruno who was charging on towards the Council's debating chamber like a storm rolling in from Rara Avis Ridge.

No one in Lustreland's history had ever discovered tobacco, but whenever the Mystic Trine attended the great chamber it was always filled with smoke. The witches and warlocks no doubt thought it added to their mysterious ambience, yet all it did for Bruno was make his eyes water and raise his blood pressure. As the chamber doors were flung open to allow him to make his entrance, scrolls of smoke were sent spiralling through the time worn banners of ancient members.

Despite watering eyes, the Second Minister still managed to glower intimidatingly at the steep, tiered seats filled with Lustreland's motley government. There were the sinister members of the Mystic Trine sitting in their fossil thrones and wearing robes over which mystic symbols menacingly rambled. There was Rimonay; small, diamond-eyed and shrivelled, installed in the position of supreme power and, just below her, Bruno's seat, much wider and with fewer cushions.

Unable to register the nuances of the charged atmosphere, one of the ushers, an opal troll, offered to escort the Second Minister to his place with all due ceremony. Rimonay waved it aside. Opal trolls were breakable and hard to come by. The last thing she needed was to send its precious shards to a master jeweller to magic them back together. (Allowing the Magic Trine to turn those turned to stone by the light of the Ligh Tofrea Sun into useful citizens had introduced complications not even the First Minister could have anticipated.)

Bruno strode to the speaker's podium, knowing that everyone else must have had their say before he arrived and seeing no reason to ask their permission.

'Dragons!' he bellowed.

Several sprites disappeared behind a row of goblins, warlocks yawned to show they weren't intimidated and the witches sniggered provokingly.

'If the members of the Mystic Trine were half as powerful as they would have us believe, there would be no need to beg favours of dragons!' the Second Minister ranted on, only pausing as a sharp glance from Rimonay reminded him that there were perils in insulting so many exponents of the dark arts.

The Mystic Trine was so called because it consisted of witches, warlocks, and any mercenary creature corrupt enough to be affiliated to them. The witches detected his brief hesitation, especially Iggata. She had the face of a tiger lily, but heart of black diamond and was the nastiest of them all.

Bruno had never crossed swords with that witch before and, however angry, still wasn't inclined to try. He had heard the rumours that she had obligingly turned the grandparents of some Mystic Trine members into hedgehogs so they could save on home help sprites. The last survey had certainly found there were more of them in the woods than was natural, and the prickly band had even started a protest movement for better ventilated nests and pension parity with refuse collecting gnomes.

There was a faint, infatuated sigh a short distance away.

Bruno became aware of Wizard Qulio gazing at Iggata as though she had just slid down on a ray from the Ligh Tofrea Sun. The man's docile eccentricity may have been ideal with changelings and educated monsters, yet when it came to recognising distilled evil he seemed to have a mental block.

The Second Minister refused to be sidetracked any longer. 'Yes, dragons! Has this chamber lost its mind?'

Oblivious to his rhetorical abuse, the Mystic Trine's sinister librarian had the inconvenient tendency to take most things literally. 'No, but I have read about a tribe of pumice trolls who leave theirs safely locked away until they need them.' She didn't know how to be sarcastic; facts and statistics governed her bibliophile existence. If Iggata's malign reasoning was like a rapacious spider's, the Librarian's labyrinthine mind was cloaked in a web that no mystic bullet could penetrate.

To conceal that he was becoming distracted from his tirade by the unexpected obfuscation and the tall, spindly Qulio standing a short distance away like a willow being buffeted by the stormy atmosphere, Bruno indicated that he should sit at the debating bench. There was no other place for him. Wizard or not, the Mystic Trine would not allow Qulio to sit with them. He wasn't mercenary or menacing enough for their company and his spells usually fizzled out before he could cast them.

When the flurry of gowns to allow Qulio through to his place had stopped, the Second Minister cleared his throat and carried on with his onslaught.

'How could any sane entity believe that the survival of Lustreland must be handed over to the whim of an anarchic reptile? And one more delinquent than a flock of harpies!'

Feeling that it was time to interject before the chamber became persuaded she was taking his side, Rimonay rapped her cane on her marble dais. 'Explain yourself Minister Bruno.'

He didn't need to be asked twice. 'Not so long ago, Dragon Sesame maliciously vaporised the pond in my courtyard because I refused to allow it to roost in my orchard -'

The First Minister was hardly interested, but had to slow the Second Minister's flow of vitriol before it got under way again. 'Why did it need to roost in your orchard?'

'It took on the challenge from some roc to find out which of them could soar high enough to see the Ligh Tofrea Sun. It was its own fault it was too tired to fly home!'

Rimonay decided that the one-sided debate was becoming ridiculous and raised her hand to stop him carrying on with the endless list of demeanours queuing up for the chance to be aired.

Having built up a head of steam, Bruno ploughed on regardless. 'Then it carried off the spire from my turret to prize open the entrance of a cave some changeling or other had got itself trapped in.'

'So what's wrong with that?' The goblin organiser of Lustreland's equal opportunity campaign demanded with enough shrillness to knock a harpy out of the sky.

Political correctness had never been one of Bruno's strongest points. 'Changelings have no business in caves! They belong in the woods with that lunatic woman who spends all her time looking after them!'

Qulio's expression fell and Bruno suddenly remembered that the wizard was a close friend of that particular altruist. His hesitation gave Councillor Kolu, the insult queen of the upper benches, the opportunity to rise. Inflicting verbal wounds on the Second Minister by thrusting in the ironic knife were the highlights of her life.

As she rose Bruno roared, 'And what's your problem?'

'Perhaps the real point has escaped the Second Minister?'

Bruno may have been able to dish out irony, but was totally oblivious of it now he had built up a head of steam scalding enough to descale a troll. 'What point?'

'And I think that proves my point.'

'Are you inferring that I'm stupid?' he threatened Kolu.

'I wouldn't dream of uttering such a slur against the Second Minister. However ...'

The goblin equal opportunities representative sensed revenge at hand. 'However?'

'But I would say that, if Minister Bruno's position were not so exulted, he has the tendency to huff and puff like a gas filled bladder, his vocabulary consists of three different barks like the Cerberus, his reasoning is as fluid as the set tar the ogres use for mattresses and, like a hydra, he has seven different ways of coming to the same conclusion - all wrong! But as he is our exulted Second Minister, I will not presume to say any of this.'

The golden skin of Bruno's neck turned bright orange with rage. 'Are you sure there is nothing else you would like to add?'

'Of course not. Who am I to say that you originated from thunder absent-mindedly striking a tree because lightning refused to own you?'

That did it. Kolu had soundly kicked Bruno in his Achilles heel. She knew he was paranoid about not being designated an element; all the lowliest elves and sprites, had their flower, mineral or vegetable. Even Wizard Qulio had an element, even if no one knew what it was.

'I have no need of an element! I have the strength to know I'm right without debating the matter with some petals or a rock! And I am right about Dragon Sesame! This chamber will never make me approve of any plot to use this creature to defeat the ogres! Just think what would happen if we fell into its debt. Dragons would have the right of residency in Lustreland. Their flaming breath would fill the air. One puff into a stiff breeze and whoosh would go all the crops, or orchards - or Halls of Government. And what if it has relatives?

Would you fancy a couple of those creatures trying to nest on your chimney stack?'

Rimonay could take no more of his high-pitched irrationality and again rapped her stick. 'There is no proof any of this would happen. Dragons have always chosen to live in places like Rara Avis Ridge where they are perfectly adapted to the thin air and damp mists. And only one Dragon lives there at the moment. Sesame has no relatives.'

Arguing with the First Minister was forbidden, but Bruno would not be swayed. 'There is nothing you can do to make me agree to this plan, and without my approval it cannot be implemented.

Why in the name of Vulcanus had that been written into the law of Lustreland's constitution? Rimonay wondered to herself. She shook her head regretfully.

'We may not be able to make you change your mind, though perhaps learning a little humility will loosen the bolt that guards your precious intolerances. The Ruling Council have come to a decision. And I agree with them.'

Rimonay seldom made threats. She was too clever to need them, and alarm nudged its way through a chink in Bruno's resolve. The Ruling Council and First Minister had the power of expulsion; the ability to banish any Lustrelander to the dimension of their alter egos, a place where the sun disappeared for half a day and there were no protecting deities or elements.

The chamber stamped in approval. This was one issue every member was prepared to vote on - except Qulio, but he didn't count.

The Second Minister heard two hard rock troll ushers coming up behind him. He knew better than to take a swing at either of them. However large his fist, it was no match for granite; trust Rimonay not to select anything more chisel friendly.

With the aid of her two tree sprites, Rimonay rose.

Having made the decision, she announced, 'Minister Bruno will be allowed to see a map before he goes in case we have to retrieve him in a hurry. I strongly suggest he does not try to resist the dimension and make a commotion. Humans are very intolerant of things they cannot understand.'

Bruno was unceremoniously escorted from the chamber to the small portal that rippled with images from other dimensions. Inside its depths ghostly dead worlds existed beside vibrant civilisations living in permanent carnival. Places a Lustrelander could only conjure up in nightmare jostled with joyful worlds bustling with activity where the idea of any other existence never entered anyone's dreams.

Rimonay could have sent Bruno to any one of them; he just hoped that she chose a world not populated by anything red or reptilian.

CHAPTER 4

It was highly unlikely the ogres could have comprehended the aggravation their threat of invasion was causing in Lustreland. For them, the pursuit of the unspeakable was enough, and an outing into the neighbouring domain would be a break from the problems building up in Darkle Deeps.

Any creature expecting to survive there needed skin as tough as turtle shell. This gloomy crater, which was separated from the translucent domain of Lustreland by Rara Avis Ridge, was too low to catch the rays of the Ligh Tofrea Sun. Although the ogres were totally suited to their land of gnarled trees, thorny deserts and rugged granite outcrops sharp enough to tear the feet off any normal being, they envied everyone else their light, and even begrudged the rara avis the faint rays that frequently touched their Ridge.

Notwithstanding, had the ogres suddenly been presented with sunlight it was unlikely they would have settled down to farm. In fact, there was a legend that the light of the Ligh Tofrea Sun would transform them into untidy blobs of hairy jelly, though it was more likely any self-respecting star would have taken one look at the ogres and retracted its rays.

The ogres had also been assured by goblins, who did not want the hairy hoards bringing down their tunnels when they tramped over them on the way to Lustreland, that they should stay in Darkle Deeps. After all, its rivers were the murkiest, its swamps the most sulphurous and its vegetation incredibly rapacious - it had even been known to take a bite out of the occasional ogre. Also, enough salt could be collected in an hour from the thick crust left when their rank sea dribbled out to pickle a year's supply of jellyfish.

Unfortunately, jellyfish were becoming scarce because these succulent, brainless creatures found it difficult to survive the increasing amount of salt in the water. The failing crop from the dinosaur bone mines had made the ogres more and more dependent on the rancid weed that littered their ponds, and the trotters of the fearsome gofferhog were only reserved for the chief ogre.

Some race memory that had lurked in the ogre subconscious with more tenacity than was normal for a mere thought persuaded their chief, Jobaloba, to suggest that they should eat each other. As an experiment, his food taster bit himself on the arm, only to contract tetanus.

Their desire for a decent meal was the chance the Hurglabat had been waiting for and it hadn't taken long to persuade the ogres that it was about time they were once again allowed to revert to their original beastly ways those ancient witches put an end to.

The army was assembled and ready to march, still oblivious to the fact that they were about to invade a domain filled with a dangerous amount of light. By the way the monster had already spewed out enough gems to encrust Jobaloba's armour, it would have been more reasonable for them to expect it to provide packed lunches when the order to go came.

The Lustrelanders must have been hoping that the ogres did not remember that they used to be their sole diet before being compelled to settle down in the huge fortress which had been bulldozed up for them by semi-intelligent dinosaurs. The only pretence to architecture this structure had was the ornamental turrets made under contract by some harpies. This was because female ogres could turn very nasty if not paid double time to do work that was beyond their mates. The harpies demanded four times the going rate as they had a better sense of style than the rest of them put together. Before the job was finished, the harpies without fast enough lift off also earned a few teeth marks from the females. The consequence of which was that building inspectors from Lustreland ordered that reinforced columns be added to support the turrets of the fortress because the ogres didn't always take their power struggles outside. The din of ogres using masonry to stone each other frequently kept the residents of Rara Ridge awake. Some less than charitable Lustreland Councillor did suggest that, in view of the situation, those inspectors should be resurrected and reprimanded, but then the fortress roof eventually fell in anyway, and exposed the main hall to the leaden sky.

CHAPTER 5

Rimonay was annoyed at being disturbed on the eve of the ogre invasion. Her wizened features were not clear in the globe of frosted crystal at first. The ashtray had served its purpose, but this purchase from a new-age shop provided Peter with a better view of his Lustreland equivalent as well as being more dignified.

Soon the old woman's cracked tones rang out like the chimes of his antique carriage clock as her image resolved itself.

'What do you want now? I'm busy!'

'Sorry. I'm just not happy with the idea,' Peter protested benignly.

'What is the matter with you, man? I thought I made the matter clear enough.'

'You don't know Bernard. He's an abnormally heavy load on life's highway.'

'I know his counterpart, Bruno. Take my word for it, you've only got the tip of the iceberg.'

'But this isn't about perches for penguins, is it.'

After taking so long to accept Rimonay, his wizened alter ego so totally different to him in appearance and reasoning, Peter was now unsettled that his other self could be so ruthless. With Lustreland's First Minister came knowledge he could have happily lived without. It was disconcerting to discover that there was another dimension peopled by the counterparts of every human being. This was a parallel existence where the twin persona of the manager in his office sat on a rock taking swings with his battle-axe at subordinate sprites, office juniors whose worlds revolved around soaps and the office party as they spun out their nebulous lives counting the paperclips pinning them to humdrum existence.

Rimonay's mouth tightened in tedium and the wrinkles that patterned her face were drawn into annoyed creases. 'I can't understand why you're so worried about the wretch.'

Peter drained the last of his brandy. 'I know Bernard can be like a huffy hippo. He's the perfect antidote to the romantic tenor, but a loveable scoundrel in his own bombastic way. I sometimes even wonder if it is him at fault and not the rest of the world instead. Priceless he is, priceless.'

'You do realise why this must be done?'

'It still sounds cruel.' Peter's chuckle betrayed his true ambivalence. 'It'll not only drive him mad, but everyone else as well.'

'You just look after your dimension and I'll look after mine. Extreme situations need extreme solutions.'

'It will take a hell of a lot to persuade Indrina not to run off for good. She might even have him certified.'

'That's your problem. I've enough to worry about here.'

'Well don't go and expire on me without sending an e-mail.'

'Oh you'll know about that when the time comes.' Rimonay's deep cackle reverberated from the frosted glass as it enclosed her image in its crazed pattern. The light in its depths blinked, and she was gone.

CHAPTER 6

High in a cave in Rara Avis Ridge a dragon rustled silken wings in irritation at the vibration leagues below its nest.

Sesame puffed a few clouds of pink smoke as its reptilian mind tried to make sense of the subterranean movement. It wasn't ogres this time. Their army had never learnt to synchronise its hairy feet, and their rock concerts may have caused the occasional landslide, but never shook the crust below Darkle Deeps.

Why should Sesame worry? Dragon slaying had been outlawed and, unlike those delicate Lustrelanders, the inhabitants of Rara Avis Ridge were able to fly off to other realms. The only aggravation the dragon was obliged to put up with was those bickering harpy neighbours.

As for being asked to deal with the ogres - the Second Minister would never agreed to it. Pity. Sesame relished an excuse to barbecue a few of the lumbering brutes. Unlike dragons, ogres weren't a protected species and evolution wasn't allowing them go anywhere but down.

CHAPTER 7

Indrina took one final slash with her shears at the ivy invading the window box and decapitated another geranium. Accepting that she would never make a gardener, the stem was dropped into the vase with its unfortunate companions before she returned to the jumbled accounts of a country estate that had driven her out for some fresh air in the first place. It was no good; the tiny writing in her client's ledger and other scraps of paper were still making her double focus. It was also difficult to concentrate ever since Dr Morgan had phoned to say that her estranged husband had turned into a fairy. Bernard had always talked in his sleep, though it was usually about the encores for his Mephistopheles, not Fairyland.

Indrina thankfully noticed that it was time to visit her daughter. Leaving the muddled invoices, receipts and randomly dated entries in the ledger, she pushed a comb through her hair and threw a scarf over her silk dress, only pausing to snatch up her husband's insurance policy to examine its small print on the train. The accountant was pretty sure she wouldn't find any clause that covered the eventuality of him turning into a fairy.

When Indrina arrived at her old home, it was just as well she hadn't brought the car. The laurel that had invaded the drive yet again must have been related to the ivy invading her apartment's window box.

Not wanting Bernard to know she was there, she picked up the carton of orange juice from the doorstep and quietly opened the front door with her key. She needn't have bothered. Their daughter, Aurora, was having a one girl rave in the kitchen with an old Take That disc and a can of Coca-Cola.

Indrina switched off the CD player and handed her the orange juice. 'Try something which doesn't rot the brain.'

'Hi Mum.'

Aurora was hardly a picture of anxiety. Indrina would have suspected her husband and daughter of having a joke at her expense if the 16-year-old hadn't been capable of thinking up something more cosmic than fairies, or Bernard had a sense of humour.

'Dr Morgan still insists it's serious?'

'Oh it is. Didn't he tell you all about it?' Aurora put the orange juice in the fridge. 'We're out of mango juice, will pineapple do?'

Indrina accepted a glass. 'You don't seem too worried?'

'Of course I am. I didn't think you would be.'

'How bad is he now?'

'Refusing to utter a note. Says he's not a common minstrel.'

'But what caused it? He was his normal bloody-minded self when I saw him a couple of weeks ago. Now it sounds as though he's turned into somebody else's bloody-minded self.'

'His agent must have been working him too hard.'

Being an accountant, Indrina felt some kindred sympathy for her husband's agent, though she had never dared protest too loudly on his behalf. 'Bernard works at his own pace. I doubt if Milligan could make him sing one bar more than he wanted to.'

Aurora stopped tossing a green salad for a moment. 'Haven't you any idea at all what could be wrong with him?'

'We all go a little mad at some time or other. It's the only way to remain sane in the long run. Your father will have to come back from cloud cuckoo land sooner or later. He can't afford to stay there.'

'Daddy doesn't have the same obsession with money as you do.'

Indrina glanced through to the main living area at the exotic ornaments, ancient awards for various singing competitions, and other expensive bric-a-brac which took Mrs Hedges hours to dust. 'It's my obsession with money that stopped him bankrupting himself every time he saw something that glittered. It's a wonder he didn't sprout feathers from his backside and become a magpie instead.'

'Well, it's probably something to do with his age.' Aurora waved a salad server accusingly at her mother. 'At least he never ran off with another woman!'

'I should have been so lucky,' Indrina muttered into her pineapple juice.

'That big, blonde soprano fancied him.'

'The only thing they could have engineered between them would have been an eclipse.'

The teenager's eyes narrowed. 'I sometimes wonder if you ever loved Daddy.'

'When you're twenty you live on a different planet. You don't come down to the real world until you're forty. Everything up till then is illusion, delusion, and nervous anxiety. Humans wouldn't get together at all if Nature hadn't dulled our adolescent brains with the marshmallow of romance.'

'Rubbish. You're just making excuses.'

'So what am I supposed to do about him?'

'As he refuses to divorce you and you won't waste money on divorcing him, you are legally entitled to have him certified.'

'You're his daughter. You get him put away and risk the wrath of his fan club. I'd only end up paying for some private nursing home if I did it.'

Aurora could see looming before her the prospect of being lumbered in middle-age with a couple of horrendous OAPs. 'You could obtain a divorce on the grounds of his insanity.'

Indrina was suspicious. 'Just what are you up to, Madam? You never wanted us to part in the first place.'

'You do feel sorry for him, though?'

'Me feel sorry for that pompous Minister Bonzo, or whoever he thinks he is? Now, if he had decided he was some virile Oberon ...'

'That character was pretty arrogant as well,' Aurora reminded her then neatly pivoted the argument onto a different track. 'I wonder if Daddy caught something when you took him back to India a few years ago?'

Indrina breathed in sharply as she remembered the overpowering aromas that dissuaded her from entering most of the temples her husband happily blundered about like a sacred cow. As long as they weren't dedicated to anything that slithered, he had been all too willing to remove his shoes and burn incense. Indrina hadn't shared this enthusiasm.

'It was probably that trip which broke up our marriage.' Then something more immediate occurred to her. 'You are keeping him away from the telephone?'

'I unplugged the one in his bedroom and hid both the mobiles. I won't let Daddy have them while he's not himself.'

'Well at least you'll be able to phone Whipsnade Zoo when you find out who he really is.'

Aurora turned the salad out onto three plates and dropped a slice of quiche onto each. 'Can you pay our electric bill? They're about to cut us off. Daddy says he's too high ranking to deal with mere money matters.'

Indrina groaned and pulled out her chequebook. 'How much?'

'Three hundred and seventy,'

Indrina stopped rummaging for a pen. 'What? It's mid summer for goodness sake!'

'Well we have to keep the heat and lights on. He feels the cold and is afraid of the dark.'

'How long has this been going on?'

'Started feeling the cold a month ago.'

Reluctantly Indrina handed over a cheque. 'Perhaps a divorce would be cheaper.'

'And can you write a small article for his fan club's website?'

'No.'

'Oh go on,' whined Aurora, 'they're very sweet.'

'I'll tell them he's turned into a fairy.'

'I'll tell Clarey and he'll give you the sack.'

Indrina thought about the odd slips of paper and crumpled receipts that client called accounts, which were now strewn over her desk. She was tempted. Instead, the accountant quickly finished her meal to get back to them.

CHAPTER 8

Hada Gonn's steady gaze smouldered like cinders spat from the deepest volcano on Vulcanus. All three and a half red eyes of Jobaloba's scarred faces glowered back. How dare this upstart adventurer tell the ogre chief that the deity they worshipped was only some greedy monster that had latched onto the underside of Darkle Deeps? At least, that was what Jobaloba assumed "opportunist" meant. This was the trouble with allowing ogres to leave the bracing sulphuric air of Darkle Deeps; there was always a danger they would blunder into some domain where they might contract education.

Having travelled so widely, Hada Gonn had come to the conclusion that anything which chose to clamp itself onto the underside of Darkle Deeps not only had a very peculiar appetite, but was pure evil.

The high priest was summoned.

Kot Kut wasn't sure what high priests were supposed to do, let alone work out why he had been chosen for the position and assumed it had something to do with his acute hearing. As not even Lustreland had a high priest, only corrupt witches and warlocks, it had seemed like a good idea to Jobaloba at the time. All Kot Kut was expected to do was listen at the sacred hole where the Hurglabat gurgled up its orders. Being asked to arbitrate in arguments as to whether the monster was a god or not was missing from the job description. How should he know the true nature of deity? The only deities he had ever heard of lived in Lustreland, and they didn't encourage worship. They just preferred to play rotten tricks on the residents for amusement.

Bludon, the ogre chief's advisor, whispered into the ear of the embarrassed high priest. The holy ogre's face lit up as though presented with enough green stamps for beatification.

'A challenge!' he declared.

Jobaloba's scowl deepened. He was never known to turn down a fight, but not on a full meal of gofferhog trotters. Irritably he reached for his double-headed axe. He would have felled Hada Gonn then and there if Kot Kut hadn't decided to legitimise the proceedings with a few rules, like both combatants having weapons.

Hada Gonn chose a mace studded with foot long spikes. A reasonable precaution when facing someone with two skulls so thick their brains were totally insulated from each other. Jobaloba had little problem with this anatomical arrangement as he didn't have the wit to hold a conversation with himself and thoughts seldom arrived in them at the same time anyway.

The ogre chief's throne of dinosaur bones creaked and the jewels in his battered armour flashed maliciously as he pushed his massive bulk up to sharpen his axe against the ancient coronation stone. He would have had himself crowned on it long ago if Kot Kut could find the tome describing what the ceremony involved. Others suspected it might have upset that giant whose drain they lived at the bottom of, not to mention the Hurglabat. As long as those two entities didn't start asking each other for rent, they were just grateful that the coronation stone gave their blades a remarkably sharp edge.

Rules or no rules, Jobaloba swung his axe in a circle, fully expecting to slice off the heretical head of Hada Gonn. However, the adventurer had not only acquired an education, but trained reflexes as well. The ogre chief missed and continued to spin with such momentum he drilled himself into the dirt floor of fortress's main hall. By the time he had pulled his feet free, he was very annoyed.

Unluckily for Hada Gonn, he had also picked up the habit of good manners and not struck Jobaloba before he could recover - there was no end to the repellent niceties the young ogre had brought to Darkle Deeps.

An ugly murmur rippled through the crowd of watching ogres which was peppered with high-pitched shrieks of laughter from a few females who had no idea when to take things seriously.

With an enraged roar and halitosis billowing from all nostrils, Jobaloba rushed at Hada Gonn. His axe struck a glancing blow and sliced the thongs of his opponent's jerkin. Just as the mime and movement sprite had instructed the young ogre, he nimbly stepped aside and Jobaloba collided with an ancient pillar badly in need of pointing up. Some of the sacred jewels in his breastplate shattered and the loosened bricks above thudded onto the ogre chief's heads. In his rage, he struck the battered stone another blow and dislodged the lintel it supported.

After the surviving members of the audience had been dug out of the rubble, Hada Gonn picked up his mace and faced Jobaloba who had been irritated at the interruption of such effete humanitarianism. He quickly regained the momentum of his murderous onslaught, slashing and whirling his axe in all directions with the conviction that his opponent had to be standing in at least one of them. More masonry was dislodged, the long table upended, and the fortress's cast iron tableware clattered against the breastplates of the remaining audience.

Having expended so much effort on this dervish like attack, Jobaloba stopped to view the inevitable mincemeat he must have made of his opponent.

There was no blood, mangled muscles or livid entrails. Hada Gonn was still standing, looking somewhat bemused at the ogre chief's state of minds.

What was Hada Gonn doing in this place? What demented impulse had persuaded him to return home and try to make the ogre hoards see reason? The last time reason had put its head above the parapet in Darkle Deeps they had charged at it with rusty swords and sent it screaming back up to Lustreland. In contempt, the young ogre tossed his mace aside, accidentally impaling the foot of Kot Kut.

Jobaloba may not have been sensitive to much, but he did know humiliation when it bit him. Unable to sink his axe into the upstart responsible for it, the ogre chief went berserk. As his mighty blades whirled, innocent bystanders lost minor appendages and the fortress more of its stones. Even the voracious wildlife in the moat outside closed its gills and sank down into the corrosive quagmire.

Hada Gonn, standing in the eye of the storm, looked on in resignation.

Eventually Jobaloba was exhausted. Hada Gonn pulled his mace from the foot of the high priest and tossed the weapon to the laughing females who juggled it with some spears. Then the failed reformer picked up his knapsack and silently strode from the fortress.

The young ogre reached the far side of the drawbridge before a wall of bristling bodies dare rush in pursuit. In their efforts to be first to slay him, some were jostled into the moat and dragged under by creatures so fierce they would have sank their fangs into the turrets of the fortress had they been able to reach.

Mime and movement training was no defence against the hail of rocks and blazing logs from the fortress hearth that followed, so Hada Gonn secured his knapsack and sprinted off.

CHAPTER 9

Isolda tossed her bleached, blonde locks with the practised air of a woman in her late fifties and called to Peter as he descended the steps to his basement home.

He had more urgent matters on his mind. 'Later, passion flower, later.'

'I might have found someone else by then,' she warned. 'There are plenty of likely lads younger than sixty who come to the bar and give me the eye.'

'And there's always the danger they could sober up.' He made the mistake of lifting his large face to grin up at her and received a wet dishcloth across it for his trouble.

'Don't you take me for granted, you great mammoth.' Isolda reached down to snatch the dishcloth back before he could confiscate it. 'I know about your two wives in Africa.'

'Plenty of men have had two wives.'

'Not both at once. And I don't believe that baloney about them being a gift from a grateful government.'

'You pick the damnedest of times for an argument, Issie. You know they both preferred each other to me, anyway.'

'Served you right. You still send them money, though, don't you?'

'As both their families are refugees, they wouldn't survive without it. You know that you jealous cat.' He tried to wave her away.

'Miaow,' Isolda snarled after him as he escaped into his subterranean bolthole.

However much Isolda might have taunted Peter about the women in his past, she knew there was little chance of finding any man half as reasonable. His eventful life had taught him that raging at the inequities of the world was a waste of time.

The experiences that Peter Olan Martin kept to himself had been more colourful than many a self-confessed adventurer's. His first teenage employment was as an apprentice engine driver when the fires of steam trains had to be stoked in gale force winds and heat waves. Though he could have stayed in that employment until diesel trains or retirement, a marriage broken up by the persistent efforts of the bride's bigoted parents unsettled him so much he decided to look for new horizons.

Peter's keen commitment to the local church encouraged a privately sponsored missionary fund to accept his application for work in Africa, his mother's continent, as a lay missionary. She had died young and his father succumbed to early onset dementia before he could tell their son anything much about her; he could not even be sure what country she had been born in.

He obediently spent a couple of years in a remote village dispensing vitamin pills, Western knowledge and pearls of Christian wisdom before realising that the tribe he had been sent to enlighten was humouring him. They apparently appreciated the vitamin pills, school room equipment and Peter's amiable company, and would have been content to maintain the arrangement.

But suddenly one morning, as fast as the sun dawned, so did Peter's awareness of how his African friends saw reality. The revelation made him shake off that emotional dependency on an unseen god and wonder why the commonsense of Jesus Christ's message needed magic to prove it.

Only until he had committed religious doctrine to the dustbin of futility did the ex missionary become aware that he possessed an odd power, the ability to step aside from the real world and comprehend dimensions more likely to have existed in the ancient pagan mind. Given his sudden doubts about religion, only to find that he had the mystic ability he would have scorned in another person, he initially refused to acknowledge that it was anything more than indigestion.

The change in their would-be benefactor was not lost on the tribe who understood what was happening to Peter, even if he denied it. This man was trustworthy and intelligent with western pragmatism, and had no affiliations that could trigger a conflict of interest. He was the ideal delegate to protect their interests in the newly formed democratic government.

Peter Olan Martin found himself being sent to represent the tribal area in the new government, and was gifted two wives by a powerful tribal elder the new regime dare not offend. He barely knew what he was doing there, let alone understand how he suddenly had acquired two wives, before he was given the position of Secretary to the Prime Minister's Secretary, then Assistant to the Agricultural Minister and, last of all, Agricultural Minister.

The consequences of desertification, local farming methods, and foreign attempts to grab land gave him more than enough to think about, so he had little time for a social life or keeping his wives company. Had he not been so occupied, he might have paid more attention to the rumours of an impending coup. But this was a secure state where the army was loyal to the popular government and no opposition party had the resources to topple it. So it came as a bombshell when the elected government was overthrown, and by an unknown army captain.

The Prime Minister had discovered too late that this captain had never belonged to his country's military personnel. Shortly afterwards there was a counter coup in which both the Prime Minister and his usurper were assassinated.

The economy and confidence of the people had been shattered, so it seemed natural to the order of things in the modern world that a semi democratic government sponsored by a major power would rise from the ashes. Most citizens were relieved to be free of the military regime, if only for a puppet president dependent on foreign aid. A situation their self-respect would never have tolerated prior to the overthrow of the government they had elected.

Before the purges began, Peter had the presence of mind to get his two wives, their families, and himself out of the country.

Despite the rhetoric and accusations about the malign influence of the major powers from other African leaders, it was a long while before a glimmer of the truth occurred to Peter, the truth he had been reluctant to face because it was so incredible. That revelation lay dormant for twenty years until Indrina prompted him to recall the coup and its implications.

After leaving his wives with enough to live on, Peter had used his remaining money to collect reptile specimens required on the shopping lists of several European zoos, before making his way back home. After delivering the animals, he became temporary reptile keeper at one of them until someone with the right qualifications applied. From there he used his impressive overseas qualifications to obtain the position of research assistant to a member of parliament, though not for long. Peter found out enough scandal to jeopardise several votes of confidence, and had to admit he preferred reptiles.

It was time to settle down and invest what resources he had saved in a small hotel, for which he was lucky enough to find an excellent chef and enthusiastic manager. The three of them developed the business which eventually incorporated an adjoining Victorian guesthouse and old staging inn's stables.

The manager and the chef were in their element, ordering staff about and buttering up the clientele, leaving Peter to juggle the accounts, which he happily passed onto Indrina so he could go back to sleeping at night. This hectic life was not for him. Reluctant to disturb the regime of his enthusiastic partners, but not wanting to move, Isolda suggested he take over the huge wine cellar which was never fully used, have underfloor heating installed, and live there. The manager and chef were both given a third share in the hotel as long as he was guaranteed his income, a permanent home, and peace and quiet.

And in that huge apartment Peter Olan Martin lived contentedly ever since, surrounded by his library and items of furniture too large to fit most normal sized rooms. There was also enough space for a bathroom twice the size of the one in the hotel's supreme suite. High windows looked out to the orchard and, with the entrance from the hotel kitchen permanently bolted and the outside door tucked away in the orchard, Peter was in a world of his own... Until the arrival of Rimonay.

CHAPTER 10

The blazing logs hurled at Hada Gonn set fire to the pools of pitch that dotted his escape route. The young ogre was still ducking rocks and zigzagging to avoid the flames by the time he reached the boundary of Darkle Deeps.

Here the hobnailed boots of the army chasing him thudded to a halt.

This was where the ground moved with every monstrous breath of the Hurglabat.

Despite his recently impaled foot, some addled understanding of his own importance had persuaded Kot Kut to lead the pursuit. Abruptly finding himself caught between an army stewing with murderous resentment and a young ogre who had just overthrown convention as well as their leader's self-esteem, the high priest's confidence ducked for cover.

Hada Gonn stopped to look back at the ogres' dismal homeland, before turning towards the distant pass of illuminating glow stones that led through Rara Avis Ridge to The Province of Light. Lustrelanders may have had contempt for all things hairy and muscle-bound, but they had taught him a lot, probably too much for his own good.

What other route could he take.

By Kot Kut's apprehensive expression, it was obvious he didn't intend to drag the young ogre back by his flame red beard, and the army sent out to avenge Jobaloba now looked more inclined to wander away and play football with the goblins working the dinosaur bone mines. The only effort that required was counting to eleven and finding a detached head large enough.

Fearful that the sound of so many huge ogre feet had roused the Hurglabat, Kot Kut went to one of the deep holes in the hardened tar crust and listened. He didn't like what he heard. The high priest limped back a few paces and then, without warning or explanation, picked up the hem of his robe and ran. Not sure if this was some part of a ritual, the other ogres forgot about the puzzled Hada Gonn and followed their high priest.

Although the adventurer did not believe that the Hurglabat was a god, he knew that it existed so wasn't surprised when huge mounds rippled the lake of tar at Darkle Deeps boundary as the monster stirred. Whatever was about to happen, Hada Gonn knew that the entity wasn't going to spit up gemstones for him to catch.

Once again securing his knapsack, the young ogre turned and defiantly strode towards the pass that led through Rara Avis Ridge.

He did not make it.

In his deportment lessons he had been taught to keep his chin up; something very difficult for ogres who tended to have heads seated deep between their shoulders so, looking straight ahead he didn't notice the hole open up before him. Hada Gonn was hardly aware he was falling until he hit the undulating ground at its bottom.

He picked himself up.

Tunnels branched off in every direction, up, down and straight on. Putrid air that must have come straight from the supreme giant's compost heap circulated through them and a leaden glow allowed Hada Gonn to see into the depths of the sinister maze. Unable to clamber out of the hole, he resolutely repacked the contents that had spilt from his knapsack and started to walk.

Ominous rumblings reverberated through the semi solid walls that belled in and out like the digestive tract of a living creature. The fearless Hada Gonn hesitated as the horrible thought crossed his mind that he was actually inside the entity which he had made it his vocation to denigrate. The idea that he could be marching straight down the Hurglabat's gullet brought the adventurer to a halt.

The walls stopped moving as though this tough morsel was now digestible.

Against everything ogre in his nature, Hada Gonn started to tiptoe. There was silence except for the faint thud of a massive heart. For the first time in his life he was scared. This was one adventure too far. All those tunnels leading upwards had disappeared and now seemed to slope down to the monster's stomach.

He was submerged in a miasma like decomposing seaweed, a stench strong enough to stun anything but a goblin or an ogre. In spite of instinct, better judgement, and everything he had been taught, Hada Gonn was filled with horrible fascination. That was why, after all, he was an adventurer.

A narrow passage had a leaden glow at its far end. Fear now under control, he carefully eased himself into it and was swallowed down towards an eerie burbling like the snoring of a million gofferhogs. The glow increased and the warm noxious odour was pulsed forward in waves as though expelled by huge bellows. Hada Gonn released his precious knapsack to crawl through a narrow gap and peer into the vast space beyond it.

Although his eyes were adapted for seeing in the dim light of Darkle Deeps, the young ogre could not immediately take in what confronted him. Filling a huge chamber was the vile, throbbing jelly of the Hurglabat. Like the layers of a decaying, greenish grey trifle it was stacked between the chamber floor and high ceiling, dribbling into every available crack.

Hada Gonn knew that if it woke, the monster would pulse through the network of tunnels he was trapped in, so tried not to gasp. Even if this wasn't a true deity, it was supernaturally unspeakable. Perhaps in his own bone-headed way, Jobaloba had been right to hold the abomination in such awe.

A milliard eyes blinked in points of green about the entity's gelatinous body and fine filaments flickered like a serpent's tongues tasting the air as it slumbered.

Fortunately none of them detected ogre.

Having seen enough to fill the rest of his life with nightmares, Hada Gonn backed out of the narrow gap. But the tunnel had closed up behind him.

There was another in the living wall of the Hurglabat's chamber, only that was on the other side of the vast chamber. Was it possible to reach it? Hada Gonn only had to dislodge one small rock and he would have no more adventures.

There was no other option. He would have to descend into the chamber and past its pulsating, gelatinous body. There was very little space between the wall and monster and he would never have contemplated the manoeuvre if he had been as gluttonous as the other ogres with the girth to match.

Then he noticed the narrow ledge just below him.

The adventurer eased through the small gap and gingerly dropped onto it. As he did so he found himself gazing into tiny, flashing eyes in the monster's jelly, twitching as though trying to pinpoint prey.

Hada Gonn froze.

Then they blinked shut.

Any other ogre would have been muscle mash in the monster's maws long ago, but Hada Gonn had learnt how to think with his feet as well as his brain. He relaxed and concentrated on the lessons of the mime and movement sprite, principally the tuition about walking on eggshells and floating like a butterfly on the breeze.

As he eased along the ledge, the adventurer's bristling beard scraped the wall, sending small clouds of dust onto the Hurglabat. Half way to the other tunnel's welcoming mouth, his calf muscles tightened with the effort and threatened to cramp at any second. Hada Gonn lost sensation in one foot. It slipped and sent gravel cascading down onto the monster.

The leaden glow filling huge the chamber suddenly blazed to a deep orange as the tiny eyes opened and the gelatinous folds rippled. Again the ogre froze like a petrified gargoyle, knowing that it was now or never. Hada Gonn massaged the feeling back into his legs and swiftly clambered the remaining distance along the crumbling ledge and leapt down into the mouth of the tunnel.

The Hurglabat shuddered and rocks cascaded from its chambers walls.

With an enraged, resonating roar, the gelatinous monster became engorged, spilling into the passages like half set mucus.

Hada Gonn tore off the jerkin that was snagging on sharp rocks and ran for his life - ogre style.

The tentacles of the monster raced after him, on and on until the bones in Hada Gonn's feet cracked in protest. Ogre brains, being small, did not require much oxygen, though there was always a limit. His deep breathing training helped as he sped onwards.

Giddy with the exertion, he was barely aware of plunging through a barrier of stench so dense it had been holding back a wall of water.

Suddenly Hada Gonn found himself splashing about in a black sea.

Black sea? Above a fiery orange sky?

No more Hurglabat?

Where was he?

Far away, on the distant horizon of a forbidding ocean was the silhouette of a continent fretted out by a livid fringe of volcanoes erupting against the dark sky.

CHAPTER 11

After dusting a few shelves and emptying incriminating ashtrays, Peter sat down to read the Guardian while waiting for his guests.

Punctual as always, Indrina parked in the hotel forecourt. After Aurora had managed to clamber out of the car without falling off her stacked shoes, she tottered after her mother across the orchard and down the steps to Peter's cellar.

The door opened immediately. As soon as they were inside he pressed the switch that electronically closed it.

Indrina was curious. 'You never had that before?'

Aurora wasn't interested in security and rushed to give her favourite uncle, albeit unrelated, a hug, almost tumbling off her heels in her haste.

Taking advantage of Aurora's show of affection, Indrina removed a plain folder from her briefcase and placed it in Peter's bureau. He watched the accountant over Aurora's shoulder like a customs officer finding the cobra in the false bottom of a suitcase, then tossed the teenager into the air as though she were a six-year-old.

Fortunately he caught her before she hit the floor.

'Mind my dinner!'

'You're supposed to be having lunch with me.'

'I have to eat a meal with Daddy or he becomes awkward, thinks his food's being poisoned, and won't eat anything at all.'

'That doesn't sound like him - The not eating bit anyway. What's wrong?'

By the ensuing silence, Peter guessed the worst. He had never liked to make comments about a friend who prided himself on his level-headed, even-handedness a little too much. Peter knew the only reason Bernard kept his head level was because the notes wouldn't come out any other way. As for even handedness - he could drop bricks equally well with either.

'Not having a breakdown, is he?'

'Something like that,' murmured Indrina.

Faced with Peter's steely gaze she admitted, 'He thinks he's a fairy.'

He raised a bushy eyebrow and tried to sound surprised. It didn't work. 'Ethereal, homosexual, or soap?'

'Well he hasn't sprouted wings yet, but this dragon seems to be giving him a lot of aggravation.'

'Mummy thinks it's funny.' The resentment in Aurora's tone was obvious.

'Never knew Bernard had a sense of humour?' mused Peter.

Indrina only wished it could have been due to one of the odd moods her husband had when preparing for a stage role. 'Oh, he's not joking. He should audition for Oberon.'

'What? Britten's? Never. That's a counter tenor role. And you know what he thinks about using his falsetto. What happened to bring it on?'

'Wouldn't surprise me if it was self-induced.'

'If it was self-induced he would have become a grizzly bear or Don Giovanni. Poor Bernie. Hasn't been overworking has he?'

Indrina shook her head and sat on the settee. Bernard only overworked other people.

'Of course, I've always suspected there was more to Bernard than met the eye,' Peter conceded.

'If he's the tip of the iceberg, I could understand how the Titanic felt.'

Peter raised a reproachful finger. 'You can often be like an iceberg yourself; no man can be totally sure what's going on beneath that surface.'

Reluctant to admit he may have been right, Indrina drummed her fingers on the arm of the settee and said nothing.

'What are we going to have for dinner then?' Aurora asked.

'You mean you're still hungry?' Peter sounded off-hand.

'Well, if you've had something done especially..?'

'She'll eat anything going,' Indrina told him. 'I'm certainly peckish as well.'

'In that case,' Peter pulled a key from his waistcoat pocket. 'Unbolt the door to the kitchen stairs, young lady, and look in the service hatch. Hopefully our lunch will be there.'

Without another word Aurora kicked off her stacked shoes and dashed off.

Indrina quietly chuckled. 'Unbolt the stairs door..? Are you expecting a raid from a tribe of suet puddings?'

'Suet puddings! Don't mention that word within earshot of the chef or she'll shove garlic in my Sunday roast.'

'You shouldn't eat-'

'I know, but my bowels go into spasms coping with the amount of lettuce and broccoli on the doctor's diet sheet. Wish I still had a digestion like Aurora's.'

'I'm worried about her. She's more interested in food than boys. Claims Bernard and I put her off marriage.'

'Such is the influence of parents.'

'Despite that, she still dotes on her father, even though he is turning quite dotty.'

'There you go again, Indrina. Why don't you give the poor fellow a chance?'

'Because he's growing more pompous and egotistical as he gets older. Bernard was impossible to live with before this happened. He said he didn't mind me being in business, then always wanted me around when I needed to dine with clients. He claimed he didn't mind when I wasn't able to attend his first nights, but wouldn't speak to me for days if I didn't.'

'Shame on you,' Peter chided.

'Shame on me?'

'Shame on you for not wanting to see. You've the intelligence to know what's wrong and do something about it. Poor Bernie hasn't. He probably wants to, but isn't bright enough. There has never been anything malicious in the man, has there? You can't deny that beneath all the pomposity he has the kindest nature of any human.'

'Then why does he manage to exasperate everyone?'

'He can't help it. He was placed on this planet to test our mettle.'

'Name the entity responsible and I'll burn down its temple.'

'You frighten Bernard, you know.'

'Oh good grief!'

'Oh yes, strange exotic lady from Shepherd's Bush, you put the fear of God into him and he doesn't know what to do with it.'

The clatter of cutlery from the far end of the cellar announced lunch.

While Peter felt obliged to keep to the fat free side of the menu, Aurora was happy to pack away anything the others left.

Indrina hardly touched anything. Peter had managed to strike a chord of conscience somewhere, albeit a slack one, and she conceded between the fish and trifle that she would have to call on Bernard at some time.

CHAPTER 12

Having no idea of how he had arrived there, Hada Gonn stared at the distant, fiery silhouette of Vulcanus, relieved that the continent was on the other side of a deep, black ocean. No living creature could have survived on those flaming slopes or breathed its sulphuric atmosphere.

The young ogre swam ashore to find his bearings. Darkle Deeps was nowhere to be seen from the grey shingle beach which disappeared into the distance. Above it, very faint in their half-light, were distant the peaks of Rara Avis Ridge.

Hada Gonn now missed his knapsack. Without supplies or his leather jerkin, he wasn't going to last long in this bleak place; even educated ogres needed protein now and then, and he might well turn out to be the first to die of hypothermia. The entrance to the tunnel he had escaped through must have by now disappeared under a crust of tar; not that he was inclined to double back through that route. The only reference he had to the known Universe was the distant peaks of Rara Avis Ridge, so he set out along the tide-line towards it, careful to avoid the murky water. The mysterious chimera lurking beneath the waves of that inky ocean sucking at the dismal shore were probably more dangerous than the mutant life forms that had evolved in the moat surrounding the ogres' fortress: it was a wonder they hadn't already detected his presence.

As he trudged on the light grew dimmer and the silhouette of Vulcanus seemed to get larger, like an untidy bat looming up from the horizon. Hada Gonn tried to ignore the possibility of the fiery continent coming closer. Unfortunately something much more menacing appeared in the threatening sky, and it wasn't a bat.

The young ogre plodded on, wondering where his next meal would come from and when it would be safe to sleep. Deportment lessons long forgotten, his head was well down so he didn't notice the large shape descending through the turbulent clouds. Neither bird nor reptile, the creature was as large as a dragon and had a flattened, fretted shape like a hideous, black lace kite.

By the time the downbeat of its wings churned up drifts of shingle it was too late.

The creature had swooped and snatched up Hada Gonn.

The ogre tried to lunge at its beak or snout. The blows never found their mark - the dark monstrosity was headless! Had he been thinking straight, the adventurer would have realised that meant it could not eat him, but ogre instinct had taken over. He was oblivious of the distance the creature was putting between them and the ground and the fact he would not have survived the fall if he had managed to free himself.

Soon, Vulcanus was directly below them, its blackened mountains erupting with sores of molten lava, burning the oxygen in the air and creating a hell Kot Kut could have preached a sermon about to put fear into his ogre congregation. The fretwork monster ploughed on through the acrid plumes and fiery bombs spat out by volcanoes.

Hada Gonn now tightly clasped the claws of the creature that he had previously tried to escape.

Singed, suffocated and traumatised, the adventurer was relieved when they crossed to the far side of that horrendous continent to reach the ocean beyond. The water here was spangled with ice flows and glittered like crazed glass. With the cooling zephyrs, sensibility returned to Hada Gonn. This must have been the home of Rimonay, Lustreland's First Minister, who was believed to have been born of frost and ice. Now Rara Avis Ridge had long since been lost from sight, her province must have been even further away.

Beyond the realm of ice was another domain filled with terraced meadows, flying horses, and gondolas being rowed through gauzy clouds. Great cities clung to the sides of mountains like complicated outcrops as though spurning the deep gloomy valleys below, and the people who had built them flew like cumbersome moths buffeted by the wind eddying between the sheer rock faces. From the gondolas, supplies were being winched down to turret tops while a cavalry of winged horses escorted a huge ornamental barque from the clouds. Hada Gonn struggled to glimpse its occupant, only to suddenly find they were over yet another ocean.

Then he began to fall.

The young ogre tried to turn over and make fists to break his fall into the water. Before he reached it, clouds rose from nowhere and cobwebs with the tensile strength of bridge cables caught him. He found himself swimming in the balmy air of a realm high in the sky, a nebulous island filled with pastel mists and bubbles; thousands of transparent spheres aimlessly hovering as far as he could see. They all had occupants, though Hada Gonn could not make them out... he was too sleepy.

Fragrant smells and sweet melodies that would have appalled any normal ogre embraced him. A couch of cloud came up to catch him.

Hada Gonn stretched and was swallowed into a blissful torpor.

CHAPTER 13

As Bernard appeared to be asleep, Indrina wandered about the bedroom, critically examining the furniture she had been so familiar with.

'You won't find any dust,' rumbled the deep voice that could terrorise choruses and intimidate world-renowned conductors.

But Indrina was neither chorus nor conductor and had done enough tours of Bernard's psychology to know its weaknesses. 'So you are awake. I know Mrs Hedges never leaves any dust. She's capable of breaking enamel dishes, cracking concrete coal bunkers and bending shovels... but she never leaves any dust.'

Bernard glowered at her, and then rubbed his oval chin. 'Where's my beard?' he suddenly blurted out.

'You never had a beard, Pudding, so don't accuse anyone of shaving it off.'

Bernard was puzzled. He looked intently at his wife's hard, glittering smile that dared him to contradict her. At that moment he did not feel strong enough to take the consequences and instead lay musing at her dark, distinguished features and pattern on her expensive silk dress. The force that gave him the power to outmanoeuvre vengeful tenors and be known by some Italian divas as 'the peeeg' was not with him. How they would have shed crocodile tears and gloated to see him in his undignified predicament, huddled at one end of the bed with the sheets fitfully pushed to the other as though waiting for the resourceful Mrs Hedges to baggage both of them for the laundry.

Bernard suddenly recoiled. 'Dragons!'

'Dragons?' Indrina realised that he was looking at the pattern on her dress. 'They are phoenixes, you lump. Pull yourself together.'

Without handles, he wasn't in a fit state to try. 'Why should I?'

'If you had to go off your head you might have chosen some condition in the book, not invented one for yourself. You certainly baffled Dr Morgan.'

'Morgan could be baffled by a spot on his nose. Anyone would think I'm ill by the way you and our daughter are behaving.'

Indrina at last became convinced that this was no act. 'Don't you remember anything then?'

Bernard's expression was stonily defiant.

'You frightened the life out of Aurora, you know.'

'How?' demanded Bernard.

'Well let's start with you insisting that the cat was some goblin which had to be run through the mangle before it could enter your presence.'

'That's a lie! I just demanded it was clean!' Bernard could have bitten his tongue off.

'So you do remember? A madman who can recall his fantasies when apparently sane.'

'I'm not mad!'

'Careful with that voice, Pudding. Your agent may want to use it again.'

'Damn Milligan! And don't you dare tell him about this.'

'You'll have to make that concert at the weekend if you don't want him to find out.'

'I know.' He slumped back. 'I can keep the devil under control.'

Indrina rearranged the pillow that must have been giving him a neck ache. 'What devil?' she asked menacingly.

'Just a bad fairy,' he murmured.

'If it was the fairy we've been meeting over the last few days, bad isn't the word. It's an overbearing martinet.'

'I know.'

'Tell me about it?'

Bernard was as wary of Indrina as a praying mantis had reason to be of his mate. 'Why should I?'

'Aurora isn't old enough to cope with your lunacy, even if she does feel sorry for you. Tell me?'

Bernard sank back on the reorganised pillow and gave in. 'I'd been feeling perfectly fine all day. Did an afternoon concert, then went to the club before going to the theatre. I only had one appearance in the first act, so afterwards slipped a coat over my costume to get a breath of air. Then suddenly I had a beard.'

'Your makeup?'

'No, no. The role was clean shaven. This was a fringe of curls running round my chin, like the face wigs the Babylonians wore. There was no moustache. I've never worn makeup like that before. It felt so peculiar. Around there people are used to seeing singers in costume wandering about so they paid no attention...'

'Go on.'

'I was suddenly overwhelmed... the traffic, the street, the smells, and noises. And most of all - the night. They were alien! I was terrified at the sight of my own reflection in a window.'

'Was it wearing a beard?'

Bernard hesitated. 'Why no. But the reflection didn't belong to me. It was as though I had become two people.'

'Not your reflection?'

'More like a doppelganger. Two personalities with a mirror history living in the same space.'

The accountant's brain wasn't programmed to tackle such irrational scenarios. 'Well it doesn't sound like schizophrenia.'

'Don't tell Morgan. That's what he's set his heart on.'

Indrina suggested carefully, 'Did you try talking to this other self?'

'How could I? I was both of us at the same time.' Bernard's tone changed. 'Then without warning ...'

'What?'

For a moment Bernard seemed like a soaring eagle desperately trying to escape being struck by lightning, only to slam into a solid cloud. 'It took over. It was lucky I had the presence of mind to hail a taxi and get home before I totally lost control. If it had happened inside the theatre, God only knows where I'd be now. Morgan might have had me committed. I just couldn't do anything about it, Indrina.'

'You need a rest.'

'But there's nothing wrong with me.'

Even though Indrina had no idea what to make of her husband's condition, her professional acumen demanded that she always sound confident. It hadn't occurred to her that he resented having to always take her good advice.

'I've a friend who lives near the town where your next concert is booked,' she told him. 'He wants you to stay with him for a couple of weeks. He's a good client, but thinks you have the best baritone voice this side of Nelson Eddy and refuses to forgive me for walking out on it. I've tried to explain the problem attached to it but, as yet, he's unconvinced.'

'You Gorgon.'

'So why not accept his invitation and prove my point?'

Bernard had no way of telling if Indrina had genuinely forgotten that a similar invitation from a client of hers had been made when he first appeared there over a year ago. Knowing her it was unlikely she had just snatched the idea from the ether. 'Who is this fan of mine then?'

'Clarey Ditton-Davis.'

Bernard exploded. 'What! How could you have anything to do with that lecher?'

'I'm an accountant, Pudding. I am not in the business of scrutinising the moral habits of clients, only their books. And you of all people should know better than to believe all you read in the gutter press after they blew up that story about the spear and Brünnhilde's backside.'

Bernard glowered at being reminded of his most public embarrassment.

Indrina rose. 'I'll phone Clarey tomorrow. He'll be going to your concert at the weekend. He can take you back to his place afterwards. It'll save you having to hang around too much, just in case you have another attack. I'll have to warn him of course-'

'Don't you dare!'

'Stop being such a chump, Pudding. He worships that voice of yours, and he's had practise at keeping off rapacious reporters.'

Bernard said nothing. He hated having to admit she was right yet again. And it was an effective way of escaping his agent for a couple of weeks.

CHAPTER 14

Lustrelanders shunned Deity Rock and the glade where its mercurial residents lurked. Ripe fruit fell from the trees and rotted because no creature was willing to risk being rearranged by indiscriminate blasts of cave deity invective for the sake of taking a quick nibble. This was apart from the odd beetle, which had little room for memory, otherwise it would have recalled that one of its number had been transformed into the massive granite guardian, petrified at the glade's boundary. It was probably the cave deities' idea of a joke. The only ones who would go near to give it an affectionate pat were trolls who thought it was someone's hibernating pet.

Not even sorcerers were exempt from the vagaries of the cave deities; the Mystic Trine tested the mettle of apprentices by sending them to Deity Rock to collect herbs for their examination spells. Any mature witch or wizard who had the temerity to believe they were immune usually ended up twenty percent shorter and with an antisocial craving for garlic sandwiches. This was the worst stigma that could be inflicted on a member of a secret society who judged the spells of their associates by whatever was mixed with the smell of cordite on their breath. Any witch or wizard using garlic to conceal ingredients was deemed incompetent.

Rimonay was the only one who didn't fear the cave deities: not even they would have dared flick a magic spark in her direction when she approached. It usually meant trouble if she came to Deity Rock - for them! And now the First Minister was about to pay another visit. The two tree sprites she usually relied on for support had fluttered off long before reaching the granite beetle, so her progress through the vegetation rustling excitedly in anticipation proved hard going.

Exasperated, Rimonay lashed out with her stick at the bushes top heavy with gooey fruit and unnatural number of spines.

Then, from nowhere, stepped a minstrel. She was short, brightly dressed, carrying a lute, and probably too foreign to know any better. Rimonay had no intention of admitting how dangerous the place was before she had helped her to the cave deities' glade.

Thorny bushes snatched petulantly at the ribbons on the minstrel's costume as she propelled Rimonay into the most feared half acre of Lustreland. The itinerant entertainer had travelled widely enough to know when a place was giving out bad vibrations so, as soon as the good deed was done and needle sharp grip on her arm released, she reclaimed her lute from a particularly fierce creeper and ran off, leaving the elderly Lustrelander to her fate.

When the bright colours of the minstrel had disappeared from sight, Rimonay thudded her stick on the portal of the nearest cave.

'Oracle! Come out you senile puff of magic!' The ground rumbled and Rimonay steadied herself on a rock to stop toppling sideways. 'That's more like it. Come up and let me tell your fortune.'

The air in the entrance of the cave rippled. A stream of smoke sinuously issued from it to make a circlet about her silver hair.

'I'm getting bored with this,' warned Rimonay. 'There's a certain wizard in Lustreland entitled to the truth, and if you carry on like this I just might be the one to tell him it.'

The smoke dropped to the ground like a suddenly sinking soufflé and solidified into a large female with the nether end of a fish. From tail to ample chin, she shimmered with the neon radiance of a deep-sea ostracod.

'To what do we owe the honour of a visit from the First Minister of Lustreland? Like me to make a surprise appearance at the Crystal Mansion, would you?' the Oracle threatened.

'Sacred Sun forbid! The last time you were there you ensured Bruno became Second Minister.'

The Oracle's large face beamed. 'Ah yes, how is the little lad getting on?'

'You know damn well he's no longer little and is about to send us all into oblivion.'

'Oh dear. Well, we can't get everything right.'

'Oh yes you can. I know it was your idea of a joke.'

The Oracle chuckled.

'So let me tell you one of mine.' There was an evil cackle in Rimonay's tone.

The Oracle wasn't sure what she meant. Rimonay knew many things, but jokes weren't in her repertoire. 'Go on.'

Rimonay limped to a boulder and gingerly lowered herself onto it. 'Everyone is worried witless about being invaded by ogres.'

'Naturally, no one wants to get upwind of an army with halitosis.'

'The dragon can easily sort them out with or without Bruno's approval.'

'What? Flouting the constitution. Shame on you.'

'But we both know they're not the real threat, don't we.'

'Do we?'

'The ogres didn't think up the idea of an invasion by themselves - They wouldn't be able to work out how to get out of a paper bag unless you gave them a sharp rock.'

The Oracle was apprehensive about where this was leading. As it wasn't down an avenue of the deities' making, several shadowy forms joined her and lurked about the cave entrance like the smoke from a smouldering bonfire waiting for the cap to be pulled off the petrol can.

'You know about the Hurglabat?' accused the Oracle.

'I'm First Minister. I have access to the seeing pool. I'm well aware of the monster clinging to the underside of this domain.'

'Who else knows?'

'No one. I wouldn't dare tell them. Lustreland is beside itself with terror at the thought of ogres. If the population knew about this creature they would turn into paralysed jellyfish and make themselves all the more easier for the ogres to digest.'

'So what do you want us to do?'

'You know.'

'Why should we bother about Lustreland?'

Rimonay gave another disconcerting cackle. 'As this thing grows in strength, not even you will be able to stop it. When Lustreland is devoured, you will either have to find some other realm weak-minded enough to put up with you, or follow us into oblivion.'

'And you intend to destroy it?'

'Don't be absurd. There is only one entity who can do that.'

'Then what do you want from us?'

'The staff of the Ligh Tofrea Sun.'

The shadowy chorus behind the oracle took on bat like shapes with chromed wings, sour expressions on their silver faces.

'You are arrogant,' rasped a voice.

'No Lustrelander has the right to hold the staff of the Ligh Tofrea Sun,' declared another.

'Wrong!' interrupted Rimonay. 'By rights it should now be in the possession of a Lustrelander - the one you chose! The only reason it isn't is because the wretch wouldn't know what to do with it.'

There was a frantic exchange of alien voices.

The First Minister yawned. 'Oh come on. I'm an old woman. I'm getting tired. Don't fob me off with some yarn that the staff of the Ligh Tofrea Sun was another joke.'

The Oracle sounded genuinely offended. 'It was no joke. We knew what we were doing.'

'Pity no one else did. Well, do I get it?'

'You must pay a forfeit.'

'Naturally.'

'What can you offer?'

'A straight swap. My life when the staff is placed in the hands of the person it was intended for.'

There was a clatter of wings as the deities formed a canopy in which to debate the stark proposal.

Eventually they parted.

There, supported by the coils of smoke that had been the oracle, was the staff of the Ligh Tofrea Sun. Wreathed with ropes of shimmering tracery, it gleamed more brightly than goblin gold.

Deal done, the deities disappeared back into their caves.

Rimonay pulled herself up and reached for the magical staff. As her gnarled fingers closed about its shaft the glorious corona and decoration faded. Her own stick crumbled and fell to the ground in a pile of ashes and the staff of the Ligh Tofrea Sun replicated it in every worn detail, right down to where it had been splintered by the vigour with which she rapped the flagstones of the debating chamber.

CHAPTER 15

By the time the day of his concert arrived, Bernard was oddly disconcerted at not having had any more hallucinations, and feeling insecure enough to wonder if he would be letting down Clarey Ditton-Davis if he didn't manage to produce one. It didn't help that he still had no idea how to deal with the magisterial Minister Bruno if he did return without screwing off his own head first and demanding to know what the interloper was doing inside it.

Down Clutton had the only cattle market in the area and a history that could be traced back through several medieval houses. Otherwise it was too bland to be swamped with weekend executive homes. The centre of the county town was also permeated with the smell of sheep, cow and pig effluent where it had its weekly market, which would have offended those noses more accustomed to carbon monoxide fumes, air conditioning, and joss sticks. Though there was a small railway station - Down Clutton had only escaped the Beeching axe because the roads had been medieval as well.

Despite being suspended in historical aspic, the residents were reasonably friendly, unlike in some remote hamlets where it is considered a moral misjudgement to marry anyone further removed than a second cousin. The parish council considered evening entertainments somewhat anti Church and should be left to the pub and nightclub and their more cultured concerts, when held in council property, take place during the afternoon. (It also saved paying staff evening overtime.)

Having steeled himself to accept that he would be accompanied by the chorus of lowing cattle penned in the adjoining inn's courtyard, Bernard was just thankful none of them was a soprano.

To his relief Albert, the pianist who regularly accompanied him, had been able to make the trip out in his ancient Ford during one of the rare phases when it allowed its engine to turn over.

An audience driven inside more by the summer heat than love of music, packed the small town hall chamber where the timbers of the gallery steepled up to support an embossed ceiling in which every sound echoed, including the chirping of sparrows that had flown in through the open fanlights. The breeze from a huge fan at the side of the stage dislodged the odd sheet of music, much to the annoyance of Albert. But then, Albert could be annoyed at anything from brass candleholders to yellowing keys: when confronted by an electronic keyboard, had been known to bellow like an affronted dinosaur.

Having gone through the procedure of sorting his music into a totally different order to the one Bernard was going to sing in, then putting on his reading glasses to sort it into the right one, only to ignore it completely when playing, Albert was ready to begin. For all his eccentricity, the pianist was a brilliant accompanist for those singers with strong nerves, and the concert of lieder, Handel and two operatic arias was to be one of the best they had performed.

The audience were model listeners. Few were regular concert or opera goers and collectively held their breath until the last bar of every song. The extra applause after each individual item, although slowing, was refreshing. Bernard was encouraged enough to brave his patrons' company during the interval. Were he not so feeling so relaxed, he might have sought refuge in the ante-room when regaled with a story about a cow that could make musical noises through her milking equipment. He manfully managed to smile politely through gritted teeth whilst wishing the strangely intense woman wearing jodhpurs and woolly hat would go and relate her tales of the farmyard to someone else. The locals were aware of the local dairy farmer's repertoire and Bernard was not relieved of her company until an obliging waitress splashed white wine down the cleavage of her faded linen blouse.

All the time the bass baritone was wondering why Clarey Ditton-Davis hadn't introduced himself. He was even more puzzled when the aristocrat still hadn't appeared after the performance. Only when the encores were over did the usher hand him a note which requested that he take the short walk to the railway station. Half tempted to risk the local pub instead, Bernard it did has he was requested and stood by its white picket fence on the other side of a platform that had once borne the yearly tread of hundreds of herds of cows. He was wondering whether to catch the next train, suitcase or not, when a Jaguar with clouded windows and sizeable dent in its boot pulled into the space reserved for the local taxi.

This was not a meeting he was looking forward to.

An elegantly tall man stepped from the vintage car.

'Forgive me, but I wanted to be sure the press did not see us meet. Some local reporters are so desperate for copy at this time of year you could become headline news - and not as a visiting celebrity.'

Bernard quickly swallowed his indignation at the charismatic presence and smooth tenor voice. 'Mr Ditton-Davis? Where were you? I didn't see you in the hall?'

'I watched from the mayor's balcony. The acoustics up there are superb and the curtain conceals one from the audience as well as the stage. I do have to be careful, you see. Many local fathers believe what they read in the newspapers and are afraid my fancy might turn to their daughters. The less they see of me, the less it occurs to them.'

Bernard wasn't sure whether to hate the man right away or wait until his jealously went into third gear. 'I see.'

'Please join me in the car. I've already taken the liberty of stowing your suitcase.'

CHAPTER 16

Rimonay removed the cover from the diamond disc and went onto the balcony where she placed it on its stand and tilted it up to face the sky. At one time the rays of the mystical, unseen Ligh Tofrea Sun would shine through it, projecting a magical rainbow across the lawn below. Now the spectrum was barely visible.

Rimonay replaced the cover over the disc and scrutinised the bleached rooftops surrounding the Halls of Government. It seemed that everyone in Lustreland had decided to cook dinner at the same time and the smoke from their chimneys decorated the sky with a duvet of scrolls.

A certain dragon, bored at not knowing whether it was to be Lustreland's secret weapon, was looping the loop, puncturing turbulent holes through the smoke: as Sesame hadn't asked for anything in return for repelling the ogres, it felt rebuffed and belligerent.

The First Minister tried to recall how she had managed to get elected to this position. It was so long ago it was an impossible to remember what act of bravery or altruism had qualified her. Now she was too ancient to see any sense in either.

Rimonay took the disc inside and closed the shutters before opening the two enamelled doors of a recess. Her study was flooded with its ghostly, pink light. Dimensions not dreamt of by other Lustrelanders swam in the patterns cast about the alcove's alabaster walls by the seeing pool.

The First Minister stood and concentrated. Years ago, her mind could immediately bring into focus the realm she wanted to view. Now, just visualising them was becoming harder. But it was vital to summon up the dimension she had banished Bruno to. However aggravating, pompous and belligerent her Second Minister, it felt odd without him, as though a voracious vacuum demanded to be filled. Being unable to bring him back after so publicly sending him away would damage Rimonay's reputation for infallibility and, worse still, persuade the realm of his alter ego that fairies actually existed. There was only a short window of time left for her plan to work. Many a witch and warlock were waiting for the chance to strand Bruno in another dimension so they could propose a member of the Mystic Trine for his position. Rimonay could only hope that the Second Minister's host in this alien dimension wouldn't manage to expel him before he could be safely returned to Lustreland.

Poor Bruno, if he couldn't cope with dragons, goodness knows what he would make of a Rottweiler when he was only fourteen inches high.

In the pink glow of the seeing pool, Lustreland's nearest neighbour swam into view. On the other side of Darkle Deeps was the Black Ocean stabbed by the fierce mountainous peaks of Vulcanus. Even from such a distance its lakes of flaming lava and skyline illuminated by perpetual volcanic eruptions looked like a nasty accident at a firework display. The shores were octagonal pillars of lava cooled rapidly by the sea where not even a griffin would contemplate nesting, and the waves lapping its shores boiled away any bacteria that had the temerity to try and survive. Many believed that dragons came from the heart of Vulcanus. But nothing could live there now, even trolls, including the basalt ones that guarded the Halls of Government.

On the other side of Lustreland, beyond the woods and vast canyon studded with the fossils of extinct sea monsters, was Frozonia; high and crowned with turrets of ice. The domain was populated by winged antelope with anti freeze for blood, distant relatives of the more refined unicorns who preferred their mists to be temperate. An ancient race of elves had carved their likenesses into the cliffs of ice before embracing extinction, and their artefacts were frequently found on the market stalls of Dipnit, the land below the towering ice terraces.

Warmed by oceanic currents, Dipnit was fertile, though the light was equally shared with darkness. Rimonay wished Lustrelanders could realise how fortunate they were to have the permanence of the Ligh Tofrea Sun.

Without warning, the monstrous realm of Galleraya invaded the seeing pool. This parasitic domain wandered dimensions, voraciously taking bites from other realms to add to its sky born dungeon. In its deceptively benign bubbles were trapped people; elfin to ogre, books; open and shut, exotic and pulp; flowers from exotic land, alien animals, and even small buildings; all suspended in clear cells as though stored in a clear honey comb by cosmic bees. The First Minister had consistently found the pickled reality of Galleraya difficult to cope with. Her greatest fear was that it could swallow Bruno while she was trying to retrieve him. The parasitic hive existed nowhere and everywhere, prowling in acquisitive vampire fashion, capturing the breeze to create bubbles throughout its nebulous labyrinth. Once absorbed, there was no escape from its sinister prison. It was the black hole of Lustreland's universe. Rimonay noted sourly that she had never seen a witch or warlock suspended in its bubble filled prison; plenty of startled goblins, hibernating trolls, and the occasional sprite who should have been quicker. Nothing was too extraordinary or malign enough to give Galleraya indigestion.

Rimonay suddenly noticed someone she knew well; the only ogre to come out of Darkle Deeps and crave education. The tutors had laughed at the idea to begin with, but Hada Gonn had been no ordinary ogre. It was everyone's tragedy that he now lay slumbering in one of the bubbles that filled the strange dominion.

With an effort, Rimonay pushed aside the image. She had to make way for a greater monstrosity. Galleraya only snatched morsels of their dimension, but there was a more terribly entity waiting to absorb everything in it.

The First Minister had detected distortions in the lay of Lustreland some while ago. Using the seeing pool to peer below her realm she found a horror beyond comprehension. Like a massive tick, the Hurglabat had clamped itself to the underside of Darkle Deeps, dragging it even deeper. There it had been biding its time for the opportunity to devour Lustreland. Now it could happen. The population had become so self-obsessed and lost the ability to notice anything while the Ligh Tofrea Sun's light was fading fast.

The Hurglabat was the last remaining reason why Rimonay could not die - just yet.

CHAPTER 17

Apart from being elegantly tall, Clarey Ditton-Davis had the sort of style that only comes with practise or enough wealth to not worry about what others thought. He was remarkably good looking in his refined way, and without the bronzed complexion some of society's elite wear like a status symbol. It was evident to Bernard why women would cluster round this honey pot like enthusiast bees. The thought that his wife was a close friend of the glamorous creature would have angered a lesser man, but Clarey's easy manner neutralised the opportunity for any tantrums on Bernard's part. The singer was susceptible to flattery, and having an elegant, intelligent man ladle praise on his sublime bass baritone voice as he chauffeured him to his country home gave Bernard's ego a level of reassurance not even his agent could manage.

After passing the gatehouse, the vintage Jaguar drove on through woodland, to a meadow where a Dutch barn came into view. Beyond that, the mansion's chimney stacks loomed over the treetops.

The Ditton-Davis country seat was the equal of any other stately home, and with that air of polite decomposition that begged for expensive maintenance. Its grounds were somewhat disorderly, which were tended just enough to suit its residents without the planting and manicuring tourists would expect. The occasional puckish face peeping from behind a privet hedge and low crumbling wall added an Alice in Wonderland touch. Bernard didn't comment. He suspected that these sprites belonged to Clarey's illegitimate brood which the press were forever getting indignant about. How many was he supposed to have sired to date? Six? Twelve? Twenty? Like the male ostrich, Clarey raised his own progeny regardless of which mother had left her eggs in the nest; he could afford to.

The courtyard of the front portico had been given over to a play area and garden. There was no way for a car to reach the entrance without knocking down the safety gate and committing infanticide, so the Jaguar was left by the stables housing a resentful grey mare and two small ponies, which probably explained the hoof shaped dent in the car's boot.

A small, neatly dressed man was trying to herd several children out of their playground like a recalcitrant flock of geese.

'Tim, Tinker, Anne, Teddy, Rowland, Matthew - stop doing that!' he scolded in a tired voice as they hurtled down a slide in a giggling crocodile.

Bernard and Clarey stood aside until the unruly gaggle had been ushered up the wide steps into the main hall. Before following them in, the singer noticed the bemused expression of a gardener. The old fellow scratched his stubbly chin as though pondering on a beetle race, and then took off his cap to scratch a stubbly, sunburned head. The rustic, decaying elegance of it all was enough to make Bernard wonder what was going to confront him inside the main door. Given the peculiar nature of his own hallucinations, he resolved to avoid looking glasses and rabbit holes.

The reception hall was huge, enough to have doubled as a ballroom at one time; now it was cluttered with adults' toys, well out of reach from infant hands. Every available alcove contained antique musical instruments, many unfamiliar to Bernard's experienced eye; some looked ancient enough for their owners to have missed the Ark. There was also an equally unlikely collection of potted vines doing their utmost to colonise the imperious staircase in an attempt to reach the domed skylight high above.

And at the centre of this glorious disorder stood Mrs Porter. By her severe look of disapproval and fitted, designer two-piece it was easy to deduce that she was neither the collector nor arranger of the hall's decor.

The small man, having turned his flock loose in an adjoining room filled with ceramics and other breakable valuables, came back and offered to carry Bernard's suitcase up the stairs. The guest thought that leaving a roomful of antiques and infants under the supervision of a 12-year-old was somewhat risky. He assumed that the establishment possessed a generous stock of Elastoplast and comprehensive contents insurance. Having a physique that should have been able to shoulder anything that fell from Stonehenge, Bernard politely declined the offer of help. He hoped it hadn't been made because of a complex attack of dry rot on the stairs or some resident ghost waiting to pounce.

Clarey Ditton-Davis and the small man escorted Bernard into a large, airy bedroom overlooking parkland.

Clarey discreetly closed the door behind them and introduced his diminutive friend. 'This is Alex, but we call him Mouse.'

The small man's turned up nose seemed to twitch as he flickered a wide, friendly smile. He was a strange creature with laughing grey eyes and hands perpetually in motion whenever he spoke in a soft, agreeable voice. Bernard fancied he should have made an excellent flute player.

'My secretary, Mrs Porter, is unable to stand the sight of Mouse,' Clarey announced so laconically Bernard was unable to take his words in immediately. 'He is an inoffensive little rabbit, but something has made her take such a dislike to him that we avoid letting them be in each others' company for too long.'

Bernard was puzzled that anyone would dislike the small man as neatly dressed as an expensive teddy bear, and could only wonder what concealed facet of his nature induced the hostility that merited such a dire warning. He was not to be enlightened, however.

'I am telling you this in case you witness any unfortunate encounters of the personal kind. I do not like guests to be embarrassed in my house. Mouse has offered to leave, but I won't hear of it. He is a very dear friend of mine.'

'Of course,' muttered Bernard. He really wanted to ask why he didn't sack his secretary instead.

He was going to learn the answer to that soon enough.

CHAPTER 18

Since being thrown out of the Council's debating chamber for trying to prevent the Second Minister's banishment, Wizard Qulio decided to keep his head down. He knew that there were several members of the Mystic Trine who would have done far worse to him for merely being able to understand Bruno without disappearing in a blue flash of frustration. Despite making a great effort, even the president of the equal opportunities committee had to admit that empathy did not come easily in he Second Minister's case. The goblin advised Qulio to stay in the woods with his friend, Juniper, and the changelings she looked after, but the wizard saw no point in drawing unwelcome attention to her as well.

Instead, he roamed places his better sense told him to avoid, only to find he was dangerously near Deity Rock. The wizard had a better reason than most to give it a wide detour and didn't realise how close he was until he saw the granite beetle guarding the boundary of the deities' glade.

About to take to his heels, Qulio heard the tittering of sprites in a nearby thicket. Despite the risk of it being a cave deity ambush, his curiosity urged him to silently go over and find out what they were up to.

Few sprites were substantial enough to risk the caprice of the local residents and these two, who turned out to be the attendants of the First Minister, were no exception, which was probably why they were waiting a safe distance from their caves, playing jacks with semi precious stones that in balmier days had been ladybirds.

If Qulio's commonsense had overruled curiosity he would have left then, but he hesitated just long enough to see Rimonay slashing at the bushes in her path as she hobbled past the granite beetle. Was it Qulio's imagination, or were the branches ducking out of her way? More disconcerting, Rimonay must have been fraternising with cave deities. This meant trouble. At first the wizard was just relieved that it wasn't aimed in his direction and secretly watched. After receiving some abuse for fluttering off on arrival, the tree sprites helped the First Minister to her carriage drawn by a slow, old unicorn.

As the wheels crunched away on the rough track Qulio came from his hiding place. Did the First Minister's secret rendezvous at Deity Rock have something to do with Bruno? Perhaps Rimonay had been upbraiding the Oracle for selecting him as Second Minister all that time ago - though wasn't likely. Bruno, with his sharp sense of right and wrong, had been a consistent, stalwart servant of government for all his bombastic swings of mood. He just had this abhorrence of dragons. It was inevitable he would blunder into trouble over one sooner or later. Unfortunately it had to be Sesame, one of the easiest going creatures in Rara Avis Ridge.

Qulio didn't want to know what Rimonay was up to and he would have been powerless to do anything about it if he did, so when the carriage was out of sight he turned to follow the same track.

Without warning a minstrel stepped from behind the granite beetle. She was as surprised at the sight of the wizard as he was to see her. They gazed at each other apprehensively. Despite being widely travelled, she had never encountered anyone quite like him before. A contradiction on two legs, Qulio was tall and very lean, a voluminous gown concealing his thinness, only apparent by the way his white beard fringed the contours of his face, scarcely encroaching on it. Because of the wizard's advancing years, it was strange to suddenly notice the limpid youthfulness in eyes too clear and pale to be old. Despite the billowing hair and soft wavy beard that reached his knees, Qulio wore the mantle of his age like a fish would feathers. A wide brimmed hat, which the wizard would only remove when in friendly company, shadowed many of these contradictions from critical eyes. Timidity was the only aura he reflected, and that was all the more noticeable because of his height.

Having taken in the sight of the unlikely wizard, the minstrel smiled.

'Sorry, didn't mean to startle you,' she apologised before realising that he always wore that expression.

'It's dangerous here,' warned Qulio. 'Be careful not to wander into the cave deities' glade.'

'I'm foreign in these parts,' Crystabel explained. 'Probably should pay more attention to where I'm going. What are you doing here?'

'Wasn't concentrating on where I was going,' admitted Qulio. 'Something on my mind.'

Crystabel followed as he hastened away. 'Really. Why not tell me about it? No one in these parts wants to listen to my songs.'

'It was just something to do with the Second Minister.'

The minstrel took the lead along the track, doing skips and half turns as she went.

'Friend of yours?'

'Yes. He's an honest soul with a stout heart, yet can be very stubborn. That's why he's been banished.'

'Sounds an odd sort of way to treat a Second Minister? But then, I've known stranger things in some of the realms I've passed through. In one kingdom they select their rulers by measuring how accurately candidates can toss a coin into the clog of the last ruler's daughter - though most others just slog it out with swords and axes.' Qulio looked horrified so she assured him, 'Don't know how lucky you are here. You're pretty isolated, aren't you?'

Qulio nodded. 'Yes, I suppose we are. We've always depended on the oracle to select candidates for the important positions and we just vote for them.'

'What made the oracle choose this Bruno?'

Now a safe distance from Deity rock, Qulio sank onto a mossy bank to catch his breath. The minstrel sat cross-legged on the ground in front of him, anticipating material for yet another ballad.

'Bruno was brought up by a truffle gatherer and his hog. He was still a youth when he encountered this giant who had blundered into Lustreland. She wore the beards of several ogres on her belt and had got it into her head that Lustreland was swimming in jewels and gold. She was in the process of raiding a goblin mine - well, trying to get her arm down its lift shaft - when Bruno came out of the wood and saw her. He had just done a profitable trade with the goblins who have a weakness for truffles, so he decided to take on the giant.'

Crystabel laughed in disbelief. 'What? A mere youth?'

'There was never anything "mere" about Bruno. 'At first, the giant wanted to eat his pig and grind its owner to pulp, yet Bruno somehow managed to persuade her that she had her arm down a salt mine. Not one of the brightest giants. He appealed to the giant's greed and claimed that the really precious gems could only be found in the deepest places. She demanded that Bruno take her to one. After explaining that it was too far for him to walk, the giant lifted him onto her shoulder and told him to point the way.

'Several flattened hamlets later, they reached the far side of Lustreland where the woodland ends and the ground drops away into infinity. "Down there", Bruno told the giant. The giant wasn't that stupid however, so she lowered Bruno over the side on the rope she had stolen from the winding gear in the goblins' mine. When he was out of her sight he crawled into a cave in the rock face, released himself, and then weighted the rope with a rock so the giant didn't feel it go slack and become suspicious.' Qulio's insecurity made him a fancy that the minstrel's eyes were glazing over, though in fact she was committing every detail of the adventure to memory. 'I'm not boring you, am I?'

'Goodness no. There's a ballad in this somewhere.'

Warming to the novelty of being appreciated, Qulio went on. 'Bruno searched the cave and found a dragon's egg shining in the darkness. It rippled with veins of fiery fluorescence in a nest of branches and roc feathers. He quickly tied together a rough net with some creepers, rolled the egg into it and used it to replace the rock weight. He tugged the rope then swung the net out so the giant could see the egg sparkling far below. She quickly pulled it up. As she did so, the dragon that had laid it returned. Just as the giant had the egg in her clutches, it swooped. Fire blazing and talons drawn, it knocked her into the abyss. She's probably still falling.'

'How did Bruno get back up?'

'As the egg fell he managed to catch the net. He held the egg over the chasm and the dragon had no option but to save him as well as its unhatched offspring. Needless to say, it wasn't very happy. It takes a dragon ages to produce an egg.

'It picked Bruno up in a claw and flew him back to Lustreland where it dropped him from an unfortunate height onto the spoil from the goblins' tunnels. They were so elated at their mine being saved they decked his rough tunic in jewels, trimmed his hair and paraded him off to the oracle who used to reside in the Crystal Mansion. Being an oracle, she already knew what had happened and declared that he be trained for the position of Second Minister.'

'Wasn't there any other vacancy? Like imperial rounder-up of warthogs?'

Qulio combed his beard thoughtfully with his fingers. 'We've never had royalty - every other citizen entity you can imagine - but never the crowned sort. Our democracy seemed to work quite well until...' His words tailed off as the futility of it all overwhelmed him. 'And, of course, First Minister had already been taken.'

'As he was so brave, wouldn't he have made a better soldier?'

'Soldier? Why a soldier?'

'Sorry, you don't have them here either, do you?'

Qulio's expression became distant as he contemplated the price Lustreland was going to pay for being too civilised. 'That's why we're about to be overrun by an army of ogres.'

'Pity your government didn't think of putting Bruno in a chariot and pointing it in their direction.' Crystabel wondered why his face fell. 'What's the matter?'

'I'm not so sure anyone is going to see Bruno again.'

Crystabel jumped up and strummed her lute. 'Of course you will, whether you want to or not.'

Qulio sighed. He had been wrong so many times, why shouldn't a mere minstrel be right.

CHAPTER 19

Bernard liked children. And, inexplicably, they appeared to like Bernard.

Despite his first impression that there were dozens of young people swarming through the mansion and its grounds, Clarey's household only had six; two belonged to the cook, one to a housemaid, and Clarey's three who were called Tim, Tinker and Teddy.

The next day the hyperactive brood inveigled their guest into never ending games, despite Clarey's intention to show him his musical instrument collection and Mouse's efforts to explain the curious habits of his exotic vines. Mrs Porter eventually intimidated the brood to bed in a manner that could have driven a flock of Little Lord Fauntleroys to rebel. Bernard found the woman's behaviour strange and he half expected her, like a tweed suited Miss Whiplash, to order him upstairs after them.

Despite his better judgement, the guest tentatively pointed out to the woman that they were only children after all.

Mrs Porter explained coolly in a tone that suggested his visitor's status was little higher than the feral pigeons roosting in the stables, 'They would never have come into being at all if Mr Ditton-Davis did not have money. '

Bernard had never learnt when to keep his mouth shut. 'What does that have to do with anything?'

'Their mothers chased after him, well aware of the consequences. They never wanted the resulting children, so the only person they now know as "mother" is that simpering little rodent who follows him around like a lap dog. Now please excuse me. I have work to do.' With that mixed metaphor, she stalked off haughtily in a way that was an insult to the cut of her expensive two-piece.

Bernard was quite deflated by the sharpness of her tongue and wouldn't have been able to answer had she waited for a reply. Well aware he should have minded his own business, he decided not to mention the conversation to Clarey, though it did make him wonder all the more why he put up with her in the easygoing household. Inevitably he began to compare Mrs Porter with another forceful woman, Indrina. He was compelled to admit that he preferred his wife. However independent, complacent and intimidating Indrina could be, she didn't quite have the poise of a polar bear guarding its ice floe.

Not daring to admit to himself how lucky he had been in marrying her, Bernard braked the train of thought before it plunged off the plateau of his self-esteem. He much preferred others to massage his vulnerable ego with flattery.

By the time Clarey had shown the singer his musical instrument collection and Mouse had given him a tour of his exotic vines, Bernard's mind was buzzing with the contradictions between the real Clarey Ditton-Davis and the things the gossip magazines wrote about him. Despite himself, he had the horrible feeling Indrina might have been right yet again. After all, there was no crime in rearing children, even out of wedlock, as long as they were cared for. And Clarey could not have been a more caring father, or Mouse a more caring mother.

Bernard was still pondering over the conundrums of the day and putting his own problem to the back of his mind until that evening when Clarey discreetly reminded him, 'Don't forget that there is a bell pull by your bed if you have any "visitors" during the night.'

Bernard gazed into his second brandy and wondered if his condition really merited that much concern. 'Thank you, but I'm sure I will sleep soundly enough.'

'You don't sleep walk do you?' Mouse chipped in.

'Goodness no. Indrina would have soon let me know if I did.'

'Good. Because it's so close, Alice opened the French windows in your room. From your balcony you could walk straight down the fire escape into the park. We would have the deuce of a job finding you if you got lost.'

'Mouse thinks of the impossible as well as the unlikely. At one time he even wanted to tag the children,' explained Clarey.

'Why not? They're always one jump ahead of you. Tinker would have caught a train to London if Tom Harrison hadn't noticed and immediately brought her back in his taxi. I'm going to take a last look at ours now. After an attack of frosty features there are always a few tears.' Mouse finished his tonic water and bustled out, leaving a strange stillness as though every door in the building had silently closed.

Bernard continued to gaze into his glass.

'Penny for your thoughts,' said Clarey.

Bernard smiled weakly. He suspected that the aristocrat already knew most of them. For a reputedly amorous man not much past thirty, Clarey seemed to have the perceptions of an older person more given to philosophical reflection than romantic urges. In Clarey's cool, milky eyes was mature wisdom and unfathomable depths not common in the superficial makeup of the promiscuous. Bernard sensed that the problem with his doppelganger had been firmly grasped by a sympathetic spirit.

His host gave a sphinx like smile. 'Don't worry about ghosts, mine or yours. Sometimes things can momentarily stray. In the end, though, everything has its time and place.'

'You believe that people have their own personal ghosts?'

'Nature probably made it compulsory.'

'The thought makes my flesh creep. Why should we need to inhabit other dimensions? This one is complicated enough.'

'Perhaps this is only a minor reality.'

'I know others think I'm pretty dense - and stubborn,' Bernard admitted reluctantly. 'The mould was set before I could do anything about it.' He shrugged optimistically. 'I might be a genius somewhere else.'

'You don't need to be,' reassured Clarey. 'With a voice like yours you never need apologise.'

Bernard smiled wryly. For once he didn't mind being humoured like a confused adolescent.

'There is a solution to every problem,' hinted Clarey. 'Every problem which will step out into the open and reveal itself, that is.'

Bernard was taken aback. 'You really believe that I'm sane, don't you?'

'Why shouldn't I?'

'Because that must also mean you believe in fairies.'

'And the Green Man, Robin Goodfellow, Queen Mab, and Morgana Le Fay.'

'But they're ...'

'Fairies. Giving elemental spirits collective names our children can understand does not mean that our ancestors regarded them as harmless phantoms.'

'I don't want to exist in another dimension, especially the one of that bombastic bully who burst through to this world. He must have discovered a few loose molecules in my brain to place his shoulder against - and wham!' Bernard caught his breath. 'He scared the wits out of me, Clarey. Who can he be for God's sake?'

Clarey went to a Chinese cabinet exotic enough to house half a dozen lung dragon eggs. He pushed and pulled several pieces of a wooden, childproof lock and opened the lacquered doors. Bernard recalled the cabinet of wonders his friend Peter had. His was full of alcohol, petit fours, and Cuban cigars. Behind the inlaid doors of Clarey's cabinet were glass bottles pearlised with age, rolled leaf packages that could have come from prehistoric tombs, and small pots with stoppers that flashed like cut gems in the sudden light.

'Have you ever thought about taking a hallucinatory drug?'

Bernard was surprised at the question. 'Surely that would make matters worse?'

'Not with the one I have in mind. It's so rare it doesn't have a name. I learnt about it in a Swiss clinic.'

Bernard didn't think to ask why Clarey had needed to attend a Swiss clinic. 'Go on?'

The tall man reached inside the cabinet, his sleeve spangled with rainbow flecks of light as his fingers closed over a small bottle. 'Strictly speaking, it doesn't make you hallucinate, just releases your consciousness from your body for a short while.'

'You mean astral projection?'

Clarey was surprised that his guest was familiar with the term and assumed it had cropped up in some opera or other. 'You may call it that. It's relatively harmless and very effective for stress. Unfortunately it is so expensive it will never be prescribed on the National Health.'

To Bernard, this sounded like the sort of mysticism Indrina's great grandfather went in for. It alarmed the singer. He had met this in-law when he was first married. The old man must have been a hundred and looked like a hammered copper effigy, not quite dead, not quite alive, his eyes glittering like the facets on the bottle Clarey held.

'I'm sure there are more deserving causes than me who could use it.'

Clarey sensed the horror Bernard had of the mystical labyrinth, however often he might have been obliged to sing about it. 'No, no. I'm suggesting a tiny dose which would only have effect for a matter of seconds, just long enough to expel your consciousness and, with it, the entity that takes you over.' He chuckled. 'You might have to chance which one of you made it back first, though.' Clarey immediately realised that he shouldn't have said that to a guest already paralysed by apprehension.

'Do you believe I was really taken over by this doppelganger?'

'Who's to say you weren't? I respect your integrity as much as I admire your voice.'

The flattery worked. Bernard went up to bed gingerly clutching a wineglass containing a dilute dose of the unnamed drug which he placed under the bedside lamp.

CHAPTER 20

The ogres didn't bother to search for Hada Gonn. They told Jobaloba that he had fallen into a lake of pitch.

Visiting goblin miners were making good progress in opening up another seam in the dinosaur bone mines and were looking forward to being paid generously from the stash of gems which the ogre chief used to stud his rusty armour. Even unpolished, their market price would more than compensate them for the sleepless nights breathing in tar fumes and listening to some underground anomaly gurgling in its sleep.

After his shift one adventurous goblin, who was curious about the sound, took a pick and set off to find out what was causing it. Jek Mun followed his instincts to the border of Darkle Deeps and Rara Avis Ridge. He peered down several holes honeycombing the tar. This was where the gurgling came from. Then he backed away from the foul miasma that rose up.

The Hurglabat was aware of Jek Mun's presence, which was no more intrusive than a gofferhog. It only paid attention to ogres hammering their way across the semi set pitch lakes or Kot Kut asking for divine assistance. So the goblin passed unmolested, too sure-footed to tumble down any hole that might have suddenly opened up before him.

Then he came across that ogre sized knapsack coated in a fine film of something obnoxious. Jek Mun riffled through its contents to find the usual emergency ration of dried jellyfish and flask of rancid water. But then the goblin pulled out something so unlikely, he wondered if it could have belonged to an ogre after all. In his hands he held a dog-eared volume printed in Lustreland, "The Nature of Divine Light". This was not elementary reading. Then he found a notebook bound in wood. It contained several maps labelled in a bold hand, which he was able to read because of his multilingual skills needed to deal with the ogres.

Jek Mun replaced the other items just in case he became hungry enough to risk eating the dried jellyfish. He tied knots in the knapsack's straps to shorten them, and then swung it onto his shoulder: being a miner, he could have managed twice its weight.

The goblin made his way towards Rara Avis Ridge, reading the notebook containing descriptions and maps of domains he had never heard of, yet which this determined ogre had managed to reach. Miners knew their limitations and felt safer burrowing in their own back yard. However, Jek Mun had become tired of their self-elected leader, Flunkin, giving orders to engage in the mindless tunnelling that would only make him richer and their hands more callused.

The goblin had heard of Vulcanus and decided not to head in that direction. He was more interested in the magic realm that was supposed to exist inside the mountain range of Rara Avis Ridge. No one had ever found a way into the subterranean domain and the creatures living on the Ridge couldn't have been less interested in its existence. But there in the notebook, clearly marked, was the entrance Hada Gonn had discovered.

The goblin didn't expect to make his fortune by following the map; he was just curious, like a bored cat.

The secret opening to the magic realm was well hidden. The miner used his rope and a crampon to lower himself down a chimney of rock and into a narrow tunnel winding deep into the mountain's depths.

Jek Mun lit the lamp on his helmet and set off.

This might have been a giant's sewer system, but there was no stench. Then the tunnel widened. Ahead was an ominous glow. The miner hesitated and, anticipating noxious gases, struck out his lamp. He needn't have worried, the light increased and the air became fresh as though he had passed through a waterfall.

The goblin walked into a cavern overlooking a mysterious realm illuminated by huge glow stones in its high ceiling. It was vast, filling the mountainous interior of Rara Avis Ridge. Jek Mun put down the ogre's knapsack to stand and stare. Spread out below him was a magical vista of meadows, woods, and waterfalls. Exotic animals grazed and gambolled and large ponderous birds flapped leisurely across the subterranean sky.

Hada Gonn had not been fantasising.

The miner reached out to pluck a ripe fruit from a tree growing from the rock face. It surely couldn't be poisonous? Not down here. He took a bite. It was as sweet as anything he had tasted in Lustreland. There would be no need for the dried jellyfish after all

Before wandering deeper into the magic realm, Jek Mun showered under a waterfall. Invigorated, though still overwhelmed by his discovery, the goblin had to make a decision. If he told the other miners about this realm they would only barge in, tunnel everywhere for precious gems and leave tons of spoil all over the place.

Should he tell the First Minister of Lustreland? No, she probably already knew about it and was wisely keeping quiet.

Why did he need to return to the mines, and back to the nagging father who had betrothed him to a goblin he had consistently disliked since his youth? And he still had Hada Gonn's notebook. Wherever the young ogre had got to, it was unlikely he had any more use for the maps. With it, Jek Mun could explore the Universe - or at least the parts where the local inhabitants didn't regard goblins as a side dish.

The miner was just about to spread out Hada Gonn's blanket for a nap under the ceiling's warm glow when the ground shuddered. It was followed by another shudder twice as violent. He quickly repacked the ogre's knapsack and dashed back up to the cavern.

Reading underground movements was second nature to Jek Mun, but this tremor made him wonder what had been tracking his progress. Had he known that he had woken a huge parasitic monster's interest in the underground paradise, he would have taken a different route, even one that led to Frozonia.

But his misgivings were too late. Unsure what was going to happen, Jek Mun waited in trepidation. It wasn't long before a massive tentacle lunged up through the subterranean realm in a rain of boulders and soil. It uprooted trees and demolished the ancient rock-faces down which waterfalls tumbled. The large glow stones were shaken from the high ceiling and crashed down onto the lush pastures.

There was an enraged roar as the tentacle shrivelled at being exposed to light. But the damage was done and the magical realm now exposed for the Hurglabat to consume as darkness descended.

Animals stampeded up to the safety of the cavern where they and Jek Mun watched the world cave in below them. The adjoining tunnels were rapidly crowded with terrified wildlife.

By the light of his lamp, the miner hastily searched through Hada Gonn's notebook. There was a map showing the route to an underground ocean. Marked clearly was a large galleon moored beside it. If the vessel had been made by a long dead race it must have been rotten by now, but there was nothing else for it. The realm below was now filled with the writhing tentacles of the Hurglabat sweeping away trees and meadows and devouring the magic realm like a monstrous gofferhog. The ground continued to shake and ceiling crumble, telling the miner that the entrance he had discovered must have collapsed.

So Jek Mun sped down the dimly fluorescing passages indicated in the notebook and the animals followed the light on his helmet. The more distance they put between them and the devastated magic realm, the quieter the tremors became until thy saw a pale blue glow ahead and felt the sweet zephyrs of an ocean permeating the air.

Reaching to the underground horizon of another vast cavern was a blue ocean gleaming under a ceiling of glow stones and, nestling against a decaying jetty, an ancient ship.

Jek Mun boarded the galleon and checked its sea worthiness. The hull had been well primed with pitch from Darkle Deeps and the old timbers were still securely bonded together.

The miner didn't know how he was going to sail the hulk on his own, but there was nowhere else to go. It would not be long before the monster devouring the magic realm invaded the caverns leading to the ocean.

The Hurglabat was annoyed that the animals had fled and there was little left in the underground domain to satisfy its rapacious appetite. After losing a tentacle to the light of the glow stones, it believed it at least deserved a small snack for the loss of the appendage.

The monster detected the trail of the fleeing animals and tentatively probed the passages radiating from the magic realm. There was enough water to protect it from the light.

Hada Gonn's map gave no indication of where the current would take them, but Jek Mun pushed out planks so the animals could join him on the galleon all of the same: if he was going to be sucked into a whirlpool or become becalmed in the middle of an underground ocean, he preferred to have company; at least some of them might have been able to swim to safety.

As soon as the galleon was loaded, Jek Mun cast off its mooring ropes. A gentle current eased the craft away from the jetty and pushed it out onto the subterranean waters.

Some distance from the shore the water became choppier, like a terrestrial ocean's. Not knowing where the wind was coming from, Jek Mun wondered if he should try to lower the sails. They were no doubt rotten, and he would probably fall from the rigging before he had worked out how to release them anyway. Tunnelling was his business, not sailoring.

High on a mast, one of the creatures held wide its orange scaled wings and cawed. The other animals became excited, filling the galleon with howls, grunts and whinnying. This attracted the attention of the voracious Hurglabat waiting below the sea's bedrock.

It pushed up an exploratory tentacle, creating a large wave.

Jek Mun felt the breeze of another sea on his face and tried to quieten the creatures as the Hurglabat probed the galleon's hull. Fortunately this pushed it out of the cavern into bright sunlight. By the time the monster made its move, miner and animals were afloat on an ocean of emerald green.

A tentacle lunged from the water to drag down the galleon.

Daylight was death to the Hurglabat's ooze and a scream of pain filled the new domain they had sailed into.

Horrified, Jek Mun and the animals watched the huge limb shrivel.

The water calmed. The sky was filled with pearl like clouds and, flying towards them, was a large, kite-shaped creature without a head.

CHAPTER 21

It was more difficult to sleep than Bernard had anticipated. Perhaps the two glasses of brandy hadn't helped. So, with the air circulating from the open French windows, he lay in the moonlight counting herons on the wallpaper.

He had just started to doze off when he was struck by a surge of icy terror.

His monstrous doppelganger was back!

Unable to tell whether he was awake or dreaming, Bernard attempted to clutch the bell rope, but his fingers kept closing around nothing. Then there was the sickening feeling of falling, merging with the mattress, and the overwhelming sensation of dreaming that he was lying in bed wide awake. He had to gain control before Minister Bruno invaded his mind again.

His blood pressure shot up with panic and real sensations at last flowed through his fingers.

The wineglass containing Clarey's potion was nearest. Bernard swallowed the draught before he lost control again. At first he was filled with a strange calmness, like a clam watching a predatory octopus pass by.

Without warning his shell was prised open. With a sudden convulsion, Bernard felt as though part of him had been wrenched from his body. He almost fainted at the thought of his entrails being splashed over the duvet but forced himself to sit up and put on the bedside light.

The only thing dampening the bed clothes was perspiration. The duvet was piled in a heap and fitted sheet in a tangle. Bernard wondered whether anyone would hear if he screamed, and then lunged for the bell rope. He missed as a furious voice came from the pile of bedclothes.

'You fool! You stupid imbecile!'

Unable to believe another part of his anatomy had learnt how to speak, let alone heap abuse on him, Bernard snatched away the duvet as though it was concealing a scorpion.

Under it was Minister Bruno.

He was little taller than fourteen inches and wearing a long robe that partially concealed voluminous trousers gathered at the ankle. The tassels of the orange girdle securing the robe to the high chested body reached down to slippers that should have been worn on daintier feet. His natural hairline began was on the top of his skull as though it had been pushed there by the habit of him arrogantly throwing his head back.

'You idiot!' The voice would have been deafening coming from a full size bass baritone. 'Let me back at once!'

Did Jonathan Swift experience something like this before coming up with Gulliver's Travels? Did that satirist have a miniature alter ego that woke him in the middle of the night to spit venom?

Bernard gawped in amazement for some time before he could respond. 'What the hell are you?'

The interloper's eyes glowered like an indignant owl's. 'Minister Bruno, you buffoon! Now stop being such a plebeian idiot and let me back!'

Rage overtook terror. 'Let you back! This is my body! My brain! Not a repository for every waif and stray who blunders about the ether! I should chuck you off the balcony!' Bernard made a grab at the small bundle of pomposity. Something pricked his hand viciously and he retracted it with a yelp of surprise. 'You hellish little..!'

Bruno was clutching a knife in proportion to his size, though quite effective. 'I am not usually violent, nor is any other Lustrelander, unlike you humans. I am only allowed to carry a weapon because of my rank, but ...'

'But what, you sawn off miscreant? I'll give you threaten me!' Bernard snatched Bruno up, his large hand encircling the Minister's trunk and pinning his arms to his sides to save his fingers from further attack. The resulting abuse more than made up for that.

'You limp-brained offspring of a goblin! Are you trying to kill us!?'

'Kill us? No, but one of us is going to be rattled about quite a bit.' Bernard at last gave himself a few seconds to collect his wits before he did something totally irrational. 'What, or who, the devil are you?'

Bruno stopped panting in anger and the enraged flush slowly seeped from his golden skin at the realisation that this was one argument he was unable to win. Compromise was not in his nature, but when some giant who urgently wants an explanation has you clasped in his massive fist, the learning process can be surprisingly fast.

'You really don't know who I am?'

'No. Tell me?'

A long silence followed. Given how loquacious the miniature tornado had been, especially with abuse, Bernard suspected that this was something he would be better off not knowing. Unfortunately his tongue was stuck to the roof of his mouth and would not retract the question.

Bruno took a deep breath. 'We are the same person. I am your other self.'

Bernard was slapped by the wet hand of sickening truth and slackened his grip. 'Rot!'

'Kill me and you would be killing yourself.'

'Kill you? I couldn't wring a chicken's neck. I couldn't even go with Aurora to the vet to have the old cat put down.' Bernard immediately realised that he had thrown away his trump card. 'Anyway, why shouldn't you die after what you put me through?'

'Neither of us can go on living after the other is dead. If you do not let me return to share your identity, I will die. I cannot survive long in this world out of it.'

'No way. You - whatever you are - had no right to invade it in the first place.'

'I had no choice. I was expelled.'

'I'm not surprised. Who'd want to keep you?'

Bruno's ego recovered sufficiently for him to declare, 'I am Lustreland's Second Minister. No decrees or laws can be passed without my approval.'

'In that case, as you are so important, whoever expelled you here can take you back. I'm prepared to run that risk.'

'There may not be time.'

Bernard increased his grip. 'I'm sure if you tell me how to go about it, we can persuade whoever sent you here that it might be a good move to make the effort.'

It was three o'clock in the morning when Bernard slipped down the fire escape clutching a less belligerent Bruno.

As the numbing horror of the situation wore off, its novelty began to dawn on the singer. Bruno had apparently been coping with it for some while, now the ties to his alter ego's reality were beginning to slacken.

'Toads, vipers, seven-headed serpents ...' Bernard heard the diminutive minister with the mighty ego cursing under his breath. Whether Bruno represented part of his nature or not, he was glad he wouldn't be witnessing the Second Minister's encounter with the fairy folk he was calling so many names from the bottom of mythology's spectrum.

Bernard blundered into something very quagmirey and thankfully not easy to identify in the shadows cast by moonlight.

'That way! That way!' Bruno snapped.

Feeling like an ox being harassed by an irritatingly large gnat, the singer retrieved his shoe and stumbled in the direction Bruno indicated.

As the silhouette of the house became concealed by branches, Bernard had to stop and pull away brambles snagging his pyjamas. No rendition of The Champagne Song had ever made him so out of breath.

Bruno was becoming frantic. 'Go on, go on!'

'Shut-up, you carping nuisance! I don't see the need to traipse all this way.'

'You must reach the bowing oak before your moon sets.'

'Why? Is it magic?'

'No you fool, there's a safety portal in its roots. All bowing oaks over 500 years old have escape roots.'

'Are you being bloody funny?' Then Bernard realised that Bruno's sense of humour was likely to be as limited as his, and this was certainly no time for appalling puns.

'How can you be so sure the tree is in this park?'

'I was shown the map before I was sent here.'

'Then how did you know I would be..?'

'All right, all right.' Bruno no longer had the wits to explain anything more complicated than simple directions. 'It's magic. Just get moving will you!'

Bernard groaned. He hoped that at any second he would wake up, sweltering and with a hangover.

He stumbled on through tangled branches and stinging nettles to reach a small, haunted clearing beneath the bowing branches of an ancient oak.

Bruno's glowing, golden skin had faded to a wan, yellowish white by the time Bernard laid him on the leaf litter.

The singer waited for a few seconds, hoping it was a trick of the moon's rays and the Second Minister would become bright red with rage at any moment or, better still, disappear.

Unfortunately, the miniature monument to Lustreland's status quo remained as real as a piece of gravel in a rambler's laced boot.

'Go away, you idiot!' Bruno scolded weakly. 'They won't collect me while a human is watching.'

Though he hardly expected any thanks, Bernard was annoyed at being dismissed by a creature no bigger than Pinocchio. He tightened the cord of his dressing gown in annoyance and stomped off, hoping he could find the house in the early light before the quagmire found him. He wondered what would happen if the pompous package expired before Lustreland realised he was there. If Bruno had been telling the truth it would have given one or two obituary writers the opportunity for the heading, 'Well known singer found in bog after Fairyland fell on him.'

Then the true absurdity of the predicament occurred to Bernard and his imagination went into overdrive. As he squelched back over the marshy spot that had snatched off his shoe he wondered if whatever did it was waiting to complete the meal.

Bernard told his mind to pull itself together, but he wasn't listening. Robin Goodfellow and Queen Mab were no longer fancies of poetry, pantomime and opera: they were peeping through the branches and fanning the air with cobweb wings to a chorus of squeaking bats. Each vixen's screech, owl's hoot and unidentifiable swishing sound came from regions the Beaker folk understood. He was going to remember every irregular note the creatures of the night made until the day he died. How he longed for Clarey to come dashing through the trees to offer a reassuring hand. Instead there arose visions of the gardeners beating the undergrowth for his remains.

Despite the nettles, brambles and bog, Bernard quickened his pace.

Then there was an eerie cackle.

Every nerve in his body turned to ice.

That wasn't Queen Mab. It sounded ancient and mineral, like a jagged diamond laughing defiance at the lapidary about to strike it. He wanted to believe that it was his imagination because his nerves were vibrating like a battery of tuning forks.

Then came a voice.

'Run little mortal, run,' it rasped softly. 'The hounds of our dimension will catch you.'

Bernard shuddered. This was more terrifying than his encounter with Bruno.

'Who are you?'

'Don't be afraid,' the voice chuckled. 'It's only an old woman having a little joke. Go back and sleep soundly. I promise you will wake up.'

'Are you a witch?'

'I am your good fairy.'

'You can't be. I just met him.'

'That Bruno? He's your millstone, sweeting. Go home and let Clarey be your council. You should stop listening to your own. It's a cauldron of confusion that will boil you to pulp.' The voice cackled again, and then faded.

Terrified, Bernard snatched up the hem of his dressing gown and ran for the silhouette of the mansion looming angularly in the moonlight.

CHAPTER 22

The Hurglabat stretched its tentacles. The monster's power was growing and it could taste the delicious apathy of the Lustrelanders far above. Even better, it could now insinuate its will into minds more complex than the galvanised buckets ogres used for brains and from which the simplest thought had trouble scrambling out.

While Lustreland remained oblivious of its growing presence, the residents of Rara Avis Ridge detected grey ripples in the borealis, even though such ascetic considerations were not first on the list of priorities for foraging harpies or nesting rocs. Life was complex enough; any further into confusion's labyrinth and they would have had to reserve tickets on evolution's shuttle.

The Hurglabat was aware of the Second Minister being drawn back to Lustreland from some dimension it was not yet able to penetrate, and that one wizened old woman seemed to be the only person who knew what was going on. The thoughts of the sprites flanking her were filled with fascinated awe as a sturdy frame hovered in the alcove of the seeing pool rippling with alternative dimensions. A slight lapse in Rimonay's concentration could have left Bruno frozen in amber at the bottom of some deep ocean or orbiting on an alien world's satellite, which would have given some slippery Mystic Trine member the ideal opportunity to replace him in Lustreland's government.

But eventually a very groggy Bruno did materialise and topple back into the reality where he belonged.

The Hurglabat dabbled a mental tentacle in the seeing pool's transitional stream and tasted worlds that could satiate its rapacious appetite. A multitude of dimensions beyond Lustreland! And all accessed through that alcove throbbing with pink light.

Rimonay could detect the Hurglabat's malign presence. It made even her iron resolve shudder a little. If sprites were intimidated by mere dimensional transfer, the threat of a monster which could suck out their life's spark would have sent them all into immediate hibernation. So no one else could know. Lustreland's economy, so dependent on the vegetation, would have ground to a standstill without its fairy folk. It was better that Lustrelanders believed they only had ogres to confront.

Rimonay would have shared the dark secret with the Second Minister if he were not as stubborn as a troll and probably talked in his sleep when his marigold sprite was housekeeping.

Before Bruno's strength and indignation could return, Rimonay's sprites took him home, steadying him in the saddle of a griffin that had compromised its Rara Avis status to become a lucrative taxi service. They left the Second Minister on the turret of his home where he fell fast asleep until a persistent thought worried him awake.

Bruno gradually became aware that he was annoyed - very annoyed! He pulled himself up and looked out over the ornamental wall.

There was something wrong. He forgot that he was angry for a moment. The light on the horizon was flickering as though a lace curtain had momentarily been drawn over it. Being catapulted between dimensions hadn't caused the nauseous feeling in the pit of his stomach; it was something much deeper, dragging at the feet of his soul with treacle tenacity. He shook his head and the thought retreated.

Bruno swallowed the contents of the flask Rimonay had tucked in his sash and immediately realised why he was so annoyed.

Predictably, the Ruling Council was furious at their plan being thwarted by a mere human, and that Bruno's demeaning experience had not made one dent in his refusal to acknowledge Dragon Sesame as an ally. It was obvious that some dirtier, and totally illegal, deed would be required if Sesame was to be enlisted in time to stop the ogres. This might have crossed the Second Minister's mind had he been thinking rationally and was willing to believe they could sink even lower.

Bruno stayed in his own corner of Lustreland nursing his badly dented self-esteem in solitude. As he had few friends capable of putting up with his high-handed manner for very long he didn't expect anyone to come calling.

The marigold sprite allocated to do those chores considered beneath his elevated status had the habit of never being there when needed or leaving everything in such a muddle that she was frequently told to get lost. There was no irritating tittering or glimmer of her brilliant petals so she apparently hadn't come back since being ordered to flutter off the last time. Bruno assumed she had gone on a nectar binge and would return in a few hours even more incapable. He did not like to admit it, but for once he would have been glad of her company. It was at a time like this a minister needed someone to witness their superior self-control. Too proud to feel sorry for himself, he wouldn't have objected to someone else doing it for him.

Instead, confident no one would witness it, he flew into a gale force tantrum. The room's contents were hurled against the walls, fairy lace cushions shredded to cobwebs, and elegant vases smashed.

When there was nothing left to break and tapestries lay scattered about the floor in shreds, Bruno sank to his knees in exhaustion. About to burst into tears and hammer the floor, he looked up through a window to see the amazed expression of his sprite. She who had fallen asleep in the vine of flowers surrounding it. There could be no doubt that the impish, orange fairy had witnessed the full extent of his childish outburst. Knowing it would only be a matter of minutes before a blow by blow description of it was circulated to every sprite, elf, gnome, and goblin in Lustreland, Bruno was frozen with embarrassment.

Taking his inability to move as a sign of brain damage, the sprite fluttered inside and gingerly touched his burning forehead. Reaching the conclusion that her bombastic guardian had at last blown a fuse and was beyond rewiring, she rescued some cushions from the wreckage, persuaded him to lie down, and covered him with a rug.

The Second Minister was obliged to remain there, wide awake, watching the Marigold sprite flitting about the room, salvaging what had not been smashed beyond magicking back together, and sweeping everything else into piles for the refuse collecting sprites. The scars on the walls were beyond her powers to repair and needed a master plasterer.

Bruno didn't move until the debris was tidily stacked and his sprite brought a sweet concoction that he was obliged to sit up and drink. The sickly substance was difficult to swallow, but he dare not refuse it; such liquids were nectar to the flower sprites. Perhaps if he behaved with some humility she would not spread the news of his tantrum too far.

The Second Minister continued to play the invalid and allowed the marigold sprite to assist him to a couch. She watched him until satisfied that there would be no more tornadoes of rage, and then silently left in a twinkle of relief.

As soon as she had gone Bruno went up to the turret where he bided his time, watching the sky to see if he could catch a glimpse of the illusive Ligh Tofrea

Sun whose rays filled it, then tossing petals from the vine spilling over the wall into the water below. Though the silver spire was still missing, he had refilled the pond.

'Wretched dragon,' he muttered to the nearest gargoyle. 'All this trouble over an aerodynamic lightning conductor.'

The gargoyle diplomatically pretended not to hear.

Below, a figure with a long stride and wide-brimmed hat was furtively making his way across the garden, at pains not to be noticed. Given the number of seeing glasses in Lustreland, anyone with common sense would have known it was a waste of time. Qulio may have had a deep well full of wisdom, but little idea of just how nosy others were.

Bruno quickly went down to open the door to the only person capable of feeling sympathy for a marauding snail with salt on its tail.

Wizard Qulio nervously slipped inside. He noticed the wreckage of Bruno's tantrum before he could pour out what was troubling him. The wizard assumed the Second Minister had just fought off a gang of troll assassins and was almost back out of the door before Bruno seized his arm.

'It's all right, it's all right.' Bruno groaned. 'I just had this spasm... you know how things are.' Embarrassed, he wandered away to rescue the only intact chair.

Sitting down was the last thing on Qulio's mind. 'You must get away from here quickly!'

The Second Minister apparently wasn't the only one stressed to snapping point. 'Why?'

'There is a trap being laid for you.'

Bruno's indignation promptly steamrollered any vestige of hard-learnt humility. 'If I don't stay here that wretched dragon will be enlisted as an ally. I cannot believe the members in the Ruling Council would stoop any lower to change my mind.'

Qulio may have been timid, but he wasn't always a fool. 'Only this time they are in league with the Mystic Trine. I was the only one to protest about it, and you know how much my vote counts for.'

Bruno was touched by the wizard's concern for his welfare. A guilty notion at the back of his mind niggled that there were more worthy causes he could have spent it on. 'Calm yourself. I'm safe enough. I hold too high a rank for anyone to harm me.'

Bruno obviously believed that Rimonay had rescued him from the roots of the bowing oak more by design than luck.

Qulio flinched from confessing just how fortunate he had been. A witch who had discovered the fine filament connecting his living substance to Lustreland would have happily tied a knot in it if the First Minister hadn't threatened to suspend her newt breeding licence.

'Please believe me,' Qulio pleaded. 'I have a dear friend called Juniper. She lives in the woods and could hide you where no one would ever find out.'

Bruno was not flattered. 'You mean the woman who looks after changelings?'

'Why yes. What harm have changelings done that they should not be cared for?'

'Oh Qulio, Qulio, I don't understand you, yet admire you all the same,' Bruno reassured him. 'Nothing will happen to me simply because I am resolved that a dragon will not hold us in its debt.' Qulio opened his mouth to protest. 'Say nothing of Dragon Sesame's benevolent nature to me. I know differently and am the only one able to see it.'

Qulio sighed. 'No, Minister Bruno. Inside your heart lodges a splinter of fear that makes you see things through a darkling lens.'

There was no way to convince the wizard without using brutal words better suited on an ogre. And before him stood the only person in Lustreland, he would never have used them on. 'Thank you for finding the courage to come here and warn me, Qulio.'

'I am the most easily frightened creature in Lustreland, but know my fear.'

'No harm will ever come to you. I promise that. Don't live in dread of what will never happen.' Bruno opened the door and looked out. 'It's safe to leave now. Take care.' As the wizard was departing he called. 'And give my regards to Juniper.'

Qulio flickered a brief smile before darting into the cover of the trees.

CHAPTER 23

A mysterious travelling merchant had invited the self elected goblin tyrant, Flunkin, to look into a seeing glass. In it he saw the gems that studded Jobaloba's armour. They were huge and much finer than anything dug from a goblin mine, Flunkin had to know where they came from. Then he saw Kot Kut in the glass. He was carrying a huge basket of jewels - What a waste on ogres! Goblins knew how to appreciate such bounty from the ground, so he sent a trustworthy crow to spy on the high priest.

For an ogre, the high priest was unusually nervous and prone to looking over his shoulder, which no doubt had something to do with the baskets of gems he regularly carried back from the pitch lakes after each religious ritual. Ogres didn't need much intellect to know that, when it came to anything that glittered, goblins were untrustworthy; the idea just had difficulty in bludgeoning its way into their cerebral cortices so it wasn't difficult to persuade Jobaloba that they could be trusted to open a new seam in their dinosaur bone mines for them. The ogres couldn't comprehend that there was any other motive; not many creatures would dare cross an ogre. When the miners arrived in Darkle Deeps, they even invited the visitors to play a game of football. Fixated on getting to the gems at whatever cost, Flunkin thought it was a good idea to humour them - depending on whose head the ogres decided to use as the football. Tyrant or not, the other miners decided it would take more than a handful of precious rocks to persuade them to join in a game of slay your neighbour with their hosts and hurried off to their campsite. This was on the lip of a dismal crag that overlooked the grey sea dribbling duckweed onto a granite shore, the ogre idea of luxury.

Night and day were very much alike in Darkle Deeps so there was never an ideal time to sneak after the high priest going about his highly lucrative devotions. From the goblin camp's vantage point, Flunkin could see the holy robe flapping into the dismal distance. Checking that none of the miners saw him leave, he furtively darted after it, towards the pitch lakes that separated the domain from Rara Avis Ridge. Adult goblins were so close to the ground in their camouflage cloaks any one could easily have been taken for a rather animated mound being pushed up by a gofferhog, although even those hardy creatures drew the line at tunnelling through tar.

Flunkin kept a safe distance as Kot Kut droned a deep chant that vibrated down through his boots and into the ground. Slowly, the pitch lake parted like a pair of voluptuous black lips. The goblin knew that a message was being pumped into the ogre's tiny mind, which his goblin brain was too complex to intercept.

Kot Kut suddenly produced a pannier from the folds of his robe and dutifully held it aloft to catch the fountain of glistening gems showered up from the hole. Flunkin had trouble containing himself at the sight of so many jewels, his eyes watering at the thought that the thick-skulled Jobaloba could simply obtain riches it would have taken goblins aeons to mine by sending out his high priest with a basket and nasal chant. It didn't matter that Flunkin had no idea how the spell worked. When it came to anything subterranean, goblins didn't need magic.

His pannier full, Kot Kut trudged back to the ogre fortress with the Hurglabat's new message for Jobaloba and his waiting army.

As soon as the high priest was out of sight Flunkin sped towards the hole that had spewed out the gems.

He peered down into a chasm and saw its depths sparkling with crystals.

Flunkin had to make a quick decision. Was it worth the risk of scrambling down the hole and back out again before it closed up, or should he wait until Kot Kut made his next trip? If the geode of the goblin tyrant's heart was ever sliced in two there would be no glittering crystals, just greed written all the way through it.

He decided to take the risk and unwound the rope about his waist and secured it to a rock before lowering himself into the hole. Surrounded by ruby, emerald, diamond, metanite, and gazzine, his hand pick became a blur as the gems were loosened like sunflower seeds by a starving magpie. What the goblin couldn't cram into his knapsack and huge pockets he allowed to fall to the floor. He could always swallow the jewels if he ran out of places to carry them.

Flunkin's acquisitive reverie did not last long. The Hurglabat had detected his frenetic activity.

The goblin was so occupied he didn't notice the lips of the cave closing.

When he paused to look up, it was too late.

CHAPTER 24

Bruno sat for some while musing over Qulio's nature, but not long enough over Qulio's warning.

The next visitor to rap the Second Minster's door was a vegetable sprite. He had a cabbage and onion expression that might have well bubbled up from a potato stew.

'Message for you,' he sniffed through the tears brought on by his own odour. 'No reply.' The sprite ambled off, no doubt back to some narcotic herb party being held in a parsnip patch.

The envelope bore the crystal seal of the First Minister which shattered in silver confetti as Bruno swiftly opened it without stopping to wonder why it had not been brought by one of her own haughty attendants.

He had been summoned to the Crystal Mansion. Only such high-ranking dignitaries as him had right of entry to that edifice. It could only mean that he was no longer in disgrace.

Bruno decked himself in his robes and chain of office. He also took his staff of office in case he encountered any of the inebriated vegetable sprite's relatives on the way through the wooded grove that encircled the Crystal Mansion. They were not malicious creatures, though forever trying to impress tourists with their ethereal antics. Most visitors were delighted by the impromptu airborne ballets but it was beneath the Second Minister's dignity to marvel at anything.

When Bruno arrived, the grove was ominously deserted.

Sprites were nosy, yet avoided being too close to weighty events because powerful fluxes of energy and spells which, although not aimed in their direction, could easily blow them away. Bruno should have realised that they were aware off something he wasn't and turned back then. Unfortunately his ego refused to comprehend the meaning of diplomatic retreat.

Bruno did notice that the emptiness of the vines and diamond barked trees seemed odd, and the petals of huge cloud flowers were so motionless it felt that they were holding their breath. The only movement came from the slender bells of some convolvulus dripping honey onto the leaves below. Even that delicious meal of nectar was being left untouched by residents with more sense than appetite.

Unperturbed, Bruno walked into the Crystal Mansion's light which emanated from millions of illuminating leaves growing from the walls.

Legend had it that this tree palace sprang from the ground aeons ago when the light inexplicably went from Lustreland. During that time of darkness it grew leaves and blossom which threw out enough light to lift the gloom in the domain until the Ligh Tofrea Sun was restored. Then the tree crystallised. Branches became supporting pillars, leaves thatched its walls and roof, and blossom framed the spaces that created windows and doorways.

Traces of its original brilliance still filled each chamber. Because the Crystal Mansion was magical, mere citizens could not enter it; only those of the highest rank were permitted to ascend the stairway of twisted roots to its main portal.

Inside, the luminous rooms were deserted. Rimonay could have been anywhere, waiting to make one of her daunting entrances, so Bruno waited in the main hall. Then he caught sight of a golden envelope. Convinced that must have been addressed to him he strode over to collect it.

The Second Minister never reached the crystal lectern it lay on.

The floor gave way beneath his self-important tread and he plummeted down through the wickedly hard roots that supported the marvellous mansion. The iridescent crystal leaves, which had been such a delight to the eye, became the jagged instruments of his descent, each handhold biting into his flesh so viciously his downward plunge seemed preferable. All he could do was hope that the well at its bottom no longer contained any water. Apart from not wanting to drown, Bruno wasn't very keen on amphibians; their conversation could be wearisome, and probably interminable if he was unable to climb out or escape along the dried up riverbed that legend said once existed beneath the Crystal Mansion. But minds more devious than his had already thought of that.

His last inexorable slide down a smooth, glass-sided funnel ensured that there was no hope of clambering up again, and any outlet at the bottom of the well had been blocked by huge rocks.

Worst of all, Bruno had no one to heap abuse on for this latest indignity, not even a boring toad, and the boulders were too massive to hurl about in a fit of temper.

Witchcraft had been at work here.

The Second Minister's Lustreland eyes were unused to the gloom and the dim light coming from the glittering rim of crystals far above only emphasised how impossible his predicament was. Bruno's self-importance insisted that no one would dare assassinate such a high ranking minister as him, and rescue would come soon enough. On the other hand, that small splinter of fear Qulio had warned him of niggled the other possibility.

Gathering together the torn folds of his gown and rearranging his chain of office, Bruno groped about to find a conveniently shaped piece of rubble so he could sit down while he waited. But every boulder in that tiny space had been fashioned with the same vicious edge of Nature's, or more likely a witch's, chisel.

Hours of discomfort ensued until Bruno's imagination began to override his common sense. He started to hear a soft voice whispering far above him. It sounded as though the sharp crystals were slicing apart each syllable before whole words could reach him. Fearing madness, the Second Minister was convinced that his senses were playing tricks on him and refused to look up.

The whispering became more urgent and there was a sudden clatter as something crashed down in a shower of splintered crystal.

Bruno leapt in alarm and looked up to see a pillar lying across the hole far above. It was supporting a long ladder of wooden rungs roughly tied together.

So he was to be rescued after all! Rimonay and the Ruling Council had only planned this farce to frighten him!

Bruno secured his staff of office in his sash before clumsily ascending the swinging rungs, swearing at the pain from his lacerated hands. Somebody was going to pay for this latest humiliation.

By the time he had clambered to the top of the hole he was in such a ferment of rage he blindly reached out for a handhold. Unfortunately this turned out to be Qulio's beard, and the wizard would have been pulled into the hole if Bruno had not found his extended hand just in time.

Qulio? It was only Qulio after all.

Amazement at the wizard's unexpected courage took him aback. 'Do you know the penalty for being in the Crystal Mansion?'

Qulio's reply was soft and reproachful. 'The penalty for me not being here might well have been your demise.'

That cut no ice with Bruno. 'The Ruling Council wouldn't have dared murder me!'

Qulio shook his head. 'I had to leave you down there for so long to be sure. And it took Juniper, the changelings, and me hours to make the ladder.'

Instead of being grateful for the risk the wizard had taken, Bruno's rage was becoming a dangerously overloaded volcano.

'We have to get out of here,' Qulio urged. 'Neither of us must be discovered.'

Bruno hauled the ladder up and replaced the felled pillar in a fraction of the time it had taken Qulio to move. 'You must hide in the woods with Juniper,' he ordered. 'They must not find out what you have done.'

'You will have to come with me.'

'I have other things to do!' boomed Bruno.

Qulio was beside himself. 'I beg you. The pact with Dragon Sesame has already been made.'

'Without my approval!'

'Isn't that why they laid this trap for you? They are going to be angry when they find you have escaped.'

'Angry!!' stormed Bruno. 'I'll show them what anger is!' He snatched up his staff and strode out of the Crystal Mansion.

Qulio hesitated. The Second Minister's mood was too explosive for any pacifying spell he knew, and the chemicals pumping through that broad body put him way beyond any herbal remedy. Qulio considered conjuring up another hole for him to fall down - a much softer one of course, but knew the hole would come off worse.

There was nothing he could do, just follow at a safe distance from the fearful vibrations emanating from the Second Minister.

CHAPTER 25

The cackling voice in his dream made Bernard wake with a start.

He was half way to the fire escape before realising it was daylight and he wasn't wearing anything. His mud spattered pyjamas and dressing gown were lying in a heap on the floor with the duvet and there were painful scratches criss-crossing his legs. At least he hadn't left any blood on the bed sheet.

After soaking his pyjamas in the wash basin and hanging them up to drip over the bath, he took a shower to remove any other evidence of his night time jaunt. By the time he was dressed, he felt confident enough to face the world and go down to breakfast.

Bernard found it difficult to deal with the embarrassment of what had happened during the night and told Clarey that his evil fairy had fled back to whatever ethereal asylum he had escaped from, and promised not to return. The way Clarey discreetly accepted his explanation with a show of charitable relief that his drug had actually worked made Bernard feel guilty. The singer reluctantly came to the conclusion that Clarey Ditton-Davis was nothing like his tabloid image and possessed a palpable warmth beneath that exterior of quiet sophistication. Deep in the aristocrat's courteous manner glowed a pool of kindness that would have been tapped dry by more mercenary mortals, and might have accounted for why he was so reluctant to sack his despicable secretary.

It was comforting to discover the true nature of his host. It lifted Bernard's mood until, when he looked down from his bedroom landing into the hall later that morning, he saw the icy Mrs Porter meet the white lightning of Indrina. That should have been an encounter to relish, though for some reason he felt apprehensive.

'You'll have to wait,' Mrs Porter was telling his wife.

Indrina smiled sweetly. 'I'll make a note of how long and put it on the account.'

'I will have to find whether Mr Ditton-Davis is receiving today.'

'If he doesn't receive me today, you'll be barricading the bailiffs out tomorrow.'

Mrs Porter glowered, knowing that she couldn't intimidate this visitor, and stalked off to find Clarey.

Indrina didn't need to look up to know Bernard was watching. 'Don't dash off anywhere, Pudding. I want to see you as well.'

Before he could reply, Clarey had dashed into the hall. Being the perfect gentleman, and sensitive to Bernard's aggravated feelings about his wife, he welcomed Indrina with warm caution. Bernard was not so well-mannered. Bailiffs or not, he bounded down to grab Indrina's arm in case she disappeared for the rest of the day.

She shrugged and patted the back of Clarey's hand. 'Shall I attend to my matrimonial faux pas first?'

Suddenly Aurora rushed in, pursued by a gaggle of children who surrounded Clarey.

'I'll just attend to the mistakes that were made out of it.'

Aurora, Clarey and the children disappeared outside to play hide and seek while Bernard hustled Indrina up to his room.

As soon as the door was closed Indrina took several letters from her briefcase.

She waved them under his nose. 'Did you know you were about to drop dead, Pudding?'

Bernard snatched the letters. Reluctant to believe what they said, he held them at a distance like a horse having trouble finding its nosebag and read them again. 'I don't know who's the bigger idiot, the hospital who checked these tests, or Morgan who took them.'

'They probably belong to somebody else of course, but they aren't going to own up.'

'I feel sorry for the fellow they do belong to. You really enjoyed coming all the way out here just to scare the life out of me, didn't you?'

'Of course Pudding. If you had a sense of humour you might have enjoyed the joke.'

'Joke! They say that I should have died of lockjaw, or hepatitis B, or rabies or something - weeks ago. You should be a widow by now.'

'They aren't sure what they mean. Some researcher wants to dissect your DNA to see if there's a knot in it.'

Bernard detested the way Indrina could purr with the sweet maliciousness of a playful cheetah. 'You were looking forward to being a widow, weren't you?'

'And you expected me to jump on the funeral pyre. No chance, you must be worth too much.'

'Can't you think of anything else but money?'

'It's my job.'

'And can't you ever think of anything else but your work? You're still my accountant so you should know how much I'm worth, down to the last penny.'

'Perhaps you wouldn't find it so galling if it became just a business arrangement?'

'You should have married your laptop.'

'All right, let me have a divorce?'

'That would save you money instead of chasing me for one.'

'Quite probably.'

'I'm fine now. Why do you want a divorce anyway?'

'No real idea. It probably wouldn't seem that different from being married to you.'

The Don Giovanni deep in Bernard's wishful thinking snarled. 'And what does that mean?'

'Nothing lover. Did I tell you about the client who swears by honey, gin and hot water to get an erection?'

'You're a fine one to talk about lack of passion! Take you to a restaurant and you add up the menu. Aurora's carp at least blew bubbles when I fed it.'

'Since when have you taken me to a restaurant? Come nine o'clock, you're too busy chasing big blondes with a spear.'

'That was an accident!'

'I never heard her complain about it.'

Bernard at last reached the limit of his ability to verbally duel. 'Why do you have to start the most idiotic conversations!'

'Why not? You've always been a fruit loop. Probably coming from a family who thrived on black pudding and Wagner.'

'Mahler!'

'With tripe, egg nog and long hikes over Precambrian bogs to walk it off.'

'My parents were no more eccentric than anyone else's.'

'Your parents laid a minefield in that dense skull of yours. It's hardly surprising we're beginning to hear explosions.'

'So what do you expect me to do about that!'

'Start admitting the fact, Pudding.' Indrina tossed the letters onto the bedside table. 'Let's have these tests done again.'

'I'm all right now. And who would care if I did drop dead tomorrow?'

'Stop feeling sorry for yourself. It's not the way to get sympathy and one day you may need it.'

'What do you mean?'

Indrina tapped the letters. 'Say these results aren't a mistake?'

'But I haven't died since they were taken?' Hardly were the words out of Bernard's mouth when he broke into a cold sweat at the thought of what had happened the previous night.

Indrina rubbed in the salt. 'These tests were taken when you were delirious. They might as well belong to your fairy twin.'

She couldn't comprehend the terror that struck her husband at the flippant suggestion.

He crumpled into a chair.

Minister Bruno must have been telling the truth.

As Bernard became submerged by tormenting thoughts, the torn legs of his pyjamas caught Indrina's attention. They were still damp and clumsily half pushed into his suitcase. She then examined the hem of his dressing gown and cast a suspicious look at Bernard who was pondering on Queen Mab, ancient bowing oaks, and how far it was to Lustreland.

'What've you been up to, Pudding? Paddling in the piranha pond?'

'What?' he murmured. 'Must've sleep walked.'

'That wasn't sleep walking. That was being chased by the Hound of the Baskervilles through Grimpen Mire.'

Without warning Bernard came to a decision. 'Show Clarey those letters.'

Indrina was taken aback. 'You want him to see them?'

'I can't explain, but he'll understand. Now please leave me alone.'

'Curiouser and curiouser.' It was at times like these that Indrina wondered if she had misjudged her husband. More used to worrying about his diet and heart, it had never occurred to her he was sensitive enough to have a mental breakdown.

If she stayed any longer she would have felt obliged to play the dutiful wife, so the accountant gathered up the letters and her briefcase to go and find out if the children had found Clarey and her daughter.

Indrina descended the main staircase as four young women arrived. She peered down though the vines to see them quickly herded into an adjoining room by the disapproving Mrs Porter. By the time she reached the hall Clarey's secretary had gone about her business.

'Poison ivy's gone,' she told Mouse who was hiding behind a large datura.

'So beautiful, yet so deadly.'

She knew he didn't mean Mrs Porter. 'What? They looked quite inoffensive to me?'

'No, the datura.'

'Thought you meant the young women.'

Mouse giggled. 'Gorgeous, weren't they.'

'I didn't know you had a mind like that. You surprise me.'

'I've surprised quite a few people in my time.'

Indrina laughed.

He proffered his arm and they crossed the hall to the room where Aurora was prancing about, trying not to fall off her shoes as she gamely danced with the two eldest children. A younger one looked on, dreaming of jelly trifle while the others slumbered in Clarey's long arms as he lay sprawled over several cushions on the floor.

Mouse trod on a plastic cup. It was like a gunshot and woke Clarey.

Reluctantly, he allowed Mouse and Indrina to escort him to the library where the brutal economics of his estate were laid before him.

By the time Indrina's briefcase had been emptied, there was no room on the table for smelling salts.

'Do you want to keep this house?' There was no compromise in the accountant's question.

Clarey momentarily reeled. 'Of course.'

'Then you will have to make the estate work harder for you. You've enough acres for forestry.'

'But firs aren't natural to this land.'

Mouse was enthusiastic. 'It might encourage red squirrels.'

Clarey laughed. 'They would probably eat you.'

'Or farm the four meadows by the river,' suggested Indrina.

'The townspeople use them for gymkhanas and fêtes.'

'Without paying any rent?'

'Well of course they don't.'

'You could sell Bracken Wood to the local authority for council housing. They're offering you enough.'

'I promised the preservationists ...'

'You won't win,' Mouse whispered to Indrina.

'I don't want to keep all this land for myself,' Clarey said. 'But as soon as I let it go it will either be built on, made into a golf course or put to forestry. This land is special.'

'Special?'

'It's ancient. From the air you can see the sight of a Neolithic village. There are at least a dozen unexcavated barrows, and a grid of standing stones radiating from the old tollgates. None of the hedgerows are younger than medieval. When at last governments do start listening to conservationists, there will be nothing left to conserve.'

Indrina gave a sharp laugh. 'You know what people really think you are, don't you?'

'A lecherous member of the landed gentry with more land than is decent unless you're related to the Queen.' Clary pulled himself up to his full, impressive height to announce, 'They can think what they want. When our children grow up they will understand the reasons. Whenever human beings touch the Earth they corrupt it with concrete and decay. Letting them destroy this land will help no one.'

'He's going mystical,' whispered Mouse.

Indrina had to give in yet again. 'Oh well, looks like another masterpiece.'

Clarey indicated the dour expressions in the Dutch masters looking down from the library walls. 'Take what you want. My father bought most of them as investments. It's a pity he preferred the ones that didn't smile like the Laughing Cavalier. He did it for the accountants, so one might as well sell them. I'd better get back to the children before Aurora is overwhelmed.' He left Indrina to estimate which picture would bring in enough to pacify the Inland Revenue.

'Think the taxman would take Mrs Porter as a down payment?' asked Mouse.

'I don't think they would take her as a bad joke,' said Indrina. 'Not much of a market for shark hide.'

CHAPTER 26

Despite several setbacks, like trying to march on high, narrow mountain passes two abreast and losing every other ogre before discovering the benefits of single file, Jobaloba's army amassed in the valley which led straight through Rara Avis Ridge and up to Lustreland. Above them a borealis curtain swam in the purple sky, and beyond that shimmered the translucent dome of their destination, so high it touched a heaven too bright for any creature to gaze at for long. The ogres had often wondered about the faint pinpricks of light in the dark over Darkle Deeps and never thought for one moment that the Ligh Tofrea Sun might have been related to them.

Lustrelanders had no idea what stars were either - apart from the Mystic Trine's librarian. As she was so weird, few people dare ask her for a book to explain it for fear of being trapped into a discussion about the quantum state of their dimension.

Lustreland's council chamber was filled with a motley assortment of proportional representatives elected by an indifferent population to sit on its steeply tiered seats. In a realm where few people shared the same interests, everyone had a member to speak for them. As a consequence, it was the safest form of government possible, a talking shop where nobody could agree on anything. Trolls overturned resolutions proposed by goblins, goblins voted down reforms suggested by sprites, and sprites, bored with the whole process, went outside to play.

Fortunately Rimonay had the power, with her Second Minister, to make executive decisions overriding everyone else's. Now he was in the middle of one of his bloody-minded spasms and the Ruling Council determined to dispose of him by any means possible, she was obliged to do business with the Mystic Trine. The representatives in the council chamber were no use in tempering the situation either and just as enthusiastic about bringing the pompous Bruno down a peg or two. Rimonay had nursed a hope that this desire was due to political ineptitude, only to accept that it was downright malice after all.

Everyone else was so desperate to enlist Dragon Sesame's help there was no debate about what was actually going to happen to the Second Minister. They just hoped the battle would soon be over and Bruno, at least, unconscious. After admitting to Rimonay that they had been responsible for dropping him down the well in the Crystal Mansion, the Ruling Council insisted they had every intention of retrieving him when everything was over. They claimed that they were just about to draw lots to select who went down to find out if he was still alive. Rimonay doubted it, but what was done was done, and she could at least look forward to their reaction when they discovered that he had escaped.

From her tower she watched Sesame perching on the pinnacles of the Halls of Government and loping up and down its scintillating, unnaturally green lawn. The Dragon was full of its own importance and wishing that its arch enemy, Bruno, could witness the sight just for the aggravation of it. No councillor, the Mystic Trine, or even Rimonay, suspected how easily a reptilian wish could be granted.

Elfin spies had brought back intelligence of the ogres' troop movements. It only confirmed that the enemy were such bumbling idiots they should have been wheel-clamped on the highway of life long ago. All the same, having gone to such pains to enlist Sesame's services, nobody volunteered to go and throw rocks at

Jobaloba while his army tried to hone the art of invasion.

The Hurglabat also started to realise that if you send out ogres to overrun any domain, you had to fit them with wheels. The monster could visualise the gems it had spewed up to their high priest flashing in Jobaloba's armour, making the two headed leader a prime target for any passing roc with mischief in mind.

But no - perhaps its hoards weren't going to be routed by a dragon after all! Rage, so volcanic that the Hurglabat's psychic tentacles could detect it from the depths of Darkle Deeps, was striding across Lustreland. The monster did not need to feed the fury, just hope it didn't trip up.

Sesame was spangled with flashing red scales, and a row of spikes along its spine drew lightning when it wheeled above the peaks of its mountainous home. Far from being an incinerating experience, the dragon found spinning in the sky and churning the clouds to trigger thunderstorms invigorating. Otherwise it was an ideal neighbour and would always recover a few boulders when a roc chick broke down the wall of its nest, or tell a griffin where to find the best sharpening stone for its beak. (Contrary to popular belief, griffins were not meat eaters; they were more partial to the shell the meat had been encased in. Though it wore many beaks down to the nostrils, it did solve the taxing problem of having to pursue prey in the first place.)

Now harpies - they were a different matter. No self-respecting fabulous beast wanted these miscreants as neighbours. They lived dozens to a cave and hated each other. The din of their bickering, shrieks and slashing of talons echoed from peak to peak, keeping the other residents awake. Sesame tried to persuade its neighbours to call in a health inspector from Lustreland but, like most neighbours, when it came to doing something nobody wanted to get involved. All the dragon could do was puff clouds of acrid smoke into the caves when the noise was at its worst. This enraged the already angry harpies. There was little a flock could do against a dragon, but they were cunning and prepared to wait for the chance to get their own back.

Sesame enjoyed its status as the only dragon in Rara Avis Ridge. The prestige this conferred allowed the fabulous creature the confidence to be very relaxed about life, which was probably why Bruno, who could be as easy going as a golem guarding the padlock to Hell, insisted the dragon was a menace to society.

Sesame was preening its scales in the privileged position of the Government lawn in preparation to do combat with the ogre army when its nemesis appeared.

He was dressed in his best robes, slightly battered chain of office, and walked with a determined, if slightly lopsided, tread supported by his ceremonial golden staff.

Bruno strode across the lawn to where Sesame was contentedly unaware of his approach. The sudden blow to its snout from the Second Minister's staff made the dragon's eyes smart in pain.

The watching councillors could do nothing and wailed in apprehension. Before the guard trolls could be summoned, Bruno let loose his enraged tirade.

'Treacherous gnomes and sadists! Murderous serpents! Poisonous toads! Did you think that assassinating me would change the vile nature of a dragon?!'

A goblin elder swallowed a loose gold filling in terror. 'How did he escape?'

'He's out of his mind,' whispered a cannabis sprite, familiar with the condition.

The ensuing brittle silence was broken by a quiet voice. 'After being put into someone else's body, and then down the bottom of a well, it's hardly surprising.'

'Qulio!' went up the groan.

'We should have put him down there with him!' declared a witch.

The councillors became aware of a rise in temperature as ribbons of orange flame licked menacingly near Bruno's beard.

'Dragon Sesame does not seem to be taking this calmly,' observed an opal troll usher. Fireproof he may have been, but was easy to shatter.

Bruno was beyond feeling anything. Having never been strong on reason, rage took over and his staff of office became the most eloquent champion of his argument. As it crashed down onto Sesame's snout again, the dragon could hardly mistake the point he was making.

Everyone stood by helplessly while the implacable rivals exchanged flame for abuse and glancing talons for crashing blows. The dragon could have easily lifted Bruno in one claw and dropped him off a precipice. Better still, it should have frizzled the fractious barrel of pomposity to a crisp then and there, flown off to vanquish the ogres and returned to collect a medal for ridding Lustreland of two of its biggest irritants in one day. Sesame had no idea why it was holding back from justifiable homicide and, instead of blazing away with the full force of its furnace, merely struck a few Lucifers in annoyance. Perhaps it was because it anticipated that Qulio would suddenly come between them, even at the risk of his beard going up in flames or being brained by Bruno's staff.

And sure enough he was suddenly there.

'Stop! Please stop!'

The Wizard reached up to stroke the dragon's bruised muzzle and persuaded it to swallow its flame.

Unfortunately, the same persuasion was lost on the Second Minister. In his own private dimension of fury, Bruno remained a one-person tornado hurling abuse at the dragon, councillors and Mystic Trine. By the time he had exhausted his anger, Sesame decided that saving any domain that had Bruno in it wasn't worth the trouble.

With malevolently flashing eyes, the dragon glared hungrily at the Second Minister, before taking off to return to the comparative peace of its cave and squabbling harpy neighbours. They'd be no medals today.

Bruno was on such an enraged high that he was deaf to the clamorous reproaches.

Qulio continued to protest that the treatment of the Second Minister had made him desperate but, as it was obvious he had been the one to release Bruno from the well in the Crystal Mansion, no one paid attention to the wizard.

The Mystic Trine's librarian scratched her stubbly chin. 'Well, it's too late to rustle up any strong enough spells now, even if we got every sprite in Lustreland to help us.'

'We could get them to pelt the ogres with light crystals,' a goblin suggested. 'That would shrivel some of them up.'

'We would never be able to carry them that far,' protested a sprite. 'What do you think we are? Trolls with lift off?'

When Qulio was out of earshot the librarian's sinister smile creased with intrigue. It was quite disconcerting, like seeing ripples appear in hammered copper. 'We'll have to entice Dragon Sesame back.'

A warlock laughed. 'You must be joking. After what the Second Minister did to it the dragon will probably side with the ogres.'

'Not if the enticement were great enough.'

Unable to persuade Bruno to flee to the woods, Qulio followed him home and cast a spell to make him sleep so he didn't attack the furniture again.

Then, as though by magic - what else? - Iggata appeared at the Minister's retreat while Bruno, exhausted by his titanic outburst, slumbered. Qulio was pleasantly surprised by her arrival. He had always secretly admired the scheming witch and threw his natural caution to the wind, which buffeted it about a little before dropping it down a goblin's chimney.

Not wanting to wake Bruno, Qulio invited Iggata up onto the turret.

His magic was limited to sleeping spells and relining non-stick cauldrons, unlike Iggata's, which was in the upside-down-waterfall league. She was quite beautiful for a witch, though her expression hard enough to strike a roc out of the sky.

Iggata had ostensibly come to find out if his beard had been singed in the fracas between the dragon and Second Minister. No other member of the Mystic Trine would have shown such concern. Qulio was as blind to her deviousness as Bruno was to Sesame's usefulness and, on top of the turret, the fragrance of the cascading blossom unaccountably made him feel deliciously drowsy.

Qulio sat on the stone bench and leaned back into the perfumed flowers while warm cobweb hues misted his vision as he slowly fell fast asleep.

'Silly old fool,' Iggata chuckled.

Her laugh attracted the attention of a passing minstrel, a short creature wearing motley and enough ribbon to dress a maypole. She carried a lute and opportunism sparkled in her eyes.

As the minstrel stopped to listen, faint words wafted down from the turret. It was an amazing conversation, so amazing most people would not have trusted their own ears. But Crystabel did have very sharp ears.

CHAPTER 27

As evening fell, Bernard sat by himself on the courtyard patio ruefully pondering whether to risk allowing Dr Morgan to take more blood tests which might prove him clinically insane. He could live with the idea of developing diabetes, heart disease, obesity, and even prostate problems, but it's not possible to slap a sticking plaster on the neurons churning out fairyland hallucinations.

Bernard yawned, it was hard work dealing with the fanciful delusions that could have only heralded from a feminine side he didn't know he had. He was a bolshie, not yet balding, blunderbuss with too many mature roles to aim at before an old age when testosterone levels and vocal timbre embarrassingly plunged. Trust Indrina to remind him that manly passion didn't always perform on cue; if only she did believe that episode with the Wagnerian mezzo soprano actually happened. Unfortunately she wasn't furious enough to sound convinced when the story broke in the press.

It was late; the children were fast asleep, Mrs Porter retired to her belfry, and Clarey and Mouse had charitably left him to his own thoughts. Bernard was beginning to wonder if Bruno the doppelganger could have only been his fancy after all. Like an asbestos blanket on a blazing chip pan, the normality of Clarey's humdrum household had virtually extinguished thoughts of the bizarre episode. Scratched shins and eccentric results to medical tests Bernard could rationalise, not the idea he was going mad.

He shuddered at the idea and rose from the wicker chair to stroll round the perimeter of Clarey's sprawling mansion illuminated by haphazardly planted solar lamps that bathed the lavender bushes in a warm glow.

Coming to a tiled glass skylight set in the bottom of an overgrown wall, his thoughts were pleasantly shattered as, from somewhere in the depths of the house, there ascended a pure soprano voice. Bernard had heard many sopranos in his time; glittering, harsh, cavernous, and resonating enough to shatter glass, but never an exquisite sound like this. The studs in the skylight were as thick as any on a busy street, yet might as well have been tissue paper given the ease with which the silver sound rose through it. This revelation was unexpected and flooded his musical sensibilities with awe and admiration. He had to know what creature could produce such vocal strength, range, and clarity.

While the heavenly notes spun their tantalising web, Bernard tried to recall the voices of the women he had seen visit the house in the hope of making a match. He continued listening until the delicious sound faded, yet remained baffled. If Clarey had wanted him to know the owner of this ethereal wonder of the world he would have already been introduced and, being the dented fairy he intermittently suspected he was, Bernard was hardly in a position to insist on being told why such a jewel should be committed to the basement.

During the following nights he made a point of being by the skylight at the same time to listen to the soprano with a range of several octaves and clarity that could be heard over the accompanying instruments. Eventually Bernard could stand it no longer. Bruno and Lustreland were now lower down on his list of priorities: he had to solve the mystery of the magical voice.

He needed the help of Kitty Callahan.

This musicologist was too gifted and discriminating to be labelled a mere talent scout with an ear for the potentially great voice. She had been the one to notice Bernard's youthful potential before he became aware of breathing exercises, Weight Watchers, and Schubert. If it were not for Kitty he would have still been singing to the razzled patrons of working men's clubs and part timing in a chip shop.

Whether the beautiful three octave voice in the cellar remained unknown because of modesty or stage fright, Kitty was the only person Bernard knew who could persuade the woman to reveal her remarkable talent to the world.

Luckily, Clarey Ditton-Davis had heard of Kitty Callahan and was happy to invite her down for a couple of days.

Even though Bernard knew Clarey to be a music lover, it still came as a surprise to find out just how knowledgeable he was. He even had a theory that the likes of Bernard's bass baritone was a recent innovation to the world of song, and probably Homo sapiens. Using historical and anthropological illustrations, his reasoning was that, as deeper voices tended to belong to larger bodied people, there must have been a time, somewhere between Ramapithecus and Jesus Christ, when bass voices were something of a novelty. Bernard was at a loss to see how their remote ancestors could have scared off a lion by squeaking at it, and had to hide his discomfort at being made to wonder if he was a direct descendant of Australopithecus robustus with an alto screaming to get out. It didn't help that Bernard's parents had also undermined their son's confidence for aspiring to become an opera singer, and even his pet mynah bird used to whistle mockingly at him whenever he sang. Having a bird as a critic as well as his parents gave the child a complex even before he found out what lamb chops were made of.

Kitty's arrival was discreet, in a taxi, and with a modest travelling case, which made her unexpected appearance all a more intriguing to the children and gardeners alike. The only person not to welcome her was Mrs Porter. Bernard wasn't surprised. He had expected the woman to dislike music as well as soft towels, spring flowers, dewy-eyed puppies, and gnaw raw meat while it was still warm.

Kitty was in late middle-age and apparently stopped thinking about fashion after the seventies. Her small-featured face, rounded out from the pointed chin that seemed to be the pivot of her head, was crowned with a mop of grey hair tucked into a large pleat. Tiny diamond earrings studded those precious ears with only the suggestion of a lobe and behind the half moon spectacles large, glittering eyes betrayed a cut glass intellect. Her immaculately tailored clothes were not in the style that attracts because she was, above all else, a listener. Kitty Callahan's own talents went far beyond the music parlour, being able to play half a dozen totally different instruments and sing tolerably well.

She also had encyclopaedic recall and the perception of a diagnosing scanner.

'You haven't done any breathing exercises for weeks, Bernard,' she immediately accused before he had chance to open his mouth.

He wasn't surprised by the comment; her powers of observation had ceased to amaze him years ago.

'Things have been a little strange, lately.'

'Have you been ill?'

Bernard blushed like a schoolboy caught with his fingers in the biscuit tin. 'Only a little.'

She laughed. 'Silly man.'

After Kitty had paid polite attention to Clarey's musical instrument collection, patted several inquisitive children almost as tall as herself on the head, and unpacked a change of clothes, Bernard was at last able to explain the real reason he wanted to see her.

Kitty listened to his enthusiastic outpouring about the extraordinary voice he had discovered with noncommittal interest.

'Well let's wait until we've heard her, dear boy,' was the underwhelming response.

CHAPTER 28

Aquelia did not often venture into Darkle Deeps. The pitch was difficult to clean from her scales, ogres saw it as a matter of machismo to do combat with serpents and, after she had constricted the stupid creatures, they were impossible to swallow. She wouldn't have been there at all, but had a strange fancy for something exotic, something that only scuttled about the unlikely living spaces this dismal domain provided. A ruppob, or gofferhog, perhaps. The ogres were usually too slow to catch them and, when they did, only their chief was allowed to eat the delicacies. After living for over three centuries in the larger cracks of Rara Avis Ridge, a serpent deserved to satisfy a few menopausal cravings.

Aquelia peered into each deep hole she passed and hissed at the putrid fumes wafting up. Whatever had fallen down them must have been decomposing for a long while. This was a waste of time. The serpent puffed out her cheek pouches in disgust, resigned that they would still be empty on her journey back to Rara Avis Ridge.

Then Aquelia's tongue flickered enthusiastically. Were her senses deceiving her, or did she smell goblin? The molecules which could only be wafted by that bipedal, burrowing species hung enticingly in the air. In Rara Avis Ridge and Lustreland she was forbidden to give a goblin so much as a hungry glance, but in Darkle Deeps - who would know the difference?

Flunkin was used to the dark and could see quite well at the bottom of the shaft which had closed over his head, enough to tell that there was something peculiar about the rocks enclosing him. At that depth they usually caved in, not emitted a long, low groan as though possessed by a living entity. It crossed the goblin's horrified mind that he was in the pit of a huge stomach. Then, in true goblin fashion, Flunkin rationalised the prospect of being propelled through some monster's intestines. There had to be another route out other than that.

Then whatever had swallowed him decided that some creatures were just too toxic to digest and a retched violently. The floor of the cave juddered and belled upwards to vomit the goblin out. Gems cannoned from the walls like a ballistic hailstorm, nicking pieces out of Flunkin.

In a final, convulsive spasm, the Hurglabat coughed with an explosive roar and the cave was turned inside out.

Aquelia stopped investigating holes in the pitch to watch in amazement as a fountain of gems with a goblin on top of it erupted from the ground.

With a long, loud wail, Flunkin landed on a mound of sharp, precious stones.

The goblin's irrational avarice immediately quelled the pain and, without waiting to check for broken bones, he scurried about, replacing the jewels that had spilled from his knapsack. He was so engrossed he didn't notice the hungry serpent looking down at him from the end of a particularly long coil.

Having crammed as much as he could into his knapsack and pockets, Flunkin then tightened his belt and proceeded to pack the sparkling booty into his jerkin. Only when he was weighed down and it was impossible for him to run did he look up and see Aquelia contemplating whether he would comfortably fit into one of her cheek pouches.

'Hello.' Flunkin gave a watery smile, automatically stuffing precious stones into the upturned cuffs of his boots without taking his eyes off her.

Flunkin was aware that serpents had a penchant for gems. They occasionally visited the larger mines and wended their ways through the chambers looking for the odd stone that might take their fancy - The goblins never protested of course. Even greed had its limits.

'Fancy making your fortune?'

Aquelia gave an enigmatic blink as though measuring Flunkin's calorific value.

He desperately held up the brightest gem he could find. 'Thousands of them. How many do you want?'

Serpents always wore the same expression; a sinisterly contented smile that could have meant they had just heard a good joke or were about to swallow the largest meal of their life.

Flunkin held his breath; the offered gem was getting heavy and his own fixed smile was causing his cheekbones pain.

At last Aquelia, open jawed, lunged down on the goblin.

With amazing delicacy for a creature the height of a mature tree and with fangs like the pikes of four troll guards, she picked the gem from his fingers and swallowed it into her pouch. Then the serpent seized the goblin by his heels and upended him. Gems scattered everywhere. Aquelia leisurely selected the biggest and brightest as well as several for their novelty value.

When she had left, Flunkin scrabbled what remained of his ill-gotten gains back into his knapsack.

The goblin wailed to himself all the way back to camp, even though he had enough gems left to buy a crown and another domain to go with it.

CHAPTER 29

Clarey and Mouse had plenty to occupy them once the children were asleep and were happy to let their guests wander.

Knowing neither Indrina nor the taxwoman would understand them, Mouse would have attempted to put the household accounts in order, but the ledgers were snatched away by a zealous Mrs Porter before he could so much as tally up the week's consumption of jelly babies. Clarey reassured him that anything outstanding would be put right by donating another Dutch master or the ceremonial silver salver to the nation.

Bernard discreetly showed Kitty the way to the overgrown skylight, hoping that the routine of the mysterious soprano would not be disrupted by her arrival. He assumed that Clarey would spend the evening visiting one of the alternative dimensions kept in his Chinese cabinet. So he and Kitty patiently waited for some sign of the magical music he had insisted would astound even her experience ear. Time passed and Bernard felt a flush of embarrassment under his collar; why did he always blush in the presence of the only woman he would have sold his soul to impress? Even in the falling dusk, she must have noticed.

Thankfully the lights went on in the sunken room, which Kitty deduced was a ballroom as there wasn't one on any other level.

After a few bars from a harpsichord, that clear voice carried upwards like a shaft of light through gauze curtains.

Bernard was too enraptured by the sound to notice Kitty's lack of kindred enthusiasm. When he eventually became aware that her lips were pursed critically and eyes squinted in disapproval he was crestfallen. 'What's wrong? Isn't that the most beautiful soprano you've ever heard?'

'Yes,' agreed Kitty, 'and I've listened to quite a few.'

'Then what's wrong?'

'You are a silly man, Bernard.' She suddenly smiled. 'I don't blame you for wanting me to hear it, though would have preferred not to.'

He was astounded. 'What?'

'The owner of that voice knows they would be better off remaining anonymous. Just you forget you ever heard it, Bernard,' and she actually started to walk away before the ethereal voice had finished singing.

He was torn between staying and pursuing her. 'I don't understand?'

She turned back. 'This is a strange world, Bernard. We think it is so enlightened compared to the way it used to be, when actually our modern sensibilities are still as narrow-minded as they ever were. But then, you probably never log onto Facebook or Twitter.'

'What are you talking about?'

'If that voice was celebrated in public its owner would be ridiculed by the tabloid press, music establishment, and bar room comics - not to mention all the online bigots now get the opportunity to air their toxic points of view.' Kitty strode off again and Bernard had to catch up.

'But why? How can you be so sure when you don't even know who she is? Who would want to ridicule perfection like that? The woman's a genius.'

Kitty stopped suddenly in her tracks and looked up at the night sky to indicate that, as far as she was concerned, the conversation was over. 'I can see a shooting star.'

'I don't understand?'

She gave a deep sigh. 'Nobody would attack a woman with a voice like that. Opera houses would double the seat prices to pay her fees, young men who normally only looked at each other would dote on her, even if she was sixteen stone and my age, and old men would demand to die listening to her when their times came, but ...'

Bernard was beside himself with frustration. 'But? What possible reason is there for a voice like that to be ridiculed?'

'It's surprising how differently a work of art is viewed once we know who actually created it.'

'So? We're not talking about Hitler's paintings. Hitler wasn't a genius - this woman is. Her background is hardly going to matter.'

'No it wouldn't - If the voice belonged to a woman.'

Incomprehension silenced Bernard until what she had said sank in. 'But a boy's treble could never have that power and range?'

'You still don't want to see, do you? You always were stubborn about admitting your little prejudices.'

'Me? Prejudiced?' the singer blustered.

'Like how you resolutely refuse to use your falsetto for fear of being laughed at.'

Bernard was now fearful of what he might hear. 'I still don't understand?'

Kitty gave another long sigh. 'Your heavenly, exquisite, unique, soprano voice is unique - because it belongs to a man!'

Bernard was silent for some time, hardly daring to use the taboo word. 'A castrato? She certainly can't be a counter tenor.'

'I can hardly tell the fellow's anatomical composition from here, though I wouldn't be at all surprised. It's possible for a whole man to sing as a soprano, though not with that scintillating clarity. And just recall the trouble modern counter tenors had in being accepted. Anything higher than their range coming from a man is bound to encounter resistance - perhaps outrage. If the voice weren't so brilliant few people outside the music world would pay much attention but, as you rightly said, this is genius and difficult to ignore. In your soprano's case, if he has any sensitivity, it's probably wise he does confine his talent to a cellar.'

Bernard desperately hoped even she could be wrong. 'You are sure?'

Her silence convinced him more eloquently than words.

He groaned. 'Oh hell.'

'Does your soprano still sound so good?'

Bernard was far away. 'Who could that voice belong to, though?'

'Leave it alone, Bernard. Living in our society so full of obsessions about virility and appearance without your full manhood must be bad enough. Just think of the gift he would be to internet trolls and witless bloggers who can only attract attention by holding extreme opinions. Our singer must be aware of what would happen if he went public.'

'But should the world never hear this voice because of a vindictive minority?'

'That vindictive minority have more influence over the way we all think than we like to admit. Our sopranist understands the quality of his voice and has made the decision not to declare it. We have to respect that.'

Kitty left Bernard sitting in the courtyard. As one tumultuous episode in his life had been dealt with, he felt another beginning to present itself.

Dark thoughts in the recesses of the bass baritone's mind glimmered into life. The pages in the volume of prejudice he refused to acknowledge began to turn. Kitty was right. This catalogue of submerged intolerances had lain in wait for the very occasion when someone like this miraculous soprano made his entrance. Bernard had to admit that he would have been one of the many to damn the singer as an unnatural creature; one of those who insisted that the most humane way to treat antique roles composed for his kind was with the female substitute where the counter tenor dare not tread. But then, he had always nursed a fancy for bosomy sopranos dressed in armour or knee breaches.

Bernard marvelled at the suppressed desires and fancies that had lurked with his other murky prejudices. He felt quite disgusted with himself for having given them a home. Something had to be done about this. He had always presented himself as such a respectable fellow. Whatever Italian divas and the rest of the world may have accused him of in the past, he had always been honest, dignified and faithful to his wife, even if all three virtues had repaid him with nothing but hallucinations and tension headaches. Gone was the advice once offered to him by a veteran bass baritone just before he retired at 80. 'We should always show intelligence when handling even the most banal role - but never think. It's better not to know what a fool the librettist is making of you. Such is life.'

CHAPTER 30

Mr Paton was an anonymous looking man. He was always dressed in powder grey suits and ties striped with pastel blue or green, and his well-manicured hands wore no ornaments. Pale eyes framed by lashless lids that could never express intensity or fanaticism punctuated a line free face which, fortunately for him and anyone else who might have seen it at an inconvenient moment, had no distinguishing features, handsome or ugly. This bland enigma never carried anything bulkier than a briefcase, even though he might have been travelling from one end of the Earth to the other. He also wore no locket with picture, or carried a wallet with family photos or monograms. He was the sort of identikit picture witnesses construct when they have nothing much to remember and source of puzzlement to customs officers if no one else.

Almost as much could be said for the two men who joined him that chilly summer afternoon for a stroll through Hyde Park. Flanked by a navy blue trench coat with trilby, and black overcoat with Homburg, Mr Paton and his companions strode out leisurely - international executives teasing over a business transaction.

'Case 147 needs better finance,' announced the Homburg. 'The government might regain power if tanks aren't sent in right away.'

Paton was not convinced. 'Won't the rebels become suspicious?'

'They're too committed to their cause to ask where the funds are coming from. It's cheaper to let them fight for our interests without knowing it than having to hire mercenaries. We've infiltrated them well enough to take over with only half a dozen assassinations. If this government gets back in there is no one we can rely on.'

'All right. We need their uranium deposits. Pity to see all that revenue wasted on the Third World.'

'They've managed to live on corn, rice and millet for so long, what would they want with power stations and bombs?' added the trilby.

'A crack at us.' The homburg laughed gruffly and caught the attention of a galloping red setter.

As its owner came within earshot, the conversation was halted until a shrill whistle called the dog back to its regular route.

'How much?' asked Paton.

'Twenty million.'

'All right. It'll be in the Swiss account tomorrow. I'll arrange the usual precautions.' Then as an afterthought, 'Use the oil account this time.'

The trilby's stride remained unbroken as he turned to look at Paton. 'Something wrong?'

'Last week some hacker managed to get the bank's computer to read out.'

'How?' demanded the homburg.

Paton gave a slight movement of the shoulders that would have been a shrug from anyone else. 'It might have been a programming error or coincidence. Doubt it was the Chinese.'

'We don't want them muscling in.'

'We'll have to cut a deal with them eventually now they're buying up Africa. This glitch was probably only taken advantage of by some pubescent hacker. Anyway, the information is useless without the dollar and gold holdings.'

'I don't like glitches like that,' agreed the trilby. 'We should transfer it again.'

'Moving that amount of capital in one transaction would attract attention. Better to ditch the account if it becomes compromised. There is no way it can be traced and we can afford to lose the fifty million. We'll be making treble that in the next arms deal alone.'

'You'd think, given how lucrative the arms trade has become, liberal do-gooders would be taking a moral stance by now.'

'Not when a country's economic stability depends on it. We've got too many senators, MPs and newspaper proprietors in our pay, and these people are easily squished if they try to blow the whistle.' Paton gave a bird like laugh. 'If there's any condition worse for the human mind than keeping it confined, it's telling it to think for itself. Fortunately for us all the new democracies have brought everyone down to the same level of self-interest. Be sure to attend the meeting next week.'

The homburg sighed. 'I suppose we have to bring the flowing robes and chain mail?'

'Of course you do.'

'All this mumbo jumbo is so childish.'

'It's our cover. You know it's necessary.'

'But no spells and chanting this time - please.'

Paton was implacable. 'If we are ever discovered it will save the network. People are prepared to accept magic, secret societies, and Satanism - but not the realities that affect their lives. The reluctance of the world to believe it is being manipulated is our greatest weapon, mark my words. Now let's call it a day before that dog and its owner come back.'

And the companions parted, each to his own route.

CHAPTER 31

As he dozed, Qulio heard singing. The voice below the turret was earthy and the words of the song questionable. The fact that he understood them quite surprised him. But the wizard had to be dreaming those rasping tones screaming at the minstrel - Iggata would never have uttered such abuse. The voice of the minstrel stopped with a sudden clang that sounded like an accurately aimed spell invoking the gong struck by the time troll.

Thankfully, pillows of cotton wool cloud carried Qulio off into the blissful realms of sweet dreams. He didn't go there very often because there was always so much to do in Lustreland, but once free of his responsibilities the guilt faded. After all, without his presence would the breeze cease to busy itself annoyingly about the Mystic Trine's magic pinnacle, would Juniper no longer remember where to collect herbs or all the changelings have toothaches at the same time?

The wizard wondered why he didn't come to this dimension more often. Here he was free of the vindictive Mystic Trine, bickering councillors and bone loss. Here the aches of decades no longer existed and timidity was a virtue. For all that, Qulio dare not enter any of the weightless crystal castles rising from this heavenly realm. Through their walls he could see deities gleaming in rainbow robes and in the pastures beyond, sparkling fountains and frolicking unicorns. Best of all, there were no witches or warlocks. They had probably created their own paradise somewhere out of time to avoid benign creatures like him and with a pension scheme he wouldn't be allowed to join.

Then it began.

Now Qulio recalled why he avoided this dimension. Every time he had been invited in it was always the same.

At first they were only a speck on the fluffy horizon, their mellifluous music so unlike that minstrel's. Melodies played on the harp of the wind unfurled like velvet ribbon as the miraculous cacophony came towards him - it never went anywhere else - heralding the familiar nightmare.

Qulio didn't try to escape. He suspected that this procession accompanied by ethereal trumpet tones must have been punishment for some long forgotten misdemeanour.

Flower petals and a drizzle of fragrant perfume engulfed the wizard. He sneezed.

Once again he was borne aloft on those billowing clouds, up to the gleaming turrets of the tallest tower where the Ligh Tofrea Sun resided. The light filling this Universe was so intense, Qulio he felt as though he would melt.

The dreaming wizard's foot lashed out and upset Iggata's small dish of spell powder as he struggled to free himself.

Then Qulio felt himself plunging down, down ... into the heady fragrance of the vine on the turret.

The minstrel had started to sing again and the witch was shouting abuse. Before Qulio's eyelids could flutter open, the harsh voice hesitated. A hard, cold hand was placed on his forehead and a blanket of mumbled words engulfed the thoughts tempting him to wake.

This spell was more powerful and dragged him down to dimensions deeper than he had been to before; so deep, Qulio had to gasp for breath.

Where was he? These depths were below no goblin realm, or even Darkle Deeps. Down here lurked something too sinister to have originated in his pastel thoughts.

The wizard was suffocating. He tried to escape the dream, but some horror refused to release him. There was a roar of rage that rose to a crescendo as the tentacles of a gelatinous monster thrashed about him. The creature's dimensions were huge, growing like a cancerous growth on the underbelly of some benighted domain.

With the courage of desperation, Qulio tried to grasp the umbilical cord that secured the monstrosity's life to the dimension it had infested. If he could only tear it free he never need have this nightmare again.

The wizard's extraordinary strength became supernatural. The monster's thorny tentacles entangled themselves and knocked pieces from the massive labyrinth it filled. With a burst of fury the monster hurled Qulio away. The wizard went spinning upwards and once again the fragrance of the vine filled his long nostrils.

CHAPTER 32

Peter watched through his cellar window as Indrina made her way past the trees in the orchard. She seemed unusually interested in selecting an early apple, and was examining it as he let her in.

'They'll not be ready for another month,' chided Peter as he let her in.

Indrina laughed and tossed him the small, hard fruit. 'You've got CCTV in the orchard as well?'

'Everywhere that matters. Don't tell Isolda.' He briefly checked his surveillance monitor to ensure that no one was taking an interest in the cellar. The problem of living under a hotel was that he could never be sure who the guests were. When he had settled there, he hadn't expected that his curiosity about international corruption would become focused on trying to discover the criminals who allowed half of his adopted tribe to be slaughtered and the rest to starve. What they had been responsible for in other countries didn't bear thinking about.

Indrina decided to bide her time before dropping the bombshell. If not done carefully the reaction from the normally placid giant would do his heart no good at all.

The accountant placed her briefcase on a large table made from the cross section of a tree. 'This is new?'

'Hmm..?' Peter was far away. 'Oh yes. To pass the time in the evenings I count its rings.'

'Where did you get it?'

'Timber merchant. It was from an old oak he felled and kiln dried over ten years ago. Was intended for panelling in the town hall, then the contract fell through.'

'How did he manage to dry it in one piece?'

'I suppose he cut it first.'

'He wouldn't have been able to use it for panels in cross section.'

Peter was on tenterhooks and in no mood to make small talk. 'Have you come here to argue mathematics with the furniture?'

'You know I see the world as a gigantic jigsaw and like to put the pieces together whenever I get the chance.'

'I had noticed.'

Indrina pulled a folder from her briefcase. She settled into an armchair then opened it. 'Peter, have you ever wondered about the power of the weapons industry?'

He sat down to face her. 'Of course. Everyone knows that arms manufacturers have enough clout to oust a president.'

'And a good many economies would go into decline if some nations didn't have arms industries?'

Peter wasn't so sure. 'Would they?'

'The wealthier nations rely heavily on weapons production and depend on there being enough repressive regimes about the world willing to buy them.'

'Go on?'

'And it takes an inordinate degree of manipulation to keep these tyrants in power.'

'I've no doubt about that.'

'Not to mention the oil industry who wouldn't be allowed to destroy the environment without people in the right places.'

Peter fixed the accountant with a penetrating gaze. 'I know my opinion of politicians isn't very high, but...'

'Governments don't have to be involved. They aren't the ones with the real power. Multinational companies are. They and the world's banks control the planet's economy.'

The penny dropped. 'You're talking about a secret organisation, aren't you?'

'Undoubtedly global.'

'Go on?'

'A contact of mine in the States accidentally stumbled on vast dollar and gold reserves.'

'Accidentally?'

'He was hacking into several banks' non-invested accounts for the executors of the estate of an eccentric old lady. She had secretly tucked away large sums of dollars in static accounts because she had some peculiar notion about it being evil to let money breed. The amount involved was considerable... but nowhere near as huge as some other massive sums of money he discovered lying stagnant. To accountants that sort of stillness can mean a very deep pool, especially to ones with dubious reputations, like my contact's. He was an accomplished hacker, but unable to find out who owned them. The account numbers had no names and it was probably only some security blip that allowed him to see them in the first place. He decided to check the bullion and fed in the phantom account numbers. The same thing happened. There were tons of the gold belonging to an equally phantom owner. Then alarm bells started ringing and he got cold feet. He stopped checking. This was something bigger than the Mafia or bankers salting away illegally invested income for a rainy day and it would have been dangerous if he was traced.'

Peter scratched his head. Having guessed where she was leading, he wasn't too sure he wanted to follow. 'The Internal Revenue must know who owns large amounts of bullion? It's not like figures. It's bulky and has to be stored somewhere.'

'That's right.'

The brandy flush drained from Peter's dark cheeks. 'What proof have you?'

'My contact may be a mature hacker, but he reached 50 because he knows when to stop.' Indrina flourished the open folder. 'It's all circumstantial.'

'What about the independent press?'

'Finding it would be more difficult than passing a wheelbarrow up the backside of a constipated civil servant.'

Peter groaned. This was too much for him to take in at once. He would have known what to do about international criminals; he had been working on that assumption for years. Now Indrina had taken away his chance to become harmlessly eccentric and make anonymous serial phone calls to various police departments. If there was an international cartel sucking the world's resources dry, what hope was there for the rain forest or Siberian tiger? Who was going to stop them when so many regimes needed to placate populations throwing off their sandals for expensive trainers and demanding concrete wonderlands in which to drive their new cars.

Peter got up to pour two brandies and handed one to Indrina before slumping into his favourite armchair. 'I joined the Green Party, y'know.'

'Thought you were a Social Democrat?'

'Liked to think I was. Creeping cynicism has taken its toll.' Peter plucked at his frizzy grey locks. 'How on earth can we identify this international cartel?'

'We can't. They must be using the cover of some unregistered organisation to communicate directly.' The accountant slowly sipped her brandy. 'Perhaps there is a way ...'

'What way?'

'I'm not telling you.'

Indrina was startled to find an angry Peter suddenly towering over her.

'You are not going to do anything dangerous! I forbid it!'

She looked up at his flushed face in momentary amazement, and then smiled sweetly. 'There is nothing dangerous in what I have in mind, Peter. Not even a calculated risk and, if it comes to it, I can calculate very well.'

He wandered away growling. If the rest of the world was stupid enough to let a secret consortium created by rich nations bleed it of its natural resources, pollute the atmosphere, and turn the oceans into open sewers, that had to be its own look out.

Being Olan Peter Martin, he couldn't hold that point of view for long. 'Perhaps there is something I can do.'

'What?'

'You're too hard-headed to understand.'

'I've always suspected you were a mystic. So was my great grandfather. You may be four times his size, but have that otherworldly aura of the psychic limpet mine about to explode its way through the shell of reality.'

Peter gave her a sideways glance, half afraid the accountant believed what she had said. 'The Green Man, standing stones, and ley lines I leave to the devotees of the magic mushroom.'

Indrina nevertheless suspected that he had taken round trips through more than one dimension. 'Your plan's not dangerous is it?'

His shaking head almost reassured her.

'Telepathy?'

'A little more reliable than that.'

Indrina suddenly realised. 'You've got a mole!'

'More of a wizened bat.'

'But what does it have access to apart from caves full of guano?'

'Anything that smells twice as bad if you like.'

'Multinational computers? International banks? Are they any good at cracking passwords?' Indrina asked eagerly.

'You mean computer passwords?'

'Well I'm not talking about runes.'

'Perhaps. Depending on what you're going to do with them?'

'There are ways to cover your tracks,' she protested innocently.' If this money is so well protected there must be umpteen passwords for each account.'

'And you would like all of them?'

Indrina watched him carefully for a moment. 'How could his mole get at that sort of information without being telepathic?'

Peter flickered an eyebrow. 'Trust me?'

She trusted the mild-mannered man more than any other living being, and perhaps it was best neither of them knew what the other was going to do. If he could come up with those passwords, she would get unrestricted access to all the syndicate's currency and gold.

Peter smiled benignly. 'It will be much easier than cracking a safe, Indrina.'

'Quite a safe with international banking involved. Governments and multinationals can't operate without it.'

'Not tempted?'

'Bernard is convinced I'm obsessed with money, but I do have some scruples.'

Peter went to his cabinet which held his stash of forbidden treats and reached for a cigar. Then he opened its other door and the sweet, dry aroma of biscuits, spices, and almond marzipan wafted towards Indrina. Her hand extended to take the jar of preserved stem ginger and fork from him.

'Don't complain about me smoking and I'll not warn you about your waistline.' He puffed his cigar into life.

'Hang diets. Why should I be so fussy about my figure when I've got a husband who was expelled from Weight Watchers? You should be more worried about your heart.'

'Well, they can't patch it up, can they.'

Indrina was taken aback. 'I didn't know.'

'Too old for a transplant. Even if I wanted one. Messy business anyway. Let the heart go to someone with a bit more mileage in them.'

'I'd no idea things were that bad?'

'So don't be too surprised when it does happen.' Peter slowly drew on his cigar. 'What would be your definition of "some unregistered organisation"?'

Indrina shrugged. 'Bent charity, perhaps a secret society, though it's more likely to be a fanatical religious order left well alone by the authorities - chasing witches is politically incorrect nowadays.'

'Secret Satanic society?'

'Aleister Crowley sort of thing. One that boasts it can control the world with magic. Gives out the smokescreen of a loony do-gooder club.'

'What makes you so sure it has something to do with the occult?'

Indrina pulled a paper from the folder. 'Judging by the movement in the accounts, we know they get together every lunar month.'

Peter beamed. 'Every full moon.' He changed the subject. 'How's Bernard?'

'Driving Kitty Callahan and Clarey round the bend most probably. When I spoke to Clarey yesterday he told me that Pudding seemed all right. The children like him anyway. They think he's got a growl like a teddy bear.'

'You will call on him some time?'

'He's fine now.' Peter frowned and she sighed. 'Oh all right. I haven't seen Kitty for years anyway, but all this running around is going to cost me business.'

'Not that much. Bernard isn't as well as he appears, you mark my words.'

This Indrina did, although she also wondered how he could be so sure about that.

CHAPTER 33

The new seam in the ogres' dinosaur bone mine was at last ready. Though the goblins were unable to see what nutrition could be had from the desiccated marrow of bones buried so long in the ground, the ogres managed to survive on them. And no one was going to suggest that they should go back to eating other people. The goblins hoped that the disreputable détente that they had cemented with Jobaloba ensured that they would not end up under his rusty boots when they marched through their region to reach Lustreland.

After watching the ogre army fighting amongst themselves for the pick of the weapons stacked in the fortress's armoury, Flunkin and his crew had kept a safe distance as they lumbered off to Rara Avis Ridge. As soon as there was no one left to notice (except the female ogres who were easily bribed to keep quiet with a few choice jewels) the goblin miners made their way home by a route which did not involve mountain passes, nesting rocs, and which had a roof too low to accommodate an ogre.

Flunkin kept his haul of gems a secret by hiding in the cuffs of his boots those he couldn't sew into the seams of his coat. Some slipped down and, as each sharp edge bit into his feet, ambition and irritation with humdrum goblindom increased to the point where he resolved to turn into a real tyrant at the first opportunity.

Goblin rulers had been magicians, wealthy merchants, and even women, yet never an out and out tyrant. Flunkin wasn't totally sure how to go about it, but with his newly acquired wealth he could buy anything he wanted, apart from the inevitability of having to face up to Rimonay for overthrowing the goblin region's democracy. Hopefully the ogres would keep her occupied while he was putting his plan into action. His mother would probably call him a pin-brained fool and his wife empty the frying pan over his head, so Flunkin would have to buy another wife - and another mother if he could find one willing to take the job. With total control of the mines, he would even be wealthy enough to rule any other part of Lustreland the ogres were stupid enough to sell him.

In his increasing reverie, the icy glare of the First Minister no longer held any terror for Flunkin.

The goblin's theft of its gems did not escape the Hurglabat, but he was just a minor crumb in the horrific banquet it was anticipating. The monster did have a use for Aquelia the serpent, though.

Having returned to Rara Avis Ridge and disgorged the stolen booty into a glittering pile on the floor of her lair, Aquelia coiled herself about it, defying any other fabulous beast to commit burglary. If Lustrelanders had known that serpents searched for the biggest and brightest gems only to try and hatch them out, they would have refused to be intimidated by them any more. The enigmatic expression of a serpent was believed to conceal sinister depths, not such amazing naïveté. As well as these strange inclinations and cravings for unlikely morsels, Aquelia could be very suggestible, as one fortunate goblin had realised, and the Hurglabat was easily able to place an idea in her marble-sized mind. Persuading her to part with one of her glittering stones was more problematic.

Aquelia flickered her tongue. A mysterious thought was telling her that she had a fancy. She wasn't quite sure what for; the increasingly scare gofferhogs had dropped from her menu some while ago and she had just missed her chance for an illegal morsel of goblin. No, it was a craving for something more mystical, like the potent juice from a warlock's summer pudding.

Few knew where the recipe had come from because Lustreland had no seasons, and this dish was made with anything but fruit. The Mystic Trine's librarian had an ancient recipe book which explained that its creation was the product of a dimensional overlap triggered by a chef experimenting after too many cooking sherries. She had tucked the book away in an unseen partition on its shelf, indexed as "Thing to try later", to ensure no one else found it. Unlike Aquelia, the librarian really was deep and sinister.

Now, where could the serpent find a warlock or witch willing to let her dip into their cauldron?

It was difficult to find pure evil in Lustreland because of the inhibiting influence of the Ligh Tofrea Sun and, for its scheme to succeed, the Hurglabat needed undiluted wickedness. Then it detected a witch who seemed pretty pleased with herself strolling the woodland borders, and the Hurglabat knew that it wasn't because she had just helped an elderly troll out of a family landslide. No one but a truly accomplished member of the Mystic Trine would dare wander alone on the very edge of Lustreland. This witch radiated pure evil and her thoughts were labyrinthine. Attempting to manipulate them was like trying to make slate shine. The Hurglabat only just managed to slot a tiny urge into the witch's mental fortress before quickly retracting its psychic tentacles so she didn't have time to realise what had happened.

Not even Iggata was prepared to attract the attention of the cave deities and took a prudent detour around Deity Rock. Normally she wouldn't have walked at all - when you had a state of the art besom, why bother with legs? But this was the nearest she would ever get to skipping with joy. She had the right to feel smug for ensuring that Qulio would not be around to interfere when Dragon Sesame was once again summoned to save Lustreland.

Then, not knowing why, the witch was aware of a fancy. Her thoughts usually knew better than to dawdle off into unmapped regions and she had no idea why she felt impelled to make her way towards the woodland strand adjoining Rara Avis Ridge. Perhaps the shopping list she had committed to her subconscious was insisting that she needed some new minerals? Spell power was dependent on their purity, and stocks were getting low.

As the misty peaks of the fabulous beasts' home loomed into view there was the rasping of scales behind her.

Iggata spun round, long nail ready to hurl a paralysing curse. The rasping stopped and a face with a fixed smile peered down at her. The witch knew that serpents were stupid, yet never underestimated their appetite.

Aquelia was not keen on being turned into some lowly monotreme or amphibian so immediately spat out a brilliant gem from her cheek pouch with such vigour it chipped on a rock.

Iggata turned the large coruscating jewel over with the toe of her cat skin shoe - suddenly aware it was the very gem she needed, even though had never seen its like before.

The witch fixed the serpent with the evil eye. 'How much?'

Aquelia was fazed for a moment. Serpents were the ones who were supposed to have the hypnotic gaze and she almost forgot what fancy had brought her all the way to Lustreland's border.

Of course! She wanted a summer pudding.

Iggata read Aquelia's mind. The witch had at least expected to be asked to hollow out a new lair, or for a joint of braised goblin. But then, serpents were stupid.

At the risk of losing a finely honed nail, the witch snapped her fingers. A cauldron appeared. Inside it was a large pudding.

Aquelia instantly snatched it up and wended her way back to her cave.

Iggata put the gem into her pouch and whistled down her broomstick. Now she had a new novelty the desire to walk had worn off.

As soon as she returned home she put the gem in a safe place and promptly forgot about it.

CHAPTER 34

By the way Kitty Callaghan accepted Clarey's invitation to be his guest for a few more days it became apparent she was more curious about Bernard's discovery than willing to admit. Well aware of how busy his mentor always was, the singer suspected that the talent scout in her knew something he did not.

He had been developing his own theory about Mouse, the strangely enigmatic nanny to Clarey's children. Could it be that his host collected voices as well musical instruments? Although the bass baritone had not been expected to sing a note all the time he had been there, Bernard did feel a little like a prize exhibit, albeit in the most pleasant possible way. Kitty was less diplomatic and insisted he work on breathing exercises and take long walks round the estate to remove a few layers from his thickening waistline.

It was on one of those resented excursions that Bernard strolled over a Georgian bridge to the folly on an island in the park's lake and up an avenue of stone beasts. An explicitly displaying satyr stood on a plinth outside the entrance to a mock Roman temple of fertility with a conical roof of scallop shell tiles. Whatever the virtues of the early estate owner, reticence had not been one of them. Little light reached the folly's interior through the embrasures in its walls and narrow portal, which was probably why two people had chosen the temple for a secret assignation. Bernard would have resisted the temptation to eavesdrop if it had not been for the high-pitched voice of Mrs Porter. Drawing closer, he also heard the cool considered tones of Clarey remonstrating with his secretary. It was apparent that they were discussing Mouse.

Mrs Porter's next words had him listening intently. 'I can't understand why you're so concerned about the little pest. He's no use to you, and certainly no use to any woman. Perhaps that's why you keep him, because he can't touch the goods in your harem.'

'Mouse has been a lifelong friend of mine.' Clarey sounded weary. 'I don't see why that should be any reason to destroy him.'

'The press probably won't play with the story for long. Just long enough to put him off wanting to sing again.'

There was a charged pause before Clarey's voice broke the silence. His tone had hardened considerably. 'You will still have to leave. You are nothing but a cheap opportunist who wheedled herself into this position to find what you could get out of it.'

Mrs Porter's pretence of disciplined correctness, which had so intimidated Bernard and annoyed Indrina, was replaced by something far more unpleasant. 'I'll see you and your pet spread over every tabloid in this country before the month's out.'

'I have no doubt you will. I'd believe that of anyone who could frame their own mother for adultery just to get their claws on the family jewels, but trying to intimidate me by attacking Mouse will not work.'

'You underestimate the interest the gutter press has in your privileged existence. Any copy connected with you is worth a small fortune.'

'Why are you so sure Mouse will be persecuted, even if he never sang in public?' The edge had left Clarey's voice and been replaced with inexplicable curiosity.

'Lack of manhood in our society is almost as shameful as poverty. The fact that the eunuch's a close friend of yours will bring the press like vultures.'

'Has blackmail always been a speciality with you, or is this just one off to spite me?'

There was no reply. Mrs Porter's stiletto heels clicked out her determination as she strode from the folly and over the bridge.

Bernard ducked from view. No troll would have dared stop this woman; even Big Billy Goat Gruff would have stepped aside.

Clarey came out and leaned against the entrance to watch her go. Bernard had never appreciated how tall the man really was until he saw his hair brush against the overhanging tiles. The singer would have needed another six inches and a back brushed wig to reach them.

When Mrs Porter was gone, Clarey pushed his hands into his pockets and sauntered off back to the house.

As soon as his host was out of sight, Bernard dashed off to find Kitty. So agitated by what he had overheard, his foot caught an uneven slab on the bridge as though the resident troll had stuck out its foot to trip him up. Having already engaged the vegetation of the estate in mortal combat, it came as no surprise that the Georgian paving stones should be equally unforgiving.

Bernard dusted himself off and was up and running, albeit with a limp and glad of those breathing exercises as he sped through the park, back to where Kitty sat on the mansion steps trying to teach four baffled youngsters to play the flute.

For all his pent-up excitement, Bernard was ordered to wait until the lesson was over. He sat on a bench like a scolded child under the bemused gaze of Mr Bollinger working in a nearby flowerbed who had at that moment decided to lean on his fork and admire the view.

Eventually the squeaks, squawks, and screeching produced by so many incompetent mouths sent the singer's sense of orientation into a downward spin. He wondered how the delicate hearing of Kitty was able to bear it. It was certainly addling his senses.

By the time the cacophony ceased Bernard was overwhelmed by vertigo and the urgent message he wanted to deliver became a confusion of nonsense. If she hadn't known Bernard well, Kitty would have wondered if her insistence on exercise had triggered a cardiac arrest in her prodigy. But she suspected that this was more to do with mind than matter, and he would be better off away from the gaze of a world liable to show embarrassing interest.

Kitty tried to steady Bernard as she helped him up to his room, and was at least gratified that he had lost several stone since she had discovered him so long ago. Nevertheless, the thought that she could be the only thing between him and a neck breaking plunge back down the stairs encouraged her to hasten the bulky bass baritone upwards. Having witnessed even heavier singers felled by choking neckties and sweltering auditoriums, that was not the sort of major accident she wanted to be under.

Once inside his room, Bernard desperately tried to blurt out what he had discovered; but the words refused to form. Then the light seemed to come and go as though reality was switching itself on and off and he experienced the cold terror that comes when the unsuspecting learn that they are about to die.

Mercifully, his evil fairy did not return, though the odd fragrance of unearthly blossoms briefly filled Bernard's nostrils and he could hear a lute. Someone was singing, not with the ethereal tones of his soprano in the cellar; this was a more robust mezzo-soprano blaring out a bawdy song.

Suddenly two sails flapped about him. Huge wings were scything the air and enormous claws encircled him. He tried to fight them off.

Then blackness.

'Is it necessary to keep him sedated?' Clarey asked.

'I need time to make some tests,' the doctor told him.

'You've seen the results of the first ones, haven't you?' Indrina asked her.

'Yes, Mr Ditton-Davis did show me.' The doctor was professionally silent for a moment as though an awkward patient had asked to see the incriminating diagnosis on her medical record. 'Until I can discover what's wrong with your husband I don't want him moved, though I'll warn the hospital just in case.'

'That's thirty miles away,' protested Clarey. 'I'll cover the cost of any equipment you need here.'

'I know. But some people manage to develop ailments that defy diagnosis as well as treatment.'

'Like plants which inexplicably thrive in some corners and shrivel in others,' Mouse added unhelpfully.

'I've never thought of Bernard as a daisy,' Indrina mused to herself. 'More like that bloody laurel bush which invaded the front drive.'

Clarey took the doctor aside. 'You will do everything you can to help him, won't you?'

'There is no immediate cause for concern, but I would like the nurse to stay here, and if you can ensure someone is with him at all times..?'

Though she realised Bernard's condition was potentially serious, Indrina could not help wondering if some unfathomable part of his personality was throwing a tantrum just to spite her. On the other hand, making her a widow was too dramatic a way to gain sympathy, even for him. However much her mother disapproved of Bernard, she would never have forgiven her for wearing an exotically patterned silk dress ever again: even though sati had been outlawed, widowhood had to be taken seriously.

CHAPTER 35

If there was anything worse than an ogre with a sore head it was an ogre with two sore heads, and Jobaloba exploded with rage after Sesame had swooped from the sky and banged his together with its talons.

The hail of clubs, rocks, and rusty battle-axes failed to hit the dragon as it hovered out of reach so the weapons crashed back onto their owners.

A delegation from Lustreland was monitoring the battle from the safety of a high ledge. The witch in their company occasionally got carried away, hurling spells at Jobaloba's stragglers to paralyse their Achilles tendons or part their beards with bolts of flame. At least the smell of singed hair masked the less fragrant bodily odours wafting up from the grunting melee.

With the fracas between dragon and ogres at its height, the ground shook as though about to liquefy.

The entity that had sent Jobaloba's hoards on this invasion of Lustreland was encouraging its troops; either that or it was coming up to finish off the dragon for itself. The ogre chief had no intention of becoming the corned beef in the resulting rock sandwich and, with the strength of ten warriors, hurled his battle-axe at Sesame. Being dangerously complacent, the dragon wasn't expecting the glancing blow that sent it somersaulting towards the cliff face where the Lustrelanders were clustered. The impact forced an involuntary jet of flame from the fabulous beast and the onlookers were scorched before it could regain its wings.

Infuriated, Sesame concentrated its fire on the narrow pass that led up to Lustreland and melted the rock. This flowed into the path of the oncoming army and set like a sheet of glass. The ogres had trouble coordinating their feet on firm ground and, on this slippery surface, they could only crawl. Some attempted to escape by clambering up the mountain and disturbed brooding rocs that sent them crashing back down in a hail of nesting boulders.

The dragon continued to pursue them. Even though Jobaloba had two heads, their contents did not make up one average size brain, and having an airborne blowtorch strike them together yet again only created sparks and increased his determination. Unlike their leader, the futility of the venture was beginning to seep through the battered skulls of his troops and the Hurglabat had to tighten its psychic grip on the tiny minds inside them.

An elfin observer gave a premature whoop of victory, only to see the ogres rally and provide Sesame with even more illegal sport in a domain where it would not normally have been allowed to puff so much as a spark at another living creature.

With the relish of a fabulous entity born to blaze, the dragon turned its blowtorch onto another quartz cliff face. The deadly treacle flowed. Many ogre boots remained in the molten river as their owners were chased all the way back to the dried up lake which fed their swampland when the rain on the mountains was torrential enough to fill it.

The dragon decided it was time for a thunderstorm.

The fuming ogre hosts who had not been completely unnerved by the onslaught watched Sesame soar high above them, looping the loop to heat the air with its fire. Even the more perceptive of them still thought rain was poured from the heavens by the supreme giant emptying his chamber pot; that being the only explanation for the stench of their swamps. It quite shattered their illusion when the rotating black clouds released a deluge and rain crashed down the mountains.

The lake furiously started to rise. The cascading water gave the ogres a tumble wash and swept them, so much lighter without their natural grime, into the channel that fed Darkle Deeps. Despite the shock of being suddenly clean and seeing the dragon collect lightning strikes on its spines, both of Jobaloba's heads managed to bellow out that his hoards would be back. In reply, Sesame swooped down and discharged the lightning into the lake's surface. The shock jolted the ogres onwards, carrying them back down into the swamps of Darkle Deeps, which obligingly replaced most of the filth that had been washed away.

Essence of defeated ogre percolated through the honeycomb of tunnels that riddled Darkle Deeps. The gelatinous Hurglabat rolled from side to side in disbelief. One dragon! The whole army of that dimension's most despicable creatures routed by one dragon! It was so enraged it was tempted to pick off any ogre stragglers.

The monstrous entity now knew it could not depend on brute stupidity to drive the remaining light from Lustreland. It looked as though it would have to do the job for itself after all. But there was still too much radiance. It would be shrivelled. So it would have to use another plan; one to influence minds more devious than the ogres'. Witches and warlocks may have been pretty clever, yet were conceited enough to raise the odd demon and commune with entities not normally encountered at herbal tea parties, believing themselves to be too powerful to experience any consequences.

Corruption wasn't only for the stupid.

CHAPTER 36

Seated on a huge tapestry saddle a large, jovial merchant rode a chimera resembling a cross between a unicorn and griffin. The ancient beast was pulling a painted wagon packed with fabrics, trinkets, perfumes, and remedies for everything from changeling's glue ear to chipped troll.

The merchant and his goods were escorted to the goblin tyrant's marquee, spacious enough to drive inside without brushing its ornate flaps.

Flunkin daren't ask why all the merchandise was decorated with fish. Now he had elevated himself to supreme tyrant he was expected to know everything.

The merchant beamed unctuously at seeing the avaricious goblin in all his ridiculous glory, 'That crown sits so well on your majesty. Didn't I tell you it was worth the price?'

Flunkin glowered. Yes, the thing had been a bargain, yet he still resented parting with so many gems for it. And he certainly had no intention of admitting that the copy of "The Elementary Guide to Tyranting" the merchant had thrown in for free had come in the nick of time as the other goblins were becoming so annoyed at his pretensions they were about to toss him down a flooded mineshaft. It only took two chapters on intimidation to save him from a very damp end. Flunkin was amazed at what a firm tone and unwavering gaze could achieve on his gullible subjects and even his mother stopped nagging, though his mixed species wife was less impressed and ran off with an elf from the waterfall region. Flunkin willed rheumatism on her, but with her lineage it was more likely she would grow gills, which probably accounted for his aggravated feelings about anything aquatic.

The merchant swung open the decorated doors of his wagon. The tyrant's attendants reeled at the sight of so many polished gems as light reflected from the ostentatious jewellery spangled the recesses of the tyrant's marquee. Flunkin had already owned more jewels than most goblins saw in a lifetime, yet this only fed his greed. Having power was no longer enough. His guards and tax collectors might terrorise his subjects, and he could spend all night in his treasury counting, but now he craved those special powers not known to goblins. He wanted to see into the minds of other creatures (preferably not serpents) and into invisible realms. As though able to read his thoughts, the merchant tantalisingly held a seeing glass before him. It was like a huge crystal egg freshly laid by a fabulous beast and quite different from the one he already possessed.

Misty patterns roamed its interior.

Flunkin leaned forward like a hypnotised chicken to watch tiny time-lapse creatures live, die and evolve into other time-lapse creatures. The marvellous device was depicting the sum of existence in its shining oval shell, showing the rise and fall of empires and movement of the plates that magically pushed apart icy and volcanic realms, while making others collide.

The old chimera, which had pulled the wagon inside the tyrant's marquee, also raised its muzzle for a look.

The merchant elbowed the creature aside and hissed. 'For pity's sake, Tov. You had time to see it before we left!'

Flunkin was too fixated on the wonder before him to hear. 'How much?'

The merchant silently counted the price out on his fat fingers.

The tyrant sat back and glowered, and then groaned and moaned.

The price remained the same.

The merchant eventually received the gems he demanded, repacked his wagon, and lumbered back into the woods on his chimera.

Once outside goblin territory, he dismounted, lifted Flunkin's casket of gems from the painted wagon - and tossed it to the ground.

'Well, thank you!' snapped the beast of burden as it shook the wagon's harness free.

The merchant pulled off the liripiped turban and brocade robe to stretch her silver fish tail. 'Oracles shouldn't have to do this sort of work.'

The bridle dropped from the chimera as the deity resumed its naturally nebulous form. 'It was your idea. I only came along to make sure things didn't get out of hand.'

The oracle laughed. 'You! The idiot who created a lump of malice so evil no cave deity could get near it - let alone destroy it - as a practical joke!'

'So, how was I to know it had aspirations?'

'All cave deities like a good laugh, but there was no need to distil evil and give it a nice warm home.'

Tov filtered up into some branches in embarrassment. 'It's not as if the First Minister is going to find out about it.'

The oracle flicked two bolts of energy at the gems and wagon. They disappeared. 'Let's just hope that devious goblin likes what he finds in the seeing glass.'

'You are aware it will give the Hurglabat a route right into the heart of Lustreland? As soon the light has gone, it's bound to surface.'

'That's exactly what it's meant to do.'

Flunkin dismissed his retinue and took his new seeing glass to the table in a curtained antechamber. He placed it on its stand and polished the surface vigorously with his jewelled sleeve.

The crystal clicked furiously in annoyance at being scratched. The tyrant leapt back and watched, wide-eyed, at the miniature thunderstorm raging inside it. Eventually the seeing glass calmed down and allowed a rainbow to push the clouds aside. Then the brilliant bands of colour were transformed into light from gems so large and flawless Flunkin lost his fear and pressed an avaricious nose against the crystal.

The goblin looked into an underworld encrusted with more precious stones than those in the Darkle Deep's cave. How could goblin miners have overlooked so much treasure?

As though given an endoscope to traverse the gullet of a troll with a jewelled interior, he was led through a labyrinth of tunnels and caverns under Lustreland's wooded boundary. At last he came to the gem encrusted caves, probably created at the same time as the Crystal Mansion. They were nestling under the very heart of Lustreland.

A map, he needed a map! As though reading his thoughts, the seeing glass displayed a diagram detailing how to reach the forbidden treasure.

Flunkin rushed off to find chalk and a slate before it faded.

CHAPTER 37

Qulio's sleeping spell on Bruno had proved unusually stultifying and when the Second Minister woke it was a struggle to remember why he was so angry. Had he been dreaming?

The air remained strangely soft against his skin until reality intruded with a long held note on a distant horn.

Now he could recall why he was angry. Everything had been real enough.

He leapt up.

Where was his wretched marigold sprite? Probably gossiping about him in some petunia patch. And Qulio? Where had he got to?

Bruno found the wizard on top of the turret with his head resting in a pillow of fragrant blossoms. His expression was so peaceful he didn't have the heart to wake him. Qulio resembled a youth who had not yet had adulthood thrust upon him and appeared to be in the middle of a beautiful dream. For a moment the Second Minister pondered over his sleeping friend and tried to guess what his natural element was. He doubted that even the wizard knew.

Bruno's contemplation was interrupted by a rowdy celebration in the distance where crowds were gathering around the Halls of Government. Fireworks sparkled above them, plumes of smoke from bonfires rose gently upwards to reach zephyrs propelling the occasional candyfloss cloud and the curls of smoke wrote volumes in the dazzling sky. Unfortunately for Bruno, he could not read them.

He stood on the turret gazing at the carnival through his spyglass. Sprites were tangling themselves in banners fluttering from high buildings and imps dashed back and forth through the milling crowds, avoiding the slaps of those they managed to trip up. After centuries of sedate good behaviour Lustreland had taken leave of its senses. Even some rara avis had come down from their ridge to watch and wonder at the fabulous red neighbour of theirs being garlanded and offered carbonised hog nuts. As the Halls of Government concealed this from Bruno's view, he concluded that the celebration meant that the ogres had been driven back, and without the aid of some delinquent dragon.

Before the Second Minister could rouse Qulio there was a knock at the door. He went down to answer it. A flower sprite was delivering a letter from Rimonay. This messenger was in full bloom and as bright as a sunbeam so, without a second thought, the Second Minister took the envelope and opened it. The ogres had indeed been beaten back to Darkle Deeps and the Council were about to meet. Bruno quickly put on his robe and chain of office and, light-headed with relief, left Qulio slumbering to follow the flower sprite.

Without warning a minstrel stepped into his path.

Losing momentum so suddenly, Bruno nearly tripped over her. 'Let me pass!'

Before he could lift the small interloper aside she asked, 'Do you still fear dragons?' in a derisive tone his sense of self-importance could not ignore.

'I have never feared dragons!'

Crystabel sighed. 'Then you've learnt nothing?'

'I know all I need to. Now let me pass.'

With a deep sarcastic bow, she stepped aside.

The Halls of Government were a string of ancient buildings of differing heights, some so old only dinosaur fossils and the gargoyles holding hands kept them up. They irregularly girdled a vast lawn, resembling a set of formidable, gappy teeth. At the centre of this amphitheatre was a beautiful lattice of crystal resembling a portal into another dimension. Its delicate framework was set with precious gems, their facets reflecting light onto building leagues away. Even by Lustreland standards, the hybrid grass surrounding it was also special. Over aeons the gardening gnomes had manipulated it into reflecting the colour that most suited the mood of the moment, like a dandy mindlessly mirroring the vacuous thoughts of the day.

Bruno carried his head so high he never glanced down at such lovingly nursed triviality. He is proud gaze was directed upwards to the bejewelled gargoyles glittering in the crisp light, and tendrils of living rock that had been trained to entwine the highest pinnacle with decorative ease. Had he looked down as he strode across the lawn at that moment, he would have had difficulty seeing it for the tumultuous laughing, singing population who had swarmed in from every corner of the Province of Light.

The Second Minister had difficulty pushing his way through the throng. His chain of office wasn't much help on celebrators too elated to be intimidated by anything. Eventually he was propelled from the chaotic hoi polloi onto the marble pavement in front of the main portal to the Halls of Government where not even the most jubilant reveller dare set foot.

Apart from its sanctity, aeons of polishing made it very slippery. So, as soon as Bruno stepped onto it, he lost his balance and toppled over. The gargoyles on the archway had to break ranks to catch him before he hit the ground. If only he had remembered his staff of office. Despite being recently bent over a dragon's snout, it would have at least saved him from the indignity of needing assistance from decorative waterspouts.

Rimonay, supported by her two tree sprites, was waiting to greet him. She was wearing the most formal of her frosty expressions for the momentous occasion and offered Bruno her ring, the domain's seal of office, which he kissed. Slowly, formally, he was escorted to the inner courtyard where the Ruling Council and the Mystic Trine were silently waiting. Bruno believed their uncharacteristic civility to be due to the defeat of the ogres and understanding of his dragon phobia. Some members who had previously regarded him as a blot on the page of Lustreland's constitution now greeted him with nervous smiles. That alone should have told Bruno there was a little more than mere amnesty involved.

Rimonay pointed to a circle of chalcedony in the ground, which was usually concealed by an alabaster lid. Its depths glowed invitingly like waxy bubbles.

Assuming that this was a privilege, Bruno stepped onto it.

'The ogre hoards have been driven off,' Rimonay announced in her pepper grinder voice. 'The victory was absolute. We do not expect to see them again for some while.'

Bruno was deeply curious to know how this had been achieved, but it would not have been politic to interrupt.

'Providence may have been kind to us, yet such gifts require a high price. I have always held you in high esteem, Bruno, even during your worst tantrums and most stubborn resolves. I would never willingly cause you harm. Unfortunately, I am also the guardian of Lustreland and do not have the right to allow your stubbornness to risk the wellbeing of this domain.'

Instead of having the sense to be apprehensive, the Second Minister looked puzzled, so Rimonay came to the point.

'There was no way Lustreland could have been saved without the assistance of Dragon Sesame.'

The flutter of huge wings at the mention of its name made Bruno aware that the fabulous creature was perching on the crenulations of a high roof.

'After you had driven the dragon off it was reluctant to have anything more to do with us. At first we thought the price it demanded was out of the question - but so was the invasion of Lustreland by ogre hoards that would quickly recall their appetite for our population's flesh.'

She stopped speaking and silently gazed at Bruno.

He didn't really want to know, yet blurted out all the same, 'What price was that?'

Rimonay's tired, glittering eyes continued to contemplate his gorgeously arrayed presence as the Ruling Council and Mystic Trine started to back away.

Rimonay's thin lips slowly parted. 'The price was you, Bruno.'

Without another word, she turned and beckoned her tree sprites to assist her back inside.

Bruno's instinctive reaction was rage. Confusion rapidly overtook that as he realised how futile it was. After all, Rimonay, in a less direct way than was usual for her, had just announced his execution.

The courtyard was soon empty and it occurred to Bruno that he had better not stay either. Sesame was airborne and swooping down towards him. Dragons were unable to land amongst trees. He had to flee to the woods and find Juniper.

But Bruno was unable to spring from the circle of chalcedony. Its warm, bubbling depths held him fast like a vat of half set toffee. All sensation left his legs and they crumpled beneath him.

Even if he had remembered his staff, he would have been unable to fight off the dragon now all legal restraint had now been lifted from it. The creature was free to tear him to pieces without so much as a small fine, and by its fast approaching expression, knew it.

His legs useless, Bruno desperately tried to haul himself free as huge wings threshed the air above him. He lashed out insanely to try and push them away but, with remorseless ease, Sesame's claw closed about the Second Minister's body, crushing the breath from him.

Clutching its prey, the dragon soared triumphantly into the sky, turning several victory somersaults over the amazed crowds before winging its way home.

At the sight of the ground so far below and the prospect of being shortly turned bit by bit into a dragon's breakfast, lunch and dinner, Bruno tried to faint. Yet, however much he tried, terror and nausea forced him to remain conscious.

As Sesame flew through the narrow passes of Rara Avis Ridge, its victim winced at the closeness of the jagged rocks and cursed himself for not waking Qulio when he had the chance. The wizard was the only one who could have reasoned with the dragon. Now, by the time Qulio discovered what had happened, Bruno would be nothing more than a mild case of indigestion. And, as if these horrors were not enough, the screeching and flapping of feathered wings below them heralded another.

At last the harpies saw their chance to get even with Sesame for smoking out their caves in mid squawk and showed every intention of snatching the tasty morsel the dragon had in its claws.

Like aerial hyenas, they closed in.

The dragon was unable to spin and lash out while it clutched the Second Minister and, after the harpies had made several abortive swoops at Sesame's claws, the terrified Bruno realised that they were after him. At such a height there was no place Sesame could put down its prey. Then it caught sight of a ledge - a likely perch for a bird or elastic limbed acrobat maybe, not a broad-beamed Bruno.

The previous traumas were followed by yet another as the iron talons were replaced by hardly a foothold overlooking a bottomless ravine while a vicious skirmish over who was going to devour him raged about Bruno.

The battle seemed to go on forever and the odd harpy took the opportunity to snatch at him, tearing his robe to shreds in an effort to dislodge his grip on the slippery rock.

Eventually half the attackers fluttered off, singed and partially plucked, while the rest roosted in resentful exhaustion about the cliff face. Then the dragon's claw closed about the Second Minister and they were airborne once again.

They arrived at the summit of a towering crag. Surrounding the entrance of a ramshackle cave was a sheer drop. Bruno's heart sank. When Sesame hurled him onto the branch and feather litter inside, it nearly stopped.

The cave was vast. The arched ceiling was like a troll's vault, rock pillars buttressing the walls that soared into the gloom and were lost before Bruno could see the tops of them with his Lustrelander's eyes.

With terror came pain, in the same way frost can burn, and the rustling and scraping of the dragon's scales made its shadowy shape even more alarming. The last thing the Second Minister wanted to do was guess who had once owned those enormous feathers and bales of down his fingers clutched in desperation. The branches and sharp rocks beneath this monstrous mattressing may have been comfort for Sesame, but not for Bruno. He dare not fidget. The dragon could see everything and he was determined to retain his dignity, however pointless. So, somehow finding the strength, Bruno hauled himself up to his full height and faced the dragon that was in the process of curling up for a nap.

'Kill me now,' he ordered.

The dragon opened one eye at the strange command, unfurled its long tail and coiled it around Bruno as if to say, "later", then went fast asleep.

Sleep was the last thing on Bruno's mind. Ideas and sensations chased away the pain until his head swam. Even though his arms were free, there was no way he could budge the tail entwined about him.

Then he remembered.
He still had his dagger.

CHAPTER 38

Bludon, the Chief ogre's adviser, clambered down into the fortress's deep basement where bizarre creatures were taking advantage of the copious ooze to evolve. He waded towards the pile of ancient stones onto which some semi literate ancestors had hewn pictograms. Carving ran in his family, though now it was limited to marking arrows by the ogre chief's bed to show him which way up he was when he woke.

Relighting his torch after some creature evolving to blow instead of suck had put it out yet again, Bludon noticed the insignia on a chest containing a collection of regalia which included a battered crown that some ancient ogre decided to use as the royal quoit. From that time things had gone downhill. The Magic Ring had threatened them with emulsification if they didn't give up eating Lustrelanders, the remaining dinosaurs constructing their fortress became extinct and left it half built and, worst of all, it was about this time female ogres had started to try and knit. They never managed to complete anything serviceable and their mates had been worried witless by what they intended to do with the needles when frustration set in.

Bludon pulled out a gofferhog skin volume and scraped the encrustations from its surface. Yes, this was what he was looking for - "How To Crown Your Chief Ogre".

There was nothing like a good coronation to raise morale after a humiliating defeat.

Jobaloba's advisor clambered back up to find Kot Kut. Now he had the pictures explaining how to go about it, surely not even the high priest could get things wrong.

Nevertheless, Kot Kut was puzzled. The pictures only depicted the crowning of one-headed ogre chiefs, long before strange substances polluting the water supply started to play havoc with their DNA. For fear of revealing his ignorance to Bludon, he simply doubled the amounts of unctions, anointing oils and crowns. Unfortunately, arithmetic was not the high priest's strong point.

After some time digging through the fortress treasury, Kot Kut discovered another crown not battered beyond use. With a few adjustments using a war hammer both of them could be made to fit Jobaloba's heads, still somewhat irregular from the beating Sesame had given them.

The female ogres were provided with enough wire to knit the coronation robe, the local banshees given a score of the royal oratorio, and half a dozen warriors prepared the anointing bath of boiling pitch - not only was Kot Kut's arithmetic bad, he was also unable to tell the pictogram for dewbush oil from the one for tar. Gems that had been spewed up by the Hurglabat were set in ceremonial armour that hadn't totally rusted away, or simply pushed into the tar that pointed up the fortress's main columns. Even the ghoul who had made its home in the dungeons was given a scrub down.

Bludon was nervous.

Whenever the high priest looked as though he knew what he was doing, something always went wrong. But Jobaloba was eager to be crowned before some interfering young ogre who could read, like Hada Gonn, pointed out that his ancestry was far from royal. If it weren't for the ogres' short term memories they would have recalled that the last surviving member of the royal line had been frizzled to a large crisp in an ancient expedition to steal the Ligh Tofrea Sun. Jobaloba had only blundered his way into the position of chief because he was very large and had two heads, neither of which understood the meaning of fear. Even the mightiest of warriors experienced some pang of anxiety when confronting a very determined dragon. Not Jobaloba. His skulls were so dense they should have blocked out most electromagnetic radiation and it was a wonder he could hear. So it was quite salutary to learn that even Jobaloba had his pain threshold, as Kot Kut was soon to find out.

The coronation ceremony began.

The chorus of banshees wailed, the ceremonial guard hammered the dais flagstones with their pikes, and Jobaloba began his long walk to the coronation stone. That was looking unsettlingly animated because it had spent several centuries in the company of Yupta Gum's chair, which had the habit of disguising itself as a huge gargoyle or enfolding anyone sitting in it in a crushing embrace. No ogre knew how it had ended up in their fortress and Bludon suspected that it was one of the cave deity's jokes, so insisted it be locked in the dungeons well away from the ceremony.

The ogre chief reached the dais and solemnly sat on the coronation stone which was throbbing with feline purrs. Kot Kut chanted to fill in the pauses while he shakily measured out the anointing potions. First the unctan flower juice; two ladles, one for each head; four ladles of jellyfish essence, and six of antigin root.

Jobaloba began to smell very fishy. His drenching in Rara Avis Ridge and blows to his head restored the use of his olfactory senses and even he noticed. But, fishy or not, all he was interested in were the crowns. Once he had those...

But no, Kot Kut hadn't finished. The high priest's assistant hauled aside a large flagstone. Jobaloba peered down into a large bath of bubbling pitch. The coronation stone rocked uneasily beneath him. Before the ogre chief could make out why he was suspended over a baptism of boiling pitch, Kot Kut pulled a lever. The ogre chief dropped headfirst into the hot sticky mess, rapidly followed by the coronation stone that pinned him to the bottom of the scalding, glutinous goo.

Bludon realised something was wrong and checked the order of service. There was no mention of plunging the monarch into boiling pitch, and then dropping a three-ton stone on him. He signalled the ceremonial guards to haul Jobaloba out.

At that point it occurred to Kot Kut that he might have miscalculated his translation for the ritual bath. After rapidly reviewing the pictograms, he realised it should have read one bushel of dewbush oil to be added to the ritual footbath.

The high priest may not have known much, but he could work out when to run.

The two-headed creature being hauled from his immersion in boiling pitch, spitting black goo and glistening malevolently, had lost interest in his coronation. There was only one person likely to be crowned that day.

Jobaloba reached for his mace.

Kot Kut's feet hardly touched the ground as he picked up the hem of his ceremonial robe and fled from the fortress.

CHAPTER 39

Clarey had difficulty believing what the doctor said. 'Shock?'

'Shock,' she insisted. 'He is in severe shock.'

'But why?' complained Indrina. 'Pudding's got the constitution of an Alaskan lumberjack. His voice alone could scare off a pack of timber wolves.'

'I've no more idea why he's in this condition than anyone else. I can only treat the symptoms.'

Aurora was sitting quietly by her father's bed. 'He will recover, won't he?'

The doctor took a deep breath. The sixteen-year-old sounded mature enough to know the truth, even if she did wear ridiculous clothes. 'I can't be sure.'

Aurora tried to choke back tears, and Mouse was quick to put a reassuring arm about her shoulders.

The doctor turned to Indrina. 'The only thing that might help your husband is - assuming he can hear you - reassurance. I understand that he has no surviving family, so you must now be the one closest to him.'

'He doesn't like me,' Indrina murmured unhelpfully. She wanted to retreat to a dark corner and review the possibility of becoming a Franciscan nun. At least that would absolve her from these ridiculous situations and upset her mother.

Clarey wasn't going to let his accountant off the hook that easily, certainly not after the years of aggravation over his bookkeeping she had given him. 'In his state of mind, he probably doesn't remember that. Try and talk to him again.'

Indrina pointed to a sizeable bruise developing on her jaw despite Mouse's efforts to soothe it away with ice and arnica. 'Like the last time?'

'But he was delirious.'

'He still is.'

Until then, Kitty had been sitting in a corner and watching with interested detachment, but could now see her prodigy's chances of surviving to become an ancient bass singer fast disappearing. 'I think Clarey's right. Bernard can be very complex, even though he does reason along tramlines.'

'I know.' Indrina looked down at her husband fitfully muttering in some alien tongue. It would not be long before he once again started to wrestle fabulous monsters and describe terrors that would have put an Epicurean off crustaceans for life.

The doctor anticipated the thought that was niggling at the back of her mind. 'Not only has he all the symptoms of being in shock, whatever caused it seems to be self induced.'

'Self-induced shock?'

'There is no other explanation.' The doctor peered over her glasses at the patient. 'The cause must be psychological, but I'm not a qualified psychiatrist.'

There was a long pause before Indrina asked, 'So you know about the hallucinations he was having before this happened?'

'I had to say something,' Clarey apologised.

'He probably does need a psychiatrist,' the doctor admitted. 'Your husband's subconscious must be a veritable labyrinth of horrible nightmares.'

Indrina sighed in resignation. 'And I always thought he was such a dummy.'

Kitty saw a chink in her resolve and came over. 'See how wrong you've been about him?'

'He does seem to react to your voice,' the doctor added.

'Yes, with his fists,' protested Indrina.

Though the family drama was hardly his fault, Clarey felt guilty that it had happened under his roof. 'I'll stay with you. Just in case.'

Aurora was more inclined to act as a second in her father's corner. 'So will I.'

During the following hours Bernard's fitful rambling increased. At every attempt Indrina made to pacify him he either lashed out at large birds swooping down or tried to throttle her. She believed it to be inevitable that anyone who held arguments with the mirror about his stage makeup would eventually end up in terminal hysteria. Indrina only talked to her laptop. That was different. That couldn't answer back - as yet.

'Will his hair fall out?' Aurora whispered to the nurse.

'Not necessarily.'

'I knew a girl that happened to and she had to wear a wig since she was fourteen. She didn't care about being bald, it was everyone else. But I know Daddy would be upset if he lost his hair ...'

Irritated by her daughter's bantering, Indrina took a handful of Bernard's hair and gave it a sharp tug. 'Your father's hair is not falling out.'

Aurora was horrified. 'Mummy!'

'That might have hurt him,' agreed Clarey.

Instead, a spark of sanity flickered in Bernard's eyes.

'Do it again.'

She did.

The singer yelped in rage.

Mouse, who had been unable to stay away, dashed out to fetch the doctor while the nurse patted Bernard's face to try and bring him round.

'Dead?' Bernard looked about him as though expecting someone from a different dimension to answer.

'Lift him up,' Clarey whispered to Indrina.

'What?'

'I'll grab his arm if he takes a swing at you.'

'He looks as though he's going to turn into a fire breathing pumpkin.'

Bernard's fist shot out at some indiscriminate target.

Clarey caught it. 'It's probably not wise to mention anything that breathes fire.'

'Perhaps he thinks he's an arch wizard trying to cast a spell on Voldermort,' Aurora suggested.

Indrina groaned. 'Leave Harry Potter out of this, can't you.'

'I think Daddy's coming round.'

Indrina wrapped her arms about Bernard's wide shoulders and hauled him up while the nurse moved the pillows to support him.

Bernard at last recognised Indrina. 'Where have you been?'

'Here all the while, Pudding.'

'Has the dragon gone?'

'The dragon has gone.'

He ran his fingers over her face to make sure she wasn't an apparition. 'You're not pretending?' It was his youthful voice, before he had learnt how to project it.

'Not pretending any more.'

'Now we can be married,' Bernard declared with bright-eyed enthusiasm.

Indrina was lost for words. At that moment he was more the man that she had married, not the collection of finicky fads and faults he became. 'You know I live in a mess and can't cook.'

Bernard's expression didn't flicker.

'I oil myself in sandalwood every night and wear vicious earrings in bed.' Surprised that she was unable to recall any more of his carping complaints, Indrina gave in to logic. 'We are already married, Pudding. There's no need to do it again.'

Bliss slammed shut its door as Bernard suddenly realised where he was. 'Well I know that, don't I!' he snapped. 'You're not having a divorce, though! '

'Why not?' Indrina was deaf to the sharp intake of breath from the others as they saw all their manipulating going the same way as the other million and one lost causes.

Bernard's features twitched with confusion as Indrina's hawk like glare suggested he was becoming a rabbit to pounce on.

Then he pushed the tangled hair from his perspiring forehead and announced fearlessly, 'I love you. I always have loved you. I never will stop loving you - And stop calling me Pudding!'

Indrina was amazed, all the more so by the realisation that she felt the same way about this insufferable prima donna so full of contradictions. She was compelled to admit to herself that Bernard was more than a bad habit after all. The shock to the accountant's acumen was going to leave her incapable of elementary arithmetic for several hours.

Clarey noticed this suspension of her professional acuity and mentally started to select the old master he would most like to donate to the Inland Revenue.

By the time the doctor reached the room, Indrina and Bernard were in each others' arms, Aurora was in tears, and the nurse wondering if she should serve sedatives all round or whether this sort of behaviour was as near to sanity this family would ever get.

Kitty was hot on the doctor's heels.

'They've made up,' Clarey announced.

She laughed. 'About time, the silly fools. They never did understand why they parted in the first place.'

Clarey thought deeply for a moment. 'I wonder what it had to do with dragons?'

CHAPTER 40

Bruno managed to ease the dagger from his girdle without waking Sesame. The dragon's snout was less than an arm's length away and, by the way it smacked its lips, the fabulous beast was dreaming of some anticipated banquet.

A dragon's only weak points are the scales that run from beneath the chin, along the underside of its neck and body to the tip of its tail. All other parts of its body are armoured and impossible to penetrate with the sharpest lance, yet those vulnerable scales on Sesame's neck were presented to Bruno like a gift. If he had to die, he preferred it to be in the attempt to climb down from the skyscraper cave sooner than being devoured by a dragon, especially by a dragon he didn't like.

He raised his dagger to strike into the satin neck.

Then hesitated.

Bruno had never been so close to those flame coloured scales that fluoresced in the dark. They were superb, like leaves of precious gems studded onto red velvet skin. Sesame's face was finely plated, mobile and strangely beautiful, resembling the diamond bark of the snake palm; the folded wings huge fans of shimmering silk stretched on rods of garnet, and the claws daggers of marbled alabaster.

After all the time they had spent bickering, it was remarkable that Bruno had never noticed what a remarkable creature Sesame was.

His hand slowly lowered the blade, no longer able to carry out his irrational bidding.

Again Bruno raised it to strike. But what for? How could he kill such a fabulous creature? A beautiful creature...

The terror of his abduction had shattered the bolts securing his true emotions and allowed in a terrible awareness. It now came tumbling out; stinging, smarting, and screeching like the pests from Pandora's Box. Bruno was ill prepared to ward them off. Had he been in his own domain, he would have stifled the unwelcome truth by throwing his weight around, but here the Second Minister's self-importance counted for nothing. He could rant, wail and dash his brains out, and no creature within earshot would blink an enamelled eyelid.

That horrible truth he could never live with after all his protestations of hatred for Sesame pulled tight the noose on what composure he had left. More tormenting than the thought of being torn to pieces, Bruno was now aware that it was not hatred for the dragon that so obsessed him, but infatuation.

Unable to live with the humiliation of such self-awareness, it would be better to die before the dragon woke.

Bruno lifted the dagger to his throat.

The blade was poised to sever his jugular veins when it was suddenly sent spinning from his grasp. Sesame's tongue uncoiled and Bruno watched the weapon tumble into the chasm below.

The dragon had been observing Bruno through its thin secondary eyelid, and its piercing gaze blazed in annoyance and wonder at his change of heart. Sesame slackened the grip of its tail and placed its muzzle between the Second Minister's suddenly empty hands, ready to seize his girdle before he could hurl himself after the dagger.

Bruno involuntarily clasped the dragon's snout, only to be knocked out by the fumes of its hot breath.

Sesame had never intended to devour Bruno, only give him a life changing fright, and was not devious enough to understand how that had triggered the collapse of the Second Minister's emotional defences.

This was going to be a good deal more difficult to cope with than his hateful tantrums, not least because odd sensations and sentiments not familiar to ancient reptiles were beginning to surface in its armoured skull.

The dragon was at a loss. What did it do next? Their kind seldom had their sworn enemies faint under their chins with apparent infatuation. Ever since dragon slaying had been banned and they were no longer compelled to defend themselves, no person had even protested mild affection for one. The law had only been passed because they reproduced so rarely and were an endangered species. Even Sesame had never been quite sure what sex it was. Now it had acquired an admirer who was not sure what species he was.

Though Bruno's change of heart was oddly flattering, Sesame was glad he was unconscious. For all the dragon's bravado, it hated scenes and much preferred to watch the Universe from a safe distance. Defeating hoards of hairy ogres and routing flocks of shrieking harpies were nothing to the complexities that now loomed.

As those alien sensations continued to flare up from the dragon's subconscious and deal what peace of mind it had left several vigorous blows, it started to realise that, however tough the crust of any creature, there was no accounting for the marshmallow inside. For the first time in Sesame's life, it was becoming victim to feelings flame and flight could not resolve. It was actually starting to experience affection for that pompous, pig-headed, irrational mortal softly snoring under its chin. Sesame knew that this had to be the first pricking sign of insanity which needed professional help.

The dragon carefully eased out of its nest and went to the cave's entrance. With one last look to ensure Bruno was still fast asleep, it silently dropped into the sky to glide back to Lustreland.

CHAPTER 41

Kot Kut hurtled towards the pitch lakes of Darkle Deeps. He had some fuddled idea about asking the Hurglabat for sanctuary from the tar-coated, mace wielding, maniac charging after him.

The high priest was familiar with the terrain, unlike Jobaloba who risked being sucked down by the occasional pool of pitch, which was something his heads should have thought about after being tipped into a bath of the noxious substance and having a three ton coronation stone pin him to the bottom of it.

The Hurglabat sensed what was going on above its domain and became irritated. Having failed to invade Lustreland for it, the wretched ogres were now doing their damnedest to disturb the monster's fitful slumber.

The Hurglabat made the ground shudder, creating waves on the pitch lakes. As the glutinous surface was disturbed, several caverns yawned open. Kot Kut thought his god was offering him a hiding place and dashed down the nearest tunnel. Any molecules with pretensions of common sense in Jobaloba's brain now fled for cover as he careered after the high priest into a network of disturbingly organic corridors and caves leading in every direction but out.

Up, down, round and round the two hurtled until, totally disorientated, they stopped to stare at each other across a rapidly widening chasm as though the Hurglabat was bored with the whole business and its very entrails were yawning. Jobaloba hesitated for a second, before springing like a two-ton grasshopper towards his prey. His huge feet just managed to make the far ledge.

It was a slippery with mucus and he fell.

Not knowing what induced him - perhaps he was more scared of the Hurglabat than Jobaloba after all - Kot Kut clutched the chief's chain mail sleeve and held on until his pursuer found a foothold and was able to haul himself back up.

This set up a peculiar conflict in Jobaloba. One head told him to finish off his quarry while he had the chance, the other to look around because he wasn't going to like what he saw. Reluctantly the ogre chief lowered his mace and allowed his gaze to follow the high priest's pointing finger. Below them, filling the vast chasm that had opened up, were row upon row of small, evil eyes glaring at the two ogres.

Jobaloba raised his mace. Kot Kut grasped his arm. The ogre chief grunted in bewilderment as the gelatinous monstrosity poured into the tunnels, cutting off any prospect of escape.

The Hurglabat wasn't really hungry and had never enjoyed digesting the juices of an ogre, but the monster couldn't have these two spreading news of its existence far and wide before Lustreland was securely in its grip. But it hadn't counted on dealing with a creature that had two obdurate minds, both still resolved to batter something to pulp. With too many eyes to aim between, the ogre chief hurled his huge mace at where he thought the Hurglabat might have kept its brain. It was impossible to guess what effect it would have. In fact, it had none at all. The mace hit the monster's vile, blancmange body like a fly falling onto a hot griddle.

Now the ceiling and walls of the tunnel behind the two ogres had closed up, the only way out was through the Hurglabat.

Kot Kut was wondering whether they would be crushed or absorbed by its gelatinous body when he remembered that he still had the bag of powder for the coronation ceremony in the pocket of his robe. This would have been liberally tossed over the monarch to soak up all the potions, unctions and anointing fluids that had been poured over him if events hadn't intervened. Kot Kut opened the bag and, under the baffled gaze of Jobaloba, he hurled the drying powder at the layers of pulsating blubber before them.

As exposure to the Ligh Tofrea Sun would have dried it out in seconds and a mere shaft of illumination was enough to shrivel off a tentacle, the Hurglabat had always been careful to keep itself moist.

When Kot Kut's powder hit the surface of its body the monster contracted violently. Forgetting the ogres, it lashed out with a bellow of rage, bringing down part of the cavern's ceiling. In its desperation to get rid of the lethal irritant, the Hurglabat rapidly expanded with a sneeze that vibrated through Rara Avis Ridge. Several griffins had to replace the walls of their nests and, for a few seconds, the harpies were unable to hear themselves squabbling.

The explosive sneeze propelled the ground Jobaloba and Kot Kut were standing on through the gap opened up in the ceiling. They were catapulted free of the Hurglabat's lair and Jobaloba landed in a deep pool of pitch where he managed to remain afloat until Bludon's search party found him.

Kot Kut fell into an inky ocean.

This wasn't Darkle Deeps' rancid sea. The water here was even murkier, and so dense he was unable to sink. The high priest floated for some while amongst boulders of pumice, looking at the jagged silhouette of a distant continent dotted with erupting volcanoes until a large, kite-shaped creature with no head appeared over the horizon.

CHAPTER 42

Qulio was woken from his slumber on the turret by a passing sprite anxious to tell him about Bruno's terrible fate.

Unable to comprehend how Rimonay could have condoned feeding his friend to a dragon, the wizard distractedly wandered from place to place trying to recall the incantation to summon fabulous beasts, and searching for the herbs that might dull its appetite.

It was some while before he noticed how oppressive the air had become, making his aura hang about him like a heavy cloak. Qulio shuddered at the sensation of déjà vu from some recent nightmare.

Having at last recovered from the effects of Kot Kut's powder in its primeval depths, the Hurglabat had sensed something in the essence of this social outcast with its psychic tentacles. Something that made its vile jelly shudder.

Then the wizard became aware of someone - or something - watching him with consuming fear and hatred. The chilling sensation was a novel experience. Qulio usually aroused in others nothing stronger than mild contempt. The thought that some entity was actually afraid of him almost made him reach for his ego. Had he known the entity involved, however, the knowledge would have more likely sent him into hibernation.

Anxiety elbowed aside Qulio's cloud of foreboding as he saw Sesame circling high above. He stopped in the middle of a rickety bridge, waving his hat so frantically he risked drowning before attracting the dragon's attention.

As Sesame landed, the updraught parted Qulio's beard and sent the Hurglabat's psychic tentacles scurrying for cover. Even monsters of that malevolent calibre thought twice about having their thoughts singed by the fiery feelings of a dragon - their reptilian minds were so deep, nobody could really comprehend the kaleidoscopic notions inside them. Having just been thwarted by a mere ogre, the Hurglabat wasn't about to try delving to find out.

Rearranging his beard and retrieving his hat, Qulio could see Sesame's confusion. He feared the worst. Yet, had the dragon devoured his friend, he was the last person it would seek out. The wizard didn't know what to think. Was Bruno injured, traumatised...? Or just been driven raving mad by the experience? The fabulous beast was confused as well and unable to place any sensible thought in Qulio's mind. The only way it could convince the wizard that the Second Minister was unharmed was to carry him back to its cave.

The flight there was not interrupted. Either Qulio did not look as appetising as Bruno, or the harpies had been beaten up enough for one week. The wizard was so thin he almost slipped through Sesame's claws and, seeing the yawning abyss and jagged crags pass beneath them, he clutched Sesame's scales so tightly it could well take a spell to unlock his fingers. If there was ever a time a wizard needed to believe in an all-powerful god, this was it. The other witches and warlocks were such an arrogant lot they assumed themselves to be the only creatures worthy of worship. Qulio thought it was a shame they would never be carried high over Rara Avis Ridge in a dragon's claws.

Even when safely inside Sesame's cave and able to prize his fingers free from its scales, it took some while for Qulio's circulation to return. Coupled with the sudden awareness that he was stranded in a hole at least a mile up in the purple sky filled with menacing, mythological creatures, was the fear that the person he had gone through such terror to reach was no longer there. Could Bruno have plunged to his death trying to escape, or even been devoured by some other fabulous beast? It was impossible to read Sesame's expression. To Qulio, the dragon's face, despite being armoured, had many and he had always taken it for granted they were benign ones.

There was a faint rustling at the back of the cave. Bruno came forward into the half light looking like the leavings of the Cerberus's dinner with his torn robe and lacerated skin.

Qulio was silent for a moment, and then angrily turned on Sesame. 'What have you done to him, you dreadful creature?'

Sesame was affronted by the accusation and thought the wizard was just getting over excited in his old age; perhaps it had something to do with all those herbal concoctions Juniper brewed up for him.

Bruno quickly interceded before the wizard vanished in one of his own badly aimed spells. 'Sesame hasn't harmed me, Qulio.'

Qulio's knees buckled in relief. He sank onto the jumbled branches and feathers of the dragon's nest, wagging a finger in agitation at the dragon before any words would come.

'Dear heavens! You don't know how thankful you should be for that!' he eventually blurted out.

Sesame looked puzzled. It fondly believed it would have been quite within its rights to beat up the belligerent Bruno.

'But I behaved appallingly,' the Second Minister remonstrated. 'I've been very arrogant with you as well, Qulio.'

The wizard shook his head. 'I didn't mean that.'

Bruno was puzzled. What other explanation could there be?

Qulio unfastened his mantle and wrapped it around his friend's shoulders. 'As a wizard, I have insight into many things other people should never know. Had I been aware of the Ruling Council's plan I could have ensured Sesame would not harm you, which was no doubt why I was not told.'

'I don't understand?'

'You can remember your family in the alternative reality you were banished to, can't you?'

'Of course.' Bruno's expression was a picture of incomprehension. 'Why is it so important? Is my wife's counterpart here some petal sprite who wants a divorce on both planes because I was abducted by a dragon?'

'No, no.' Qulio fitfully pushed the strands of tangled white hair from his face. However much more sanguine Bruno might have seemed, he was still as awkward as an overweight porcupine trying to back out of a sack. 'It also has no idea.'

Bruno's face fell. 'It?' he droned. 'Just what is my wife?'

Qulio visibly flinched. 'Dragon Sesame.'

Bruno looked as though he had just woken up under a landslide.

'What?'

'Dragon Sesame in that world is Indrina, your wife.'

The dragon had been perching perilously near the entrance of the cave and toppled backwards at the revelation. It plunged some distance before having the presence of mind to spread its wings. As soon as it was sure it was the right way up, Sesame flew off to find some remote, volcanic peak to sulk on.

CHAPTER 43

Few are so committed as the newly converted and Bernard's empathy for the problems of others was beginning to blossom like a confused peony in its first flush. Though the resemblance was more to a well-meaning orang-utan behind the wheel of an MG trying to deliver coconuts to starving babies. Everyone, bar Kitty, was holding their breath at this frightening prospect for the world's good causes, anxious to see which turning his new outlook on life would blunder down.

Thankfully Bernard remained his vain, self-assured, and easily irritated, self especially if disturbed before noon.

'Go away girl, go away!' he snapped as Aurora pulled the bedclothes off him.

His daughter was unable to take in the change which had apparently transformed her father from a high-handed grizzly bear into a milder mannered badger. 'It's safe to get up. The children won't be jumping all over you. Mouse has taken them into town for new school uniforms.'

'What? All in one car?'

'They used the park ranger's land rover, and they always do what Mouse tells them. He's a funny little man, but very sweet.'

'Your mother was wrong.'

'About what?'

'You never read Harry Potter. You just used the covers to hide a Mills and Boon.'

Aurora eyed him suspiciously. 'We all thought you were delirious when she said that?'

Bernard smiled artfully. 'I wasn't obliged to go deaf as well.'

'You crafty old ...'

'You know damn well she would have eaten me alive if she thought I was still capable of answering back.'

Aurora leapt onto the bed beside him. 'Just when did you know what was going on then?'

He grinned. 'When she pulled my hair.'

'I should tell her,' she threatened, 'unless...'

'Unless?'

Aurora thought calculatingly. 'A new pair of heels and Barry Manilow CD.'

'Barry Manilow!' snarled Bernard. 'If you can't have the puerile tastes of a genuine adolescent, you could at least choose a real baritone.'

'They're far too loud and he's prettier than you are.'

'You can have a dress. You've already got too many stupid shoes.' Bernard snatched the bedclothes back. 'No Barry Manilow.'

'I want some heels!'

'They're for dense girls with nowhere to go. You know your mother wants you to be a number counter when you grow up.'

'I'd rather be a fairy like you.'

He pushed her off the bed. 'Is Kitty still here?'

'Oh yes. Though I don't know why. It's not as if you're going to have a relapse and become your normal self is it?'

'Cheeky minx!' Bernard threw a pillow at her. 'Where's your mother?'

'Pouring gin on the cornflakes to get up enough courage to come and see you.'

'Courage? Why should she need courage?'

'Well you have been a swine to her. It was your nagging and perpetual whingeing which drove her out in the first place.'

Instead of erupting, Bernard uncharacteristically thought it over. 'Then why didn't you tell me that before she left?'

'I did, umpteen times, but you were never listening. You never listened to anyone. Will you get up if I fetch you a cup of tea?'

'Yes, a weak one. And bring Kitty. Tell her I want to know if she's found anything out about Mou-' Bernard stopped.

Aurora knew who he meant. 'If you want to know anything about Mouse and Clarey, old Mr Bollinger is the one to ask. He was here when their parents were alive. He's a chatty old fellow if you're civil to him.'

'Don't you worry about my manners. And don't you dare mention-'

'I won't. Not a living soul. Why should I care what you're up to?' Aurora threw the bedclothes over his head and pranced out.

By the time Kitty arrived with his tea Bernard was washed, dressed and ready to tilt at windmills. Kitty had already guessed which ones they were. Then Bernard told her about the conversation he had overheard between Clarey and Mrs Porter. She reluctantly agreed that it would be interesting to know what Mr Bollinger had to say.

As Bernard had regained his usual stride of a sprightly rhino, Mr Bollinger heard the singer coming several hedges away. The old gardener gave a dry chuckle and knocked the earth from some daisy roots.

Bernard found it was easy to get him chatting. Well past retiring age, Mr Bollinger liked nothing more than to lean on his fork and watch the world go by at a more hectic pace under the two younger gardeners and their work experience students. His was the haven of the shrubbery, lavender bushes, and poor man's orchid, with no time for of all those fancy imported weeds which had to be pampered at the beginning of their lives, and then fought back with saw and secateurs when they started to grow into the Himalayan forests their ancestors originated from. Noah Bollinger preferred to know his plants would be tame from seedling to compost heap, though he did make allowances for the sea holly, a barrier of which kept the deer off the gardens. Anything else that vicious found itself being fed through the shredder.

'The old men liked their gorse bushes and stinging nettles.' Mr Bollinger grumbled disapprovingly. 'Hunted things they did. Claimed it was more sporting than farming because it gave the creatures a chance. Though I don't see what difference it made to them whether they got shot sooner or later.' He removed his cap to reveal the line where the suntan ended and the stubbly red skin of his head began.

'The old men?' inquired Bernard casually.

'The fathers of Mr Clarey and his friend, Mouse. Weren't bad days when them two left this world I can tell you. There couldn't have been two more suited as business partners than them. Both loved money, killed their wives off at an early age and hated their sons.' Mr Bollinger muttered to himself as he nudged up a few weeds.

'But the estate belonged to Clarey's father?'

'That it did. That fellow was a noble bastard if nothing else. But he was in so deep with his business partner he was stuck with him. Some do say they eventually took a mutual dislike and polished each other off. Though to me it seems a mite difficult for the one who died first to commit murder. The Hon Ditton-Davis that was. The other went soon after. Locals do say they gallop through Hurdle Lane after the foxes, still arguing and shouting abuse at each other. And for all that, even after the way they'd been neglected, those lads of theirs still gave them a grand send-off.'

Bernard tried to conceal the fact that he was hurting with curiosity. 'They were neglected?'

Noah Bollinger shook his head like a wise old hedgehog. 'Did treat them terrible. Fathers thought they would toughen the pair up, make them brutes like theirselves. Sent them to private schools before they were ten. Made them box and play rugger. To make matters worse, one of them lads had this beautiful voice. Local choirmaster spent hours training him. Like a butterfly fluttering about the beams of the parish church it was. Old ladies used to burst into tears when they heard him sing. Famous cleric came from London just to hear it. Wanted the boy to be trained in one of them choir schools there, but his father weren't going to let his son be any sissy choirboy. The lad was packed off to a school where they had cold showers and an ex army PE instructor. That boy was a delicate lad.' The old gardener stopped to watch some starlings bounce across the camomile lawn.

'Go on,' urged Bernard.

'Boy couldn't have been much more than eleven when it happened. Game of rugger it was, with the older boys and some masters. Kicked he was. Could never grow to sire children after that. His father took him out of school and kept him locked up in the house for fear of anyone finding out. Wouldn't have anything to do with his son after that. If it weren't for that other lad ...' Noah Bollinger shrugged. 'Cook managed to smuggle the choirmaster in when the men were away, but that child weren't allowed out of the house from that time until their fathers both died; must have been 18 by then. Rumour started that he'd come from abroad - Italy or somewhere, though I've never seen the lad take a tan. Nobody outside except the choirmaster knew a thing about him.'

'And you.' Bernard gave a conspiratorial smile. 'What would you think if that lad still had a fine soprano voice, Mr Bollinger?'

As the old gardener scratched the back of his neck it sounded like sandpaper on rust. 'Tain't regarded as natural for a fellow to sing in a high voice, but if God wanted it that way, I don't see the harm in it.' He kicked some clods of earth from his old garden fork and started teasing up the tilth of the flower bed with its three remaining prongs. 'We do need some rain. Them children won't part with my hose while the weather's like this.'

'Difficult to argue with those children,' agreed Bernard, remembering a game of ludo that had developed into guerrilla warfare.

Mr Bollinger smiled wryly. 'Now that other lad certainly made up for his friend's misfortune. Always able to turn a pretty head he was. Though there were never anything nasty in him like most philanderers. And those lads love them children better than most parents could. But I'll be glad when their holidays are over and I can have my hose back.'

Curiosity satisfied, Bernard left Noah Bollinger pecking at the dry soil and muttering to himself about the weather and buttercup roots.

CHAPTER 44

Qulio was so relieved that Sesame had remembered to open its wings as it plunged from the cave, it didn't occur to him that he was trapped at the top of a mile high sheer drop without so much as a decent spell to cure vertigo. Turning his anxious gaze from the mountain peaks stabbing the purple sky he noticed Bruno fitfully examining the rips in his once opulent robe.

'Try and be patient. Sesame will come back soon. You've had a terrible fright, but it will wear off.' Qulio didn't believe a word he said, yet thought he should at least make the effort.

At that, Bruno began staring straight ahead as though anticipating another trauma he would not be able to cope with.

Qulio was growing more and more perplexed by the situation. 'Stop trying to go mad for a moment and listen to me. The Ruling Council no longer has any reason to persecute you and the dragon did no harm when it could have done.'

The Second Minister wasn't listening, so the wizard gave up and cast one of the few effective spells he knew and sent him to sleep.

Qulio sat for hours at the entrance of Sesame's home caressed by the exotically perfumed breeze laced with the rank odour of monsters' nests, and occasionally dodging from the view of the odd harpy gliding through the mists changing colour with the Rara Avis Ridge dawn.

The sight of the Ligh Tofrea Sun's lengthening rays sent a quiver through Qulio's reverie and sparked a deeply buried memory into life. With detached interest he watched a teardrop fall from his cheek into the rocks below as he was engulfed by a delicious warmth. Without warning the wizard became aware of powers he was frightened to think about. He snapped out of his dream just in time to prevent himself from tumbling down into the chasm. For a moment Qulio thought that he had been saved by a sprite tapping his shoulder even though such heights were far from their natural habitat.

Once again he settled down to watch the curtains of auroral light created by residual magic high in the atmosphere and pillars of pearlised cloud rising from the borders of Lustreland. Beautiful as it was, there was something missing. Over Darkle Deeps was a dull, deadening haze that seemed to be nibbling away at the half-light of Rara Avis Ridge like a cosmic caterpillar.

Qulio shuddered and pulled his robe tight about him.

Then there was a voice.

'What are you doing?'

The wizard jumped and lost his balance, only to be pulled back from the fastest mile any person was liable to make unaided.

What monster or fabulous creature had been secretly lodging in the back of Sesame's cave?

But it was only Bruno, and any monster in him seemed to have vaporised along with his blunderbuss indignation and obsessive dislikes.

'I was thinking,' confessed Qulio. 'There isn't much else to do apart from tidy up the place and I suspect Sesame prefers to live in a muddle.'

'Thinking? What about?' Bruno asked brightly.

'Just those things I've never dared think too deeply about before,' he evaded at his friend's newly aroused and inconvenient interest in others.

'Tell me?'

Qulio was fazed. 'My stupid life - And when it will ever end.'

'But that won't be for a long while yet. Wizard Mentala lived to be twice your age.'

Qulio looked bemused for a moment. 'I am twice my age.'

'What?'

'It's a long story.'

Bruno wasn't deterred by Qulio's reluctance. 'Tell me? We could be stuck here until the time troll retires. I'll get it out of you eventually anyway.'

'Oh all right.' The wizard gave a resigned, ragged sigh. 'It was ages ago, when I was a boy - I was once a boy. It seems so distant now.'

Bruno noticed an odd glow about Qulio. He put it down to the lack of reality pressure at that height. In Rara Avis Ridge entities could blink in and out of existence like magical mayflies, only living long enough to taste the dimension. And there seemed to be an unusual number of them flickering about the wizard as he spoke. Perhaps, with the drop in reality, his spells were anxious to try their paces.

Spells were the last thing on Qulio's mind. 'It happened when I was a student and had to collect some herbs near Deity Rock. I was afraid of going there of course. Anyone attracting the attention of the cave deities always gets rearranged for better or worse, but I had to have the ingredients or I would have failed yet another test. Having spent so much time nursing sick animals and trying to learn a little wisdom from a wise old griffin, I'd done terribly in my exams. That griffin could have taught me everything I needed to know, I'm sure. He was an irascible old soul, yet I loved him dearly.

'The Magic Ring - as the Mystic Trine was then called - were very severe in marking spells. I suppose it was their way of knocking into shape so many unsuitable candidates. Any child who carries the mark of the clouds must become an apprentice sorcerer, however unsuitable they are. That's the law. Sending us to Deity Rock to collect herbs was probably one way of ensuring they didn't return - not as trainee wizards anyway.' Qulio sighed. 'The cloud mark is only a small blemish at first. As you grow, the mark expands, like petals bursting into flower, though an ancient sage did suggest it might have been more to do with some disorder inflicting our twin selves in the other dimension.' Qulio pushed up his baggy sleeve to show Bruno the pattern encircling his thin arm.

It looked like something between an ugly stain and failed effort of a trainee tattooist.

Bruno glanced at it before gently pulling the sleeve back. 'Yes, Qulio. It does look more like a flower than a cloud.'

Aware the remark was intended to console, Qulio flickered a thin, thankful smile before going on. 'Anyway, I made it past the granite beetle and went as near to the caves as I dare.

'I pushed a few sprigs of the herb into my basket and was about to run off when I noticed a small elfin girl standing by a cave entrance. She was crying, so I couldn't leave her there. I asked her what the matter was. She explained that her pet serpent had slithered into the cave and was refusing to come out. Like everyone in Lustreland, she was terrified of the dark and was afraid to go in and fetch it. So was I. I told her that serpents liked the shadows and it wouldn't come to any harm. It probably much preferred to live in a cave anyway. I looked after many sick animals who needed homes; why didn't she adopt one of them? She was a very stubborn little girl, and probably part sprite. You know, the sort who curl up in pea pods, then leap out and give you a fright when they are being shelled. But I couldn't refuse to go into the cave for her. And she did promise to come with me if I held her hand. I prayed the serpent was as tame as she claimed and would come when she called - its name was Charity, after all. But serpents can be strange creatures.'

Bruno fidgeted uneasily. Serpents were another reptilian species he had aggravated feelings about. Qulio didn't notice. Bruno could tell by his wide eyes that the wizard was reliving every second of this nightmare.

'I was reluctant to let the cave entrance out of sight, even though there was a dull glow in the passage lighting the way. As long as the walls became no brighter, I knew the cave deities weren't paying any attention.

'Having gone so deep without being discovered, I felt a little bolder and the small girl's grip on my hand relaxed.

'Then I realised that her grip had relaxed because she was becoming nebulous.'

Bruno hadn't expected the story to take this ominous turn and held his breath as the wizard went on.

'Before I could run back out the cave closed around me. The walls grew brighter. I shook in terror - I was as a big a coward then as I am now. The little girl had, of course, vanished.

'The cave became filled with voices. I had heard of some trespassers demanding straight out what they wanted from the deities, and sometimes receiving it. But was happy enough with what I already had. I wasn't even anxious to pass my exams and become a qualified sorcerer.

'Then a voice said, "But he won't do. He's too afraid."

'"He can learn courage," insisted another. I would have told them I didn't want to if my tongue hadn't cleaved to the roof of my mouth. Then another voice declared, "He is the one. This domain will never produce anyone better. Immature or not, there is no other choice. He will have to be given an age which suits his wisdom."

'I can't say I wanted to know what was going on. Whatever they were going to do, it did not sound very pleasant.

"'Say something, boy," one of the deeper voices demanded. Like an idiot I gurgled, "Have you seen a serpent?" in the hope they would think I was stupid and let me go, but no one can fool a cave deity that easily. They started to ask me questions. Not the sort you get in exams; I was interrogated about what decisions I would make in the most amazing situations - hundreds of them. I answered as well as I could and eventually they seemed satisfied. The walls became infused with a warm glow. Then they said they were going to entrust me with something-' Qulio stopped as though gulping for air.

'Go on,' Bruno told him. 'I won't ask what it was if you don't want to tell me.'

Qulio's gaze wandered to the craggy horizon of Rara Avis Ridge as though some vengeful entity was perching on it. 'I want to tell you, but can't. Let's say it was something to do with the Ligh Tofrea Sun.'

The wizard turned to face Bruno. 'I explained that I was very honoured to be trusted with the special gift they wanted me to have, but was far too young for such responsibility. They told me it was no problem because they were going to do something about that. Terrified of what that was, I pleaded with them to let me go.' For a moment Qulio appeared frozen in an amber capsule of time, unable to move, think, or exist. Then the horror that had transfixed him slowly leached away. 'When they did...' He paused painfully. 'I'll never forget that walk back to the entrance of the cave. My limbs were stiff and it seemed such a long way up. When I eventually reached the light I was dazzled. It was some while before my eyes could adjust to it. The novice's short tunic I had been wearing was now a long, blue robe shot through with gold thread, like the ones the water diviners wear, though heavier. Not only was I stiff, I was much taller. I could now see over bushes I previously could barely reach the branches of before and creatures, who would usually pay no attention to me, sat up on their haunches and gazed in disbelief. Then there was all this white hair. The weight of it hung from my chin and head like a quilt.' Qulio studied Bruno's horrified expression for a few moments before explaining, 'They had robbed me of my youth in exchange for a gift I did not want.'

Bruno hadn't been expecting anything like this; he had always thought Qulio's view of many things idealistic and immature. Now his viewpoint had changed dramatically.

'What did you do?'

Qulio gave a diffident shrug. 'Spent years hiding in the woods, too afraid to show myself. My guardians and the animals must have thought I'd been killed. They were kind folk. I watched the search parties they sent out to look for me. I wanted to tell them what had happened, but was afraid that the cave deities would inflict some dreadful spell on them as well. Eventually I came to know Juniper, and then things weren't so bad.' He sighed. 'That all happened so long ago I've lost count of the years. What is worse, I never age. I've probably lived twice my years over, but as an old man. If I had been an elfin lout who knew nothing more than how to dig a hole and fill it in again I would have been spared all this.'

'You don't have to go on if it upsets you,' Bruno consoled, though he desperately wanted to learn more.

'All this meant that, although I would never be a competent sorcerer, I still had to become one because I bore the mark. I would have much preferred to be a hermit.'

'I'm not surprised.' Then something occurred to Bruno. 'If you have been living with Juniper for so long, she must be very old as well?'

'Because she cares for the sprites' unwanted offspring - the ones who turn out to be too mortal for comfort - they pool their powers and give her longevity. Like me, she never ages, though was never robbed of her youth.'

'So, in effect, you never really grew up?'

'Before that happened I was a precocious child. Being plunged into old age creates a lot of problems I didn't know how to cope with, like how to present myself to the Magic Ring as a mature wizard. I couldn't tell them what had happened either. As it wasn't a spell of their own making and weren't capable of casting it themselves, they would have probably tried to blacklist the cave deities for professional misconduct. I simply couldn't be responsible for the problems that would have caused. They didn't want me around of course, and I wanted nothing more than to leave, but they have so much power yet totally lack in compassion, I had no choice but to stay and remonstrate with their high-handedness. Quite a few unpleasant spells came in my direction after that I can tell you. I've often fallen asleep in Juniper's cottage, only to wake up several hours later deep in some cave. Somehow they found out how much they terrify me.'

Bruno put his arm reassuringly round the wizard's shoulders. 'But why? You were no threat.'

'I offend them. It is beneath their dignity to listen to reason. At least, I thought it was good advice when I tried to explain that it's all very well being able to conjure up whirlwinds over Rara Avis Ridge, or turn waterfalls upside down - but where was the point? To them the reason doesn't matter, only their all consuming, introverted mystical art. That's why they were helpless when it came to driving the ogres back. Despite their cleverness, they were incapable of casting a practical spell when it really counted. They should all be in those dinosaur bone mines the ogres have nearly worked out. All except Iggata of course.' Qulio noticed Bruno's circumspect expression. 'Oh she's all right. Just a little hard on the surface. Iggata is really quite warm-hearted underneath.'

Bruno wanted to call him an old fool, but was no longer sure whether that applied.

He was saved the embarrassment of lying by the screeches of harpies hurling abuse, quickly followed by the downbeat of huge wings that filled the cave and with a vortex of plucked feathers.

There was something glittering in Sesame's talons. Edged by scrolls of gold and studded with clusters of jewels, it was the richest robe the Second Minister had ever set eyes on. A girdle shot with filaments from the web of the firemoth was matched by dazzling shoulder tassels which held up the weight of the ruby encrusted sleeves like two teams of obliging dragonflies. The raiment was too exotic to have come from Lustreland, yet it was unlikely that Sesame had flown to another domain to snatch it from some alien dignitary's washing line.

There was only one explanation as far as Bruno was concerned. 'Where did you steal that from?'

Qulio was unable to stifle a giggle at the absurd accusation. Dragons had no need to steal anything. People were only too pleased to hand anything over to make them go away.

'Oh, I'm sure Sesame never stole it. And, after all, your own robe is a little tattered.'

The dragon thrust the garment at the Second Minister with resentful bad grace.

'I've never laid eyes on such richness.' Bruno carefully put it on. 'It fits well enough to have been made for me.'

Qulio thoughtfully stroked his beard. 'Perhaps it was.'

'What makes you say that?'

The wizard ran his fingertips over the gems reflecting small, mocking flashes of light onto his own drab gown. Were he to ever meet Cinderella there would be much empathy about ugly sisters of any gender. From the depths of Qulio's vast compassion and wisdom, he was unable to find an explanation for Bruno being able to escape his just deserts on so many occasions, and then be allowed to strut like a phoenix with its new suit of feathers.

As though stung, the wizard suddenly winced and withdrew his hand.

'Why, what's the matter?' asked Bruno.

'I'm sorry,' Qulio murmured.

'Sorry? What for?'

'I was envious.'

'There's no need to be.' Bruno removed the robe. 'Please take it.'

Qulio was horrified. 'No - You don't understand! Put it back on. It was made for you.'

'I don't want you to resent me.'

Qulio smiled. 'Don't apologise because I can't keep my demons under control.'

'You? Demons?'

'Those who have wisdom thrust upon them, also have demons. They were another gift from the cave deities.'

CHAPTER 45

Iggata flicked a spell at the smouldering fire. It flared up, dappling the walls like an army of shadow puppets. She was feeling bored, frustrated, and manipulated. In reality, no one would have dared manipulate a witch of her calibre, yet she craved power like some women crave motherhood. All right, she had raised her share of succubi and caused enough illegal tornadoes to have had her sorcery licence suspended, but that was only petty stuff. Iggata now felt a surge of the unspeakable tugging at her attention, although she was too experienced a witch to entertain it without a magical mallet at hand.

Unsure why, she delved into her store of rare minerals. Feeling the vibrations from each jewel, the witch was drawn towards the one Aquelia the serpent had traded for a summer pudding. Until then it had been quite inert, pretending to be a primordial mineral. Now it was calling to her.

Iggata picked up the stone with gold tongs and placed it on a cast iron dish which she lowered onto the fiercely glowing embers of the fire. As it heated up, fumes insinuated their way about her laboratory, snaking into every corner and analysing the ways of the witch. Eventually the entity inhabiting them was satisfied. They returned to the dish on the fire and clung to the jewel like a small, throbbing blancmange. Iggata had a strong stomach, but sensed she wasn't going to like the shape it was about to assume and raised her wand. Before she could utter a spell, nebulous tentacles erupted into the chamber. She became aware of a gelatinous monstrosity resembling badly stuffed pancakes; and eyes, layers and layers of tiny, malicious eyes.

The witch should have easily resisted those thoughts being pushed into her mind. It was only an apparition projected from the gemstone after all and had no power. If only she didn't feel so sleepy and start dreaming about being sucked down into a labyrinth of tunnels that twitched and twisted with the movements of the vile entity filling them. Through the mucus filled honeycomb echoed the dull thud of the heartbeat from a creature that clung to the underside of Darkle Deeps, with every intention of spilling into the domain surrounding it.

Iggata felt the cacophony of sound the Hurglabat made when it slurped and burbled as the rock it had invaded groaned uneasily, aware that it was being consumed by a malignant cancer.

Iggata's subconscious should have been repelled; instead it revelled in the monster's power. This was the entity an upwardly mobile witch could hitch her broomstick to.

Of course, had she been awake, the witch's common sense, however twisted, would have warned her off. There was a line between general wickedness and suicidal megalomania. The ideas infiltrating her subconscious however, were alluring enough to persuade any caster of spells to set fire to her state of the art broomstick and look into her crystal ball to watch her own existence being snuffed out.

Iggata suddenly woke in mid snore. She had inexplicably fallen asleep on her centaur skin rug. The images from the fire were still playing on the walls, telling her that she should remember something.

Didn't she just have a visitor? One who entered her mind, looked around, and then silently made its exit without leaving a calling card? She couldn't remember. All the volumes of spells and every ingredient used in them were still on their shelves so there hadn't been any burglary.

Those fumes must have made her imagine it. Nothing mortal would have dared enter her thoughts for long without losing its sanity. Even cave deities were particular about what minds they projected themselves into.

Now, what was it she had to do? Propose that plan involving the ogres, Qulio and the Ligh Tofrea Sun to the Mystic Trine - They were bound to applaud it!

CHAPTER 46

Bernard felt oddly elated as he left the taxi to stride under the restored coaching inn archway and through the courtyard. From there he bounded across the orchard at the back of the hotel with all the daintiness of a dancing hippo.

Despite his visitor being recognised by half the hotel guests who saw him and coming into full view of his CCTV, Peter waited until the knocker thudded before letting him in. Bernard's arrival had been characteristically public and he did not want to reveal that his basement had enough electronic surveillance to deter the fumes from the kitchen above.

Once safely inside Peter's apartment, the large man hugged Bernard as though he had given up hope of ever seeing him again.

'Dear boy, how are you?'

'I'm fine. The doctor says I'm as healthy as I'll ever be,' was the ebullient response.

'You look fit enough to take on Wagner.'

'I could wrestle Wotan with one hand behind my back.'

'You'd do better performing him.'

'Oh no.' Bernard laughed. 'The last time I carried a spear I had that accident with a large blonde soprano, which tempted some broadsheets to sink to the level of the tabloids.'

'You're lucky Indrina didn't use that as grounds for separation. Could have been the first divorce filed because of an inadvertently wielded spear. It's just as well they take the edge off those things before letting the cast handle them.'

Bernard's mood was too buoyant to pay any attention to the aspersion about his clumsiness. His face lit up. 'Hasn't Indrina told you?'

Peter's large, brown features glowed with innocence. 'Told me what, dear boy?'

'We're back together.'

Peter said nothing, just looked bemused.

'Oh, I realise how pig-headed I've been. I will change, though,' protested Bernard.

By the youthful enthusiasm in his friend's face, Peter was prepared to believe him. 'You'll take things easy now? Not expect too much of her?'

'Of course. I feel totally different since they diagnosed it as only trauma brought on by some deeply suppressed experience from the past. Believe me, I had plenty of those. In some working men's clubs I probably wasn't conscious enough to be aware of them. But it could well account for the other odd things that had been happening to me.'

'Indrina did mention something about them.' Peter ushered him to an armchair.

'I thought I was going mad.'

'So did Indrina and Aurora.'

Bernard suddenly fell quiet and stared blankly at the antique Dutch tiles on the fire surround.

'What's the matter?'

'It all seemed so real,' Bernard eventually admitted.

'What did?'

'That night I ran across the park in the moonlight to find a bowing oak.'

'A what?'

Bernard hesitated. 'I haven't told anyone else - I daren't.'

'You know you can tell me. Who am I liable to speak to? I haven't been to the opera since your Mephistopheles, and Indrina can read your mind anyway.'

'Oh no, for pity's sake don't tell Indrina!'

'Of course I won't, dear boy, of course I won't.'

It was obvious Bernard ached to confess his secret. 'You know those hallucinations I was having?'

Peter nodded diplomatically. 'Yes.'

'Well, the first night I spent at Clarey's he offered me a small dose of this drug. I don't know what it was, but when I drank it something happened. This goblin who had been taking me over materialised. He said he was part of me, an alter ego who was Second Minister of a place called Lustreland. There was also a dot of guff about dragons, ogres and sorcery - real fighting fantasy stuff. You know I would never touch one of those stupid computer games, don't you Peter, but I can't think of where it all came from - it could hardly have been the Ring of the Nibelung - you know me and Wagner...'

Peter tried not to let his expression tighten. 'Go on?'

'This Bruno character insisted that the only way to save both our lives was to take him to an ancient bowing oak where he could return to Lustreland.'

Peter forced a laugh. 'Really? You evidently both made it.'

'No, seriously Peter. It scared me. But that isn't all. My shins still have the scratches from those brambles and Indrina noticed that my dressing gown was torn.'

Peter thought it was best to change the subject. 'You are allowed to drink I suppose?'

'Just a little, thanks Peter. I still have to take tablets, and had enough trouble convincing everyone I was fit enough to travel by myself. Clarey and Mouse do fuss. They've been very good to me you know.'

'Indrina said you were being well looked after. Will you be staying there much longer?'

Bernard smiled secretly into his brandy. 'Something interesting has turned up.'

Peter pretended to half listen, pausing for a moment to contemplate a sporting print hanging on a nearby beam.

He eventually turned back to Bernard. 'What was it?'

'I've discovered a male soprano. I asked Kitty Callahan to come and hear it for herself.'

'Good God,' muttered Peter with enough lack of surprise to make the singer suspicious.

'What's the matter?'

'Who is it?'

'I think it must be Mouse, Clarey's friend. He's undersized and looks as though he could be underdeveloped.' Peter was awkwardly silent so Bernard went on. 'Actually, he's got a good light tenor when he speaks, same range as Clarey in fact. That could be training. This singer has a range of over three octaves. When I first met Mouse there was something about him that puzzled me. I couldn't put my finger on it.'

Peter chuckled. 'Mind that finger doesn't get caught in a Mouse-trap.'

Having anticipated his disapproval, Bernard ploughed on regardless, 'But this voice could-'

The large man contemplated the brandy slowly swilling round in his glass as his suddenly raised finger stopped his friend's flow of enthusiasm. 'Odd subject, the castrati. When I was a lad, a lay clerk lent me a book about them. It was very Victorian and proper; explained everything but what a castrato actually was. Reticence no doubt something to do with only "whole" men being worthy in the sight of God.'

'That was centuries ago.'

'Should have thought it was a funny sort of god then and there. That didn't occur to me until much later, after I actually came to know a eunuch.'

'No, really?'

'Well, one who didn't mind the world knowing it. Saved him from National Service. He was grateful for that.'

'What was he like?'

'Totally normal. Had a wife. More passion in that marriage than most others I've come across, including mine.'

'Must have lost his testicles after puberty.'

'No, he had the condition at birth. Probably why he was so loving - not enough testosterone to make him belligerent.'

'Oh come on ...' groaned Bernard.

'Well just look at you.'

'I'm not having any operation, however much sweeter tempered it's liable to make me. There are too many mezzos as it is.'

'Oh you wouldn't lose anything else you developed during puberty, except your bloody-mindedness.'

'I wouldn't want to be a laughing stock.' Bernard stopped himself. 'Do people really still laugh about men without gonads?'

'Are stand-up comedians misogynists? Was Himmler a racist?'

'But the castrati did revolutionise music - Rossini thought too much.'

Peter took a mouthful of brandy, and then chuckled. 'Canaries with the lung capacity of turkeys.'

'You make it sound so simple.'

'Simple? There's nothing simple about sexual non-development. Given the frequency with which some children are brought up as girls only to discover they are actually boys, surprisingly little is mentioned about it. Happens enough to supply dozens of choirs.'

Bernard grunted in disbelief. 'Oh come on.'

'About one in a thousand. It is the most common birth defect. Society just hasn't got around to making an issue of it. It's too busy on social networking sites entertaining its hang-ups with all the other taboo subjects it never dared talk about before.'

Bernard shrugged as though he had never held a prejudice in his life. 'But why?'

'Because you can't raise armies with people of indeterminate sex. Some primeval, robber baron probably noticed that women were not inclined to indulge in mortal combat for the sake of burglary, so the male hormone became a sacred totem.'

Bernard could feel the gravity of the discussion pushing him under so took the coward's way out. 'I bet Kitty would be able to answer that.'

Peter waved him down. 'Goodness no dear boy, you must have already bewildered her enough.'

'You can't bewilder Kitty. She knows everything.'

'Including how to promote the only castrato this century is liable to hear?'

'Well, I suppose it's something that you believe he's genuine.'

'If he wasn't he could be comfortably singing as a counter tenor. Then I don't pretend to know that much about the music world. Seems an odd sort of place to me.'

'It is. So was the chip shop where I worked, and the launderette where I washed the tea towels. Anywhere inhabited by human beings is an odd sort of place.'

Peter looked at him in surprise. 'Goodness, dear boy, you've started to think.' Bernard looked crestfallen. 'But do please go on. You may stumble across the solution to the Unified Field Theory.'

The irony was wasted on Bernard. 'I don't know about that, but we might have discovered another Farinelli. Have you any idea of the impact this could make?' Peter opened his mouth to protest. 'I know how narrow-minded people can be, but ...' Bernard's enthusiasm momentarily flagged. 'You don't think it's a good idea do you?'

'Not knowing the feeling of the male soprano you intend to confront the world with - I assume that is what you had in mind?' Bernard said nothing so he knew he was right. 'I think you should be very careful, bossy boots.'

Bernard huffed and puffed to himself for a moment. 'But we're not going to sell his soul to a recording company, and Clarey will have to give his permission before we can do anything.'

'Just you leave everything to Kitty.'

Bernard groaned. 'Oh why does everything have to be so complicated?'

CHAPTER 47

Goblin miners dropped with exhaustion and the troll lumberjacks hardly able to keep up with the supply of timber needed to support the rapidly growing tunnel. Flunkin ordered his workers on, regardless of any Lustreland cellar it might undermine. Given the whims of their tyrant, the miners were just relieved that they weren't heading towards Darkle Deeps even though the clay in that direction was easier to dig. They did encounter several natural passages veering off in the direction of Rara Avis Ridge, but as precious minerals did not glint at their far end, no one was tempted to investigate, and Flunkin's overseers had a devotion to duty a Ptolemy would have demanded in his slave drivers.

The goblin tyrant frequently inspected the miners' progress, just to be sure he was present when the gem-encrusted caverns were discovered. It also kept him away from his mother who had proved far more difficult to replace than his wife. She had soon recovered from the novelty of him being tyrant and started to nag again. Previously she had scolded him for being too dull-witted to know one end of a pick from the other, and so naive he would have allowed the first tinker who offered to value the family silver to run away with it. Now he was accused of being too highly-strung and having a suspicious nature. It was about time the ancient goblin at the bottom of the World Well threw back the lid and beckoned down the domineering matriarch.

Flunkin's reverie of resentment was broken by a cry from the far end of the tunnel. He leapt up from his portable throne. Either the miners had come to the wall of chalcedony that the map in the seeing glass had indicated, or there had been a cave-in. Fortunately, the troll timbers were too robust to allow the roof to collapse so the tyrant pulled on his helmet and dashed to the end of the excavation, beckoning his bodyguard to follow just in case the sight of so many precious gems gave some miner the same idea above his station that had occurred to him.

The draught from the nearest ventilation shaft was making the miners' lamps flicker and the predicted barrier of chalcedony glow soapily in the dancing light. Flunkin ordered the least exhausted miners to break through the wall. Armed with diamond tipped picks, they assailed the warm, bubbly stone like griffins attacking a vacated turtle shell. Soon there was a hole large enough for Flunkin to squeeze through. He huffed, puffed and then held his breath to topple untidily into a chamber under a ceiling speckled with glittering lights.

This had to be the magical hoard!

Excitedly, the tyrant ordered the miners to pass through ladders and scaffolding to lash together into a tower. He seized a pick, mounted the rickety structure and aimed several vigorous blows at the gems in the ceiling.

The crystal lattice set in the Halls of Government's lawn shattered. A rain of glittering fragments cascaded onto the goblins.

Two gargoyles peered down from their vantage points on the Halls of Government buildings, looked at each other, and then let out a beak vibrating wail. Several basalt trolls patrolling the jumbled complex of buildings clattered over to find out what the commotion was about.

They gazed, aghast, at what remained of the precious crystal lattice set into the Halls of Government's magic lawn and tried to make out what a gang of goblin miners were doing in the hole at its shattered centre. Did they fall from the sky? But even the trolls knew that goblins spent most of their time underground and couldn't fly.

Eventually working out that Flunkin and his followers had actually burrowed their way into Lustreland, the guards lurched into action, attempting to grab the goblins as they scuttled up through the scintillating rubble in an attempt to escape over the lawn. The shattered crystal dust was swept from the miners' jerkins and the rims of their helmets as they dashed about like chickens released from a crate that had fallen off a farmer's cart. More trolls arrived and lumbered after them, destroying what remained of the crystal lattice and adding to the crushed minerals by colliding with each other.

The gargoyles continued to watch the floor show, wondering whether to join in. They hadn't seen so much fun since the Mystic Trine tried to conjure up mini trolls abrasive enough to scour out their cauldrons, only to come up with granite bees that couldn't sting, but certainly throw a punch.

By the time the gardening gnomes arrived, their lawn had been reduced to a trampled mess covered with glittering confetti, which was all that remained of the crystal lattice.

CHAPTER 48

Peter decided to break his rule about using the door from his basement apartment to the hotel above, and he and Bernard rose like two substantial ghosts, up the back stairs and through the steam filled kitchen.

The chef and her staff were too busy to notice the interlopers. Even Isolda, a wine waitress in the dining room, had no time to pay attention to the love of her life, though the customers she was serving were more interested in identifying Bernard as the new arrivals were shown to a table by the maître d'hôtel.

With wry amusement, Peter watched the singer lap up the attention. It was just as well the man had a splendid voice, otherwise he would have made a splendid one man pantomime horse.

In an attempt to make Peter jealous, Isolda asked Bernard to autograph her order pad. She tucked the signed page into her cleavage then, with malicious affection, pinched Peter's ample cheek before leaving.

Bernard tried not to sound surprised that his friend apparently had a sex life. 'You know her?'

'The light of my existence and doom of my digestion,' Peter admitted. 'That was Isolda. She was a sort of nasturtium ginger the last time you met her.'

'Of course.' Bernard laughed. 'I gave her a photograph.' He swigged back his whisky.

'She keeps it over her bed.'

'Really?' Bernard wasn't yet tipsy enough to ask how he knew.

'I suppose I should trade her in, but she's taken out an insurance policy on me and you know I find it impossible to disappoint a woman.' Peter beckoned a waiter. 'Fancy a meal?'

Bernard was oblivious to the inference that anything was liable to happen to his friend. 'Why yes. I don't suppose they do anything vegan, do they?'

Peter beamed proudly. 'Dear boy, the chef could cook something Martian if you asked her.'

For an eerie second Bernard wondered what Lustrelanders ate. His ears briefly buzzed and thankfully the thought left.

The next two hours saw the ruination of Bernard's efforts to lose weight, and Peter ate as though oblivious of his heart condition.

Afterwards, with enough wine and whisky inside them to keep any toper mellow for a couple of days, Peter and Bernard strolled into the nearby village to take the air and intimidate the traffic by standing in unison with a group campaigning for a zebra crossing. As soon as a local reporter had noted the celebrity's support for the cause, the couple strolled back along the canal tow path where the last horse working on it just managed to avoid them.

As Bernard had consumed a considerable amount of alcohol on top of the medication he had been taking, Peter saw him safely onto an evening train, and then phoned Clarey to ensure there was someone waiting at the other end to pull him off in case he slept past the station.

Bernard's departure opened up a quiet space for all Peter's perplexing problems to tumble into.

As dusk fell, he wandered through the orchard, wondering what Bernard's reaction would be if he ever discovered Indrina's part in the hunt for the criminal manipulators of the world's economy. It would have probably been akin to the confusion the singer's alter ego was experiencing over a dragon.

Indrina's plan had left Peter's mental grasp of the economic gasping for oxygen. His business acumen was formed in the age of the cash till and ledger. It would always be beyond his comprehension how tiny gold wired chips, small as snowflakes, could pick up so many countries by their financial appendages and hold them to ransom. At one time empires were won on the blade and barrel of brute force, now their sum totals could be tapped out and transferred by anyone technically savvy enough to break codes. He hoped Alan Turing, wherever he was, relished the poetic chaos that had sprung from his projections for the computing age.

Night fell and Peter returned to the cellar where he lifted his crystal sphere from its case and perched it on its stand. He leaned back in his armchair and concentrated.

The creased features of Rimonay reluctantly appeared.

She gazed at him with studied disapproval. 'What is it?'

'Have to open a nasty box of tricks.'

She was more tetchy than usual. 'So why is that my problem?'

'Remember our deal. I need you to ferret out someone.'

'Who?'

'Probably a secret society.'

'I need more than that. What do they do?'

'Meet every full moon.'

'What else?'

'No idea.'

'Who are they?'

'No idea.'

'I might as well chase snowflakes.'

'It's important.'

'Nothing is more important than what is about to happen in Lustreland. Are you ready?'

'Yes, I couldn't avoid it if I wasn't.'

'I'll keep to my side of the bargain, but you'll have to give me more than "probably a secret society",' insisted Rimonay.

'That's just a front. Must be enough intimidating, magical mumbo jumbo involved to scare off any genuine cranks.'

'Anything else?'

'Try looking for efficient, anonymous minds; several nationalities. They'll be focused on armaments, mineral and agricultural resources and, of course, obscene amounts of money. We need the passwords they use to access the organisation's banking accounts. They'll be committed to memory and undoubtedly uppermost in their thoughts.'

'Not many humans dotty enough to believe in magic have those sorts of profiles.'

'Oh, these criminals don't believe in magic,' Peter warned.

'They will ... They will ...' Rimonay cackled as her image faded from the sphere.

CHAPTER 49

'The Ligh Tofrea Sun,' Iggata hissed. 'The source of the light that fills Lustreland. Isn't that what you wanted to invade them for? Isn't that what makes Lustrelanders believe they are so superior? And what have they ever done to deserve it? Would they share the Ligh Tofrea Sun if they knew how to? No, they don't even know what it is, let alone where it is... except for one person.'

Bludon, Jobaloba's adviser, nudged him to start taking interest.

The ogre chief could least count up to, 'One?'

'Not a cave deity you would never be able to catch. A real person as solid as you are.'

The witch's enticing revelation at last started to elicit a reaction.

One of Jobaloba's heads gurgled greedily while the other growled orders for his unspeakable hoards to stand down from what they knew all too well would be a second futile attempt to invade Lustreland. It came as a relief after being barbecued by a delinquent dragon.

Bludon flinched apprehensively as Jobaloba poked Iggata with a thick, bony finger. 'Go on, go on, witchy.'

Nobody poked a witch with Iggata's powers and got away with it.

But before she could turn the ogre into something comparatively pretty, like a bumblehog or toadstool maggot, the voice of another witch tuned into her psychic wavelength warned, 'Take it easy, Iggata. Don't go and ruin things now it's working.'

Iggata bit her tongue to prevent it casting the spell, and replied instead, 'He's the only non-deity to have the knowledge - and a coward. You shouldn't find it too difficult to get the secret out of him.'

'Who he?' growled Jobaloba.

'I shouldn't really tell on another wizard.' She hesitated in mock coyness. 'He is such an inoffensive and sweet creature. You must promise not to hurt him - too much.'

'Who, who, who?' went up the roar from the ogres, dislodging a few tiles from what remained of the fortress's roof.

Iggata raised a hand to quieten them. 'Alright, alright, I'll tell you.'

Bludon was probably the nearest thing to a realist the ogres had ever produced. 'How can we be sure you're telling the truth?'

'He told me himself. He's a little sweet on me you see. He revealed that the cave deities had passed the secret of the Light Tofrea Sun on to him. I wasn't able to get him to tell me any more, though.' Her tone hardened. 'Some bloody minstrel kept making too much din.'

'He tell us. Who he?' demanded Jobaloba.

Iggata sighed as though fighting internally with some good fairy who had taken a wrong turning into her conscience, before confessing, 'Wizard Qulio.'

'Wizard? He make bad spell for us.'

'Not him. He doesn't know one end of a wand from the other.'

'How he come here?'

'Just leave it to me.' Without further ado, Iggata snapped her fingers and vanished.

The ogres spent some time searching the fortress for her before working out that witches did that sort of thing every now and then.

In contrast to the ogres' roofless pit of a home filled with a jumble of unpleasantly steaming bodies, the Mystic Trine's magical roost perched on a slender stem of chambers and spiralling staircases. This architectural hotchpotch overlooked Lustreland with the intention of daunting those unfortunate enough to live in its corkscrew shadow. Over the millennia, turret upon turret had been added to the peculiar structure and were miraculously held in position, defying the forces of gravity that otherwise operated in Lustreland and thereabouts. As the influence of the Mystic Trine waned, their bizarre residence spiralled higher and higher into the flight paths of griffins and rocs to spite the fact. Like most frauds who love ostentation, the display was markedly lacking in taste and, had it belonged to anyone else, would have been demolished as a dangerous structure long ago.

The tower's interior chambers were cluttered with piles of equipment used in failed spells and it was left to a lone apprentice to tidy up as best as he could. Though this youth bore the mark of the cloud, it was not distinct enough for him to insist on his birthright, so he was compelled to bide his time until it either fully developed or disappeared altogether. The apprentice made sure everything had the right label, scorch marks on carpets and wall hangings were concealed, and the results of failed experiments were given good homes.

As the main chamber moved higher into the sky and the lower rooms fell into disuse, the apprentice needed a flying carpet to reach them: the Mystic Trine had long since given up bothering with sensible stairs.

In their council chamber sat a circle of conspirators silently contemplating each other, the occasional rara avis that nearly collided with the room, and a plot as murky as any swamp in Darkle Deeps.

Iggata suddenly materialised to the unlikely sound of tinkling wind chimes.

A tide of congratulation swept about the chamber. Iggata was not just their wickedest member, she was the only one who dared brave the stench and beard a hoard of ogres in their own fortress.

An elder rubbed his gnarled hands. 'Now we have him. At long last we can be rid of that lily-livered altruist.'

'And redeem our standing in Lustreland's Council,' a more ambitious young warlock reminded them. 'As soon as the ogres learn the whereabouts of the Ligh Tofrea Sun, they'll try to seize it and be destroyed like the last time. Just as well they're not literate enough to remember their own history.'

The Mystic Trine's librarian wiped the fumes of the censer from her glasses. 'Well, our records aren't so intact that we know exactly what did happen,' she cautioned. 'There is no definitive proof that its wavelength would be fatal to an ogre.' Much to the annoyance of the others, the librarian had a way of making sense. They put it down to the fact that she had been contaminated by living so close to shelves of books. It was inevitable that some unmagical knowledge would rub off. 'There is too much of the intangible about the Ligh Tofrea Sun for my comfort,' she warned.

Iggata sneered contemptuously. 'Intangible?'

The librarian was the only one who did not flinch from the witch's verbal venom. 'Yes. However much I've read, I've never been able to discover exactly what it is.'

'We know it destroys ogres. Why should we bother what it looks like?'

'It might be some sort of white dwarf.'

Knowing making personal comments about anyone was irrelevant to the way the librarian reasoned, an elder commented, 'Why not a giant?'

'No, no. A white dwarf is a heavenly body humans have in their dimension.'

'What for?'

'I don't know what they use it for. I just know it's very dense.'

'Like an ogre?' mused a witch. 'Their human counterparts certainly seem to prosper.'

'No, they're nothing to do with heavenly bodies, I'm sure.'

'How do you know?'

'I read it somewhere.'

Another elder sensed the conversation was drifting away from the matter in hand. 'If the Lustreland Council were to discover Witch Iggata's plan and our part in destroying the ogres by using Qulio, they would probably revoke our flying licences.'

Iggata sneered. 'After the way the Ruling Council agreed to treat that oaf Bruno they've no right to sit in judgement.'

'But beware the First Minister. She may be old, but is devious and once a good friend of Bruno's. I've recently been getting garbled messages in my seeing crystal. I think it's trying to tell me that the Second Minister is still alive.'

'Well, if you were a dragon, would you eat him?'

The librarian concurred. 'It was a mistake to believe any creature could be that hungry. It probably dropped him before it reached its cave.'

'Whether Bruno's dead or alive,' declared Iggata, 'he's unlikely to be in a fit state to stop us. The only thing we need think about is making sure those stupid ogres manage to kidnap Qulio. Poor precious, petrified Qulio.'

Through the psychic tentacle it had wound up through the twisting stairs of the Mystic Trine's tower, the Hurglabat purred contentedly. These warlocks and witches actually believed that this was a plot of their own making: not one of them doubted it for a second. Perhaps it should have used them instead of ogres in the first place.

Only the apprentice heard its eerie purring and sensed something unpleasant slithering about the

Mystic Trine's roost. He immediately jumped onto his carpet and flew off, never to return. Cloud sign or not, he found the monster's flesh crawling gurgling more nauseating than putting that giant three-headed moth out of its misery. If this was magic, there was a lot to be said for turning the soil and bringing in the parsnips.

CHAPTER 50

The last car passed through the security gates of the Victorian mansion and the high voltage fence surrounding its grounds snapped on abruptly enough to leave several nights pickings for a lazy poacher. Having parked their cars in tidy formation before the main entrance, the crocodile of mysterious men carrying long orange robes and plastic imitation hauberks filed into the large hall that had once been the estate's church. Each of them solemnly bowed before an elevated altar bearing a pentagram enclosed by two crescent moons: this symbol had more to do with pragmatism than fear of vengeful divinities.

A hooded figure with outstretched hands stood on the dais, towering over the congregation.

'All business will be conducted during the interval after security clearance,' he announced.

As business was all this congregation had gathered for, there was a chorus of groans and shuffling of feet.

The voice from the hood was not impressed. 'Arrange yourselves, gentlemen and switch off your mobile phones. First a prayer to Zoroaster.' Someone muttered that they did that last week. 'This is a different one.'

The assembly wearily switched off their electronic gadgetry, donned their robes, and clattered about with plastic chain mail.

Eventually, the first round of prayers, nasal chanting, and sacrifice were over. At last the gathering was at liberty to furtively discuss the stratagems of secretly funded wars, bribed and rapidly disposed of minions, and resources being manipulated away from the countries that rightfully owned them. Transactions seldom took long. Everything had to be committed to memory and, at that time of night, most of the male minds were already filled with other inclinations.

The congregation reluctantly finished its coffee, fastened its robes, and returned to the mystical mumbo-jumbo. Some, against all common sense, subconsciously hoped they were being spied on to make the absurdity of it all worthwhile.

A large bronze charger had been placed on the altar and several smaller dishes containing enough magic powder to make the lords of Hell sneeze were laid out on a side table.

Despite a sotto voice that asked if he could conjure up a hamburger, the hood announced his grave intention of using the potions to call up a spirit from the other side of the grave. Time was beginning to drag and discontented murmurs from members who had no inclination to meet long dead relatives echoed about the hall. After an appeal for more commitment to what they were doing the congregation became a little quieter, though expressions of acute boredom or profound longing for the mistress they had left in a warm bed remained.

On and on the hood droned as though he really believed something would form in the wispy smoke girdling its way about the ceiling timbers. His concentration was so focused that when a shape did start to emerge he wasn't surprised.

Everyone else was horrified at the manifestation.

'Stop it you son of a bitch!' a terrified voice yelled, though it wasn't until a full throated chorus of protest went up that their mesmerised priest realised something was wrong. His hood fell back to reveal a gaunt, glazed expression of amazement more suited to a stalker of graveyards.

It was ironic that the first time this committed cheerleader for the lower domains showed his skeletal features it was in fright at a ghost. For there, idling in the plumes of smoke, was the phantom of what once might have been a woman. Its features were so wrinkled, only its glittering, diamond eyes betrayed that it was alive.

In a flurry of sacred robes, the medium sprinted from the chamber in panic at what he had conjured up.

However hard-headed and cynical, his congregation knew that this dreadful apparition was no conjuring trick. Terror surged through the hall as a claw like hand reached out for a victim to drag down into the grave with her.

It was all the security guards could do to control the ensuing stampede and prevent anyone from leaving until the fittings of the old church had been dismantled and the grounds combed to find out what had been responsible.

They never did, of course.

CHAPTER 51

Deep in the woods, Juniper and several changelings sat patiently trying to comb the debris of Sesame's nest from Qulio's beard.

'I've nothing against dragons,' Juniper chided, 'but they are such untidy creatures.'

Qulio smiled apprehensively. 'Now Bruno's in charge, I think things are going to change.' His friend raised an enquiring eyebrow. 'Bruno likes everything to be tidy. He's not going to allow anything to soil his new robe.'

'Oh my goodness, I do hope they don't start arguing again.'

Qulio's silence spoke volumes.

Juniper understood. For someone who had been the source of so many rumours she was really quite homely with a jolly, round face, laughing button-like eyes, and bright, puckish smile. Short and plump, she always seemed to be in motion; one moment surrounded by pots and pans in a steam filled scullery, and then bustling her changeling charges inside to their meals, before hoeing the vegetable plots and evicting marauding caterpillars.

The changelings she had adopted were not ugly or badly behaved, just a little too strange in nature for most other folk to want them. Which was odd, because none of them possessed the mischievous malice of many offspring. They did not squabble or fight and doted on Juniper, who was so happy with her brood she would not have swapped them for the children the spirits had intended them to replace.

The only foundling to give Juniper a headache was Qulio. She did not like him being out of her sight for long. Although he was the kindest, wisest creature she had ever known, he would find himself in situations only braver folk had the strength to get out of. Qulio was all heart and no nerve and, despite the length of his legs, didn't always know when to run.

Juniper persuaded Qulio to stay in the woods where he would be safe, and very soon the local sprites were clustering about her home like butterflies drawn to nectar. The changelings they had deserted suddenly became petted and played with. Juniper's washing dried twice as fast in the breeze made by the fluttering of their wings and her herbs and vegetables doubled their growth. The only disadvantage of having Qulio around was that the fairy folk would not leave him alone. His warmth of wisdom was a refreshing change from the ethereal lives they led and listening to him made them feel more substantial. Although they didn't have the sort of problems the wizard could solve, they basked in the glow of his company in a way that made Juniper wonder all the more about his true nature. When he was around it was much warmer, the blossom was at its best, and even the occasional party of goblins came up from their mines to eat their lunch nearby in the sweet smelling air. For all the years Juniper had known Qulio, she was beginning to believe that she would never learn the truth about him.

All the comings and goings attracted a wandering minstrel. Curious to know if she had any gossip, Juniper invited Crystabel into her cottage where they nattered for so long the changelings wondered if they would ever see their next meal. Crystabel explained that she had come into the woods to learn the sounds of rare birds and get away from the stifling air of Lustreland. Being a minstrel who travelled from domain to domain, she had noticed that the Ligh Tofrea Sun was not as strong as it used to be, though any Lustrelander she had mentioned it to assured her she was mistaken.

'Perhaps their eyes have adapted without them knowing?' suggested Juniper.

It was obvious that many stomachs were rumbling for their next meal, so Crystabel thanked Juniper for her company and went on her meandering way to listen to each trill, whistle and screech that echoed in the branches above.

After walking for some while the minstrel heard familiar voices through the acoustic veil of bird song and murmuring of sprites. They belonged to the couple she had heard on top of a turret not so long ago.

The whispering of the sprites became more urgent.

Crystabel spied on the secretive pair from the cover of some bushes, wondering why they should meet so furtively, but they were a witch and wizard and, after all, that was the way with their sort.

When the couple started to walk off the Minstrel secretly followed out of spell casting distance. And she followed... and followed.

The terrain grew darker and the last of the sprites would go no further. Above towered the crags of Rara Avis Ridge, blocking the light from the chasm below.

The witch and wizard wended their way down path of glow stones, which created a luminous trail that faded as it reached the border of Darkle Deeps and the pass vitrified by Sesame when routing the ogre army.

Why should these two partners in magic need to travel so far on foot when besoms would have been much faster? Then Crystabel glimpsed the face of the Wizard. He had obviously been hypnotised and, as soon as they approached the border of Darkle Deeps, the witch left with a turn of speed which was magic.

Without faltering, the Wizard walked across the slippery surface that would have brought down an ogre in seconds.

It was too late for Crystabel to leap forward and haul Qulio back by his long beard. Several ogres were waiting for him on the other side of the pass. One of

them had two heads and breath so bad it was visible in
the dank air.

CHAPTER 52

Bruno snatched up an armful of branches and tossed them from the cave. 'Why do you have to be so untidy? Don't you believe in making your bed at least once a year?'

Sesame ruefully watched those dearly departed pieces scatter themselves irretrievably on the breeze. They had made up the most comfortable spot of the nest. At this rate, the only part left would be the feathers Bruno slept on.

The dragon's inadvertent house guest ranted on. 'How do you manage to survive in such a shambles? And I keep telling you to move that beak sharpener just above the cave. The sound of those rocs and griffins grinding away at it sets my teeth on edge. It's like living in a sawmill!'

It was at this point Sesame wondered if the harpies were still interested in having the Second Minister for lunch or, better still, perhaps he could browbeat them into being sweeter natured. The dragon had certainly had enough of his nagging. If this was affection, it didn't seem much different from being struck over the snout with his staff of office.

Before then, the enigmatic creature's expressions had all seemed the same to Bruno. Now he could read them as fluently as Qulio. 'Don't look so puzzled. It's for your own good. Living up here in the mists isn't good for you. We should find somewhere milder.'

Sesame liked the swirling mists and being able to look down on its neighbours, yet knew the Second Minister would never give in. The dragon couldn't understand why Bruno wanted to stay in the cave if it was so damp and untidy. He had obviously been much happier in his two storey box in Lustreland with its turret and fishpond.

There was only one solution.

Sesame folded down the flaps of skin which protected its sensitive hearing from the occasional rara avis having yet another attempt to break the sound barrier, and picked up Bruno and his jewelled robe. Though the dragon was deaf to the abuse, it could feel Bruno throbbing with rage. It was careful not to prick him with its talons in case he burst.

The Second Minister soon became exhausted and fell silent, so the harpies did not notice the glinting of the fabulous beast's fiery scales as it glided through the narrow canyons. The dragon was more concerned about those psychic tentacles twitching through Rara Avis Ridge and trying to latch into its mind. Though easy going about most things, that was really beginning to annoy it.

The dome of light crowning Lustreland came into view and the dragon hovered at the domain's boundary in disbelief. Sesame flickered its secondary eyelids to make sure it wasn't seeing things, but dragons never hallucinated. They leave it to others to hallucinate about them.

But there was no mistake; crawling over the huge luminescent bubble was a faint, sinister web of wriggling filaments.

Sesame cautiously went closer. Bruno may have raged himself into a stupor, but had to be returned before he built up another head of steam. And he had to be delivered safely - that was the agreement.

The dragon had no option. It soared as high as it dared with its passenger, and then plunged through the writhing web. The net of hellish angel hair tried to ensnare the dragon, but a blast of flame ensured they got through.

Bruno passed out.

To prove that no - well very little - harm had come to the Second Minister, Sesame went on to the Halls of Government, soaring over the lawn sequined with the debris of the crystal lattice. The dragon alighted in the courtyard beyond, and set him down, only to have Bruno come round just in time to irrationally wind his arms so tightly around its muzzle it dare not take off again.

A high pitched admonishment penetrated the venerable silence of the Halls of Government. 'Stop that! Stop that at once! Leave that dragon alone and behave yourself!'

There, flanked by her two tree sprites, was Rimonay.

Bruno suddenly snapped back to sensibility and released Sesame with a start.

'Haven't you learnt anything at all? Just look at the state of you!'

Bruno dare not obey for fear of the fright he would give himself.

The pitch of Rimonay's annoyance lowered to frustration. 'I'm beginning to think there was little point in all this after all.'

Uncharacteristically speechless, the Second Minister could only look confused.

'I needed Sesame to give you a nasty fright,' she admitted. 'It was our secret. That hypocritical, self-righteous Ruling Council didn't know anything about it. They're even more useless than you are and were happy to see you devoured. Unfortunately, you're the only one with the courage to resist corruption on any level. It's a pity your blunderbuss of a brain has always been like a clam and needed prizing open a little to let the breeze of sweet reason in.'

Words still beyond him, Bruno sat on the ground clutching his opulent robe in one hand and the other clinging to one of the spines on Sesame's head.

Rimonay rapped the pavement with her stick. 'Leave that dragon alone, you fool! You can't keep it. Nobody falls in love with dragons. Not even other dragons. They find it too difficult discovering what sex they are in the first place.'

One of Rimonay's tree sprites had been following the proceedings with keen interest. 'Then how do they-'

'Who cares! That's the dragons' problem. Fairies shouldn't need to know about such things.'

Bruno released Sesame and the dragon cautiously backed away before he changed his mind.

'Get him inside, you two,' Rimonay ordered her tree sprites. 'Clean him up. Pinch him if he gives you any trouble.' She watched her diminutive aides manoeuvre the mighty Bruno into her residence. 'You can go now, dragon. If the ogres are still intent on mischief the Mystic Trine insist that they can cope this time.' Sesame was reluctant to leave. 'Don't worry. A couple of enforcers will be over to slap an injunction on those harpies if they don't keep quiet. They'll calm down unless they want their wings clipped.'

That wasn't uppermost in Sesame's mind, and the dragon puffed out a few perplexed smoke rings.

Rimonay hoped this didn't mean that her worst fears were about to be confirmed. She half closed her eyes and returned the glittering gaze of the fabulous creature.

Its thoughts were crystal clear to the First Minister. She slowly nodded. The terror was returning faster than she had expected. The heart of Lustreland must have been breached the moment the crystal lattice had collapsed.

'All right dragon, but now you must leave well alone. You will be no match for this entity.'

Sesame had already worked that out and flapped its huge wings to catch a passing zephyr.

As the dragon soared into the sky Rimonay, stick clicking, hobbled inside.

The sprites took some time to primp, clean, and manicure Bruno to their own demanding standards. They exchanged his tattered clothes for a clean robe, girdle, and drenching in a pine scent the tree sprites thought wonderfully aromatic, but which took the Second Minister's breath away after he had become accustomed to the warm odour of Sesame's cave.

At last presentable, he was escorted to their mistress with all due dignity.

The overpowering smell of pine almost bowled Rimonay over as well, but she reassured him, 'It's easier on the nose than privet and wears off eventually. Come over here, damn you, and say something.'

Bruno was unable to utter anything other than a faint, 'Why?'

'You're my deputy, aren't you?'

He nodded.

'By rights you should take my place when I'm dead. We couldn't use you as you were, could we?'

Bruno lowered his gaze in embarrassment.

'You had to be taught sense or disposed of. I couldn't risk you blundering about in one of your pointless tantrums at a time like this. Reason must be brought back to Lustreland or it will perish. Nothing is inevitable if an effort is made to prevent it. And you are the one who is going to make the effort.' Rimonay turned to her sprites, 'You can put the robe on him. Let's see how he looks now he's organised.'

Bruno allowed the sprites to dress him in the magnificent robe while the First Minister tapped her stick on the floor with approval, muttering something about that dratted dragon flying off with the garment while it was still hanging on the web of the spider who had been commissioned to embroider it. She wasn't too happy that Bruno had been so bloody-minded as to lose weight either.

'Designed by the goblins in Pumice Hill, that was. Since the law against dragon slaying was passed, nobody needed them to forge armour any more. It's sword proof, and might even stop the odd shaft of magic if you ever fall foul of the Mystic Trine. I've had to wear a magic proof vest made of the same material since becoming First Minister. Probably prevented me from rapidly evolving into something amphibian on a good many occasions.'

'I didn't know that?'

'For a thick-skulled, stubborn martinet, you can be an innocent oaf at times.'

Bruno tried to look defiantly dignified, but still remained as baffled as when he was contemplating his feelings about dragons, so he turned to admire himself in the wall of reflecting crystal that ran the length of Rimonay's chamber.

'Somebody's bound to try and kill you sooner or later,' Rimonay explained as though that might have been a novelty to him. 'Stop playing the peacock!'

What vanity Bruno had managed to keep smouldering after his various indignities vaporised like snowflakes in a furnace.

Rimonay realised that she may have gone too far and her Second Minister's ego was crumbling back into its shell. For a moment he appeared to be on the verge of becoming as introverted as a cauliflower sprite with a phobia about bursting into flower because it knew no bloom could be less ethereal. An errant thought that Bruno might be a cauliflower sprite crossed her mind, yet she knew not even one of those could be that substantial. As an infant he had been found in a turnip field and was probably some hybrid abandoned by embarrassed elfin folk. Even the First Minister had never had the heart to tell him that. It was demeaning enough that he had been reared by a truffle hunter and his pig.

Rimonay suddenly rapped her stick on the floor, as much to break her contemplation as make Bruno jump. 'You've got work to do! Pull yourself together.'

Before she could explain what that was, a breathless blossom sprite hurtled in, wings beating so fast they were barely visible. They stopped so suddenly at the sight of the severe featured Rimonay she dropped like a gossamer wrapped brick into Bruno's arms. Enveloped in a cloud of pollen, he sneezed violently, catapulting her towards the frosty First Minister who had the self-control to hold her breath. The wide eyes of the frightened sprite looked into the icy glare of the ancient matriarch and her foliage quivered.

'What is this?' demanded Rimonay. 'Why are you drooping like an ogre's breakfast?'

'It's the Ligh Tofrea Sun! It's suddenly getting dimmer!' the sprite piped.

It was difficult to deny what she already knew. As soon as the rest of the population noticed the result would be panic throughout Lustreland. There seemed little prospect of staving of the inevitable with prevarication.

'Are you sure? You frilly fairies can get hysterical over nothing, you know.'

'But I notice it. My petals are very sensitive.'

Rimonay beckoned her attendants to assist her and prodded the blossom sprite outside with her stick. 'Don't step on the chalcedony or my guard frogs will get you.'

The fairy fluttered into the air, not daring to look back to see if the tree sprites survived the journey. Bruno followed, thankful he was no longer the focus of attention.

In the courtyard they scrutinised the sky for the monster that might have been devouring the star they had never seen. Yet every tree and spire on the horizon seemed to be in its rightful place and all the bushes, flowers and vines were still in permanent bloom. Beyond the Halls of Government, Lustrelanders still bustled about their business. But, like the blossom sprite, Rimonay was all too aware that something was missing without needing to use her sensitive's sight. The light had lost its distinctive sparkle and the glimmering sheen of radiance that gave Lustreland its name had leached away. In its place was a flat, yellowish tinge which many other lands would have been satisfied with.

For the Province of Light it could only mean one thing and Rimonay knew she at last had to admit it. 'You might be right.'

'She is! She is!' insisted the tree sprites.

'All right then.' The First Minister turned to Bruno. 'You can have one of my sprites to help you. See to it.'

With that, she hobbled back inside.

After standing with his mouth open for some while, Bruno's ego crawled out of its shell and took a look around. The blossom sprite lightly touched down and peered up at him with a mixture of insolence and expectation.

He peered down at the sliver of impertinence and a glimmer of his old self bellowed, 'Boo!'

She fluttered off in a cloud of pollen.

'See to it?' Bruno muttered to himself. 'Find out what's happening to the Light Tofrea Sun. What is the Ligh Tofrea Sun? Where is the Ligh Tofrea Sun?' He held up a finger as though anticipating inspiration, and then saw the wide eyes of the tree sprite Rimonay had delegated him. It was the one interested in the breeding habits of dragons and every intelligent thought rising through the cortex of his brain retreated, so Bruno sent him off with a message for Sesame in the hope that would douse his curiosity. Then he returned home on the elderly griffin that provided non- airborne council members with a taxi service in exchange for board and lodging more suited to his great age than a pinnacle in Rara Avis Ridge.

As soon as he alighted, Bruno dashed inside to riffle through his library. The dust that flew from the ancient bindings betrayed how seldom he referred to those tomes of knowledge, and how infrequently his marigold sprite dusted them. Now less inclined to believe he already knew everything, Bruno searched through the volumes for a mention of the Ligh Tofrea Sun until realising that he needed an index spell, the sort that obligingly sent sparks out to tap the relevant book on the spine and open its pages for the reader. He could hardly expect the Mystic Trine's Librarian to cast one for him, even though she did stand out from the others of that organisation by first looking something up before forming an intolerant view on the matter. And her gaze, usually concealed behind mirroring lenses rippling with mystic symbols, worried Bruno. He had the eerie feeling that she read her volumes by emitting wave lengths of magic too short for a cat to detect. He shuddered and impulsively pulled a massive tome from under a pile of scrolls.

Something faintly twinkling and orange fluttered from the shelf like a swatted moth.

It was his marigold sprite.

Bruno blinked in amazement at the apparition. Her petals had become transparent and the veins of her foliage were like cobwebs. With a sickening jolt he realised that she was fading with Lustreland's light.

His grasp of medicine was as limited as his ability to understand others, so all Bruno could do was lay her on a bed of cushions, puzzled as to why the sprite had returned to him when she must have thought he was quite mad.

However many dimensions, quantum or magic, actually existed, Bruno's present reality was more terrifying than anything he had ever experienced. If he failed in his mission, would all the other dimensions linked to his dwindle away as well, or just implode back into the atomic haze they had sprung from? Rimonay may have bullied him into making sense of his world, but it was only now he realised that he was in the eye of a gigantic, reality consuming, whirlpool. For all his belligerence and bluster, what was he good for in a situation like this? Only Qulio seemed to know what life was about. But then, he could understand why a bowl of oats resented milk. The wizard may not have possessed a magic index, but he did know more than he was willing to admit about the Ligh Tofrea Sun.

Bruno had no choice - he had to find Qulio.

CHAPTER 53

Curled up in what remained of its nest, a fabulous creature with flame coloured scales listened to the world below groan under the pressure of the parasitic entity growing beneath its domain. Sesame could detect the monster's tentacles radiating out under Rara Avis Ridge and towards Lustreland while its vile body remained safely under Darkle Deeps.

The dragon could stand it no longer. With Bruno gone, it was at last free to satisfy its curiosity and do the very thing Rimonay had warned against.

Sesame left the cave to glide silently over the ground it had vitrified during its battle with the ogres. It was virtually dark, but the dragon could see corpses bobbing in the small lakes left by of the deluge. Under Rimonay's rules of combat, the dragon had taken care not to kill any of Jobaloba's army, and these ogres had not died of a slight chill. The shrivelled flesh on huge skulls grinned hideously past beards bristling with fright, and eyes bulged in disbelief as though some monstrous spider had suddenly sucked the juices from them. Sesame had never seen anything like it before; not even witches and warlocks had wicked enough dispositions to inflict this sort of carnage.

Sensing that the culprit was still lurking in ambush, the dragon alighted on the cliff face just above the mass murder to examine the crime scene. It didn't want to end up as a couch cover in the monster's subterranean parlour, but was horribly fascinated by the minor massacre. Should the fabulous beast risk its scales in a closer inspection?

The Hurglabat silently gurgled in anticipation as it sensed its arch enemy. It would never get a better opportunity to rid itself of the troublesome creature, and there was more substance to suck from a dragon than a gristly ogre.

The Hurglabat remained motionless. Then slowly, insidiously, through its network of passages, tentacles seeped up to the dark pass down to Darkle Deeps.

Sesame cautiously placed a claw in one of the puddles where a corpse bobbed and nudged the cadaver with its snout. Two more claws came down and it took a tentative step.

The Hurglabat waited for the dragon to fold its wings and uncoil the tail it had corkscrewed about a rock protruding from the cliff face just in case. At last Sesame felt secure enough to put down the final claw, release its tail and unfold its wings.

Immediately the ground lifted. Saw-edged tentacles filled the air. A gelatinous bulge rose from their milling centre, row upon row of eyes rotating about the slimy folds in the monster's massive body, and then a gigantic beak opened to reveal maws lined with jagged teeth to devour its adversary.

Any other creature would have frozen at the sight, but Sesame was quicker than the Hurglabat and blasted a shaft of flame down its gullet.

The monster contracted with a prolonged screech of rage that echoed throughout Rara Avis Ridge and even made the ogres in their fortress hesitate from their despicable enterprise and flinch in terror.

With one downbeat of its wings, Sesame was airborne, blazing away at the writhing tentacles as it rose.

Rimonay was right. This entity was too much, even for a dragon.

The fabulous beast circled out of the Hurglabat's reach to watch it sink vengefully back into the ground, shredding several ogres' corpses as it went.

How was Rimonay going to rid Lustreland of that monstrosity without help? She would need a battalion of dragons. Sesame went home to retrieve the branches

Bruno had scattered and rebuild its nest, reassured that she had some wonderful plan, too devious for a straightforward dragon to comprehend, to deal with it.

CHAPTER 54

Clarey Ditton-Davis perused the sheets of music before him with a wistful smile.

He smiled. 'Written for the castrato. Now sung by female sopranos, mezzo-sopranos, contraltos, counter tenors, and even baritones.'

Bernard internally flinched at being the last accused. Clarey's quick smile reassured him that it was not a personal attack.

'It was a cruel business for unfeeling times,' Kitty reminded the aristocrat. 'In those days art mattered more than the mutilation of poor peasants' children.' She noticed Bernard's sour expression. 'However, my learned friend here believes that art can stop wars, cure bigotry, and no doubt suspend objects of beauty in the ether with no tangible means of support.'

Clarey knew what the musicologist was hinting at. He had been expecting it ever since she arrived. 'How much do you know?'

'That you have a sopranist possessing a range of over three octaves singing his heart out in the cellar with probably only the family ghosts as an audience.'

'And?'

A flush of embarrassment rushed to Bernard's cheeks. 'And,' he hesitated. 'Your resident scorpion, Mrs Porter, is blackmailing you by threatening to reveal to the gutter press that Mouse is this prodigy.'

Clarey gave a slow, almost calculating, smile. 'Oh, Mrs Porter isn't blackmailing me. She intends to do it. She somehow obtained a poor quality recording of the voice. You probably didn't notice her leave early this morning with our mini and a flea in her ear. It's only a matter of time before the phone calls start.'

To Bernard, Clarey was sounding infuriatingly diffident over the matter.

But this turn of events seemed to galvanise Kitty's resolve. 'I see. That changes things somewhat.'

Bernard wasn't so quick on the uptake. 'How?'

'The only option Clarey has is now obvious.'

'What option?'

For a moment Clarey wondered how the owner of the remarkable voice he so admired could be that dull-witted. 'To forestall her, and announce the existence of this "prodigy" before she declares it to the media. Time is on our side. I just wish I had the stomach for it. At least she's likely to shop around for the best deal and, without photographs, it won't be easy.'

To Bernard's relief, his host seemed to lose confidence, like a big game hunter who had lost the nerve to pull the trigger as the rhino charged. 'And you haven't the heart?'

But Kitty found Clarey's trepidation interesting.

Bernard never noticed such subtle interactions between other people. His train of thought, like long held notes, ploughed a straight furrow. 'What are you going to do?'

'I've never minded the other scandal too much,' Clarey admitted. 'It was strangely flattering, though did raise the hackles of local fathers with nubile daughters. This is something else. Modern society expects promiscuity, however much it claims to disapprove of it. The male without his "manhood" is virtually a non-person. Why the idea so frightens a species that has at last learnt to talk rationally about death I do not know. We live in a community that has struggled, and mostly managed, to accept atheism, homosexuality, equal opportunities for women, illegitimacy, rights of animals, and non-racism. But you produce a man who can sing naturally in a voice as high as any woman's, however beautifully, and -' He shrugged.

'It's not unnatural,' Kitty insisted. 'Most men have that potential. Fashion makes them keep their voices low in the same way women are expected to take HRT, look like emaciated wraiths, and keep their voices high.'

'That's not the real point, is it. How can such a voice be valued? With the available hormone treatment, some would say it should never exist in the modern world. Have you any idea how much soul searching went into the decision not to extinguish it while there was still the chance?' Clarey sank into a chair like a suddenly collapsed clotheshorse.

It was the first inelegant move Bernard had ever seen him make. 'Are you all right?'

The tall man gave a strained smile. 'It's nothing to worry about. I sometimes hear this buzzing noise when I become agitated.'

'Is there anything wrong with your hearing?' Kitty sounded concerned.

Clarey laughed. 'It's probably too finely tuned, like that wonderful voice both of you are so enthusiastic about.'

'The decision to save it was justified. Everyone must pay some price for their natural gifts, even women.'

'A woman cannot lose her womanhood.'

'A man cannot lose his manhood. Your sex is written on your chromosomes and those genes cannot be erased.'

'Still not the point.'

Bernard had been left some way behind. 'How come?'

'You keep out of this, you troublemaker,' Kitty told him.

Bernard looked like a scolded basset hound.

Clarey laughed. 'You cannot cut anything out of a woman that would make society accuse her of being anything less than a woman. The one positive thing about belonging to the "inferior sex" is that a woman doesn't have to prove she's a man.'

'But there's no stigma in being a woman today,' Bernard blustered unconvincingly.

Kitty detected the sudden surge of liberal ideas scribbling themselves on the postage stamp of Bernard's social awareness. 'You be careful about changing horses in mid stream and middle-age, Bernard. The high horse of morality is difficult to dismount once set in motion.'

Bernard grunted. He was determined that he should be seen wearing a more tolerant face before advancing years ossified his unyielding view of the world.

Kitty smiled indulgently at his transparent reasoning. The problems his upbringing had been responsible for were stamped on his character as permanently as fingerprints. Curing them would have been more difficult than charming away warts. Until parents were brought to book for the mismanagement of their children, there would be many more Bernards.

Kitty turned to Clarey. 'Shouldn't Mouse join this conversation?'

'No, he will trust my judgement, whatever I decide.'

'Well, I suppose if you can live with being county's most desirable man, he might be able to live with being the world's greatest singer.'

Clarey paused uneasily. 'You're not joking are you?'

'Listening to that voice made me wonder just how many Farinellis the modern world might have produced. They'll always be those who carp on about it of course.'

Bernard sensed that she was at last genuinely on his side and took a very audible deep breath.

'And you must be seen to support him all the way.'

This was something the singer had taken for granted, but not into account. 'Well, why ...' he blustered as though some intangible threat to his manhood had raised its ugly knee, 'of course.'

Seeing that he was now becoming unsure, Clarey thought it only fair to offer him a way out. 'I'll quite understand if you don't want any part of it.'

Bernard deftly knee-capped his phantom. 'I insist on being part of it. Everyone has to stand up and be counted at some time.'

'Careful you don't add up to one and a half, Bernard,' warned Kitty. 'We don't want this to develop into a circus.'

'I intend to be my usual dignified self, whatever happens.'

There was no safe answer to that so Kitty changed the subject. 'I'll make sure the right bookings and recording sessions are arranged. Clarey can no doubt hire a personal escort.'

Bernard was amazed that the real world might dare to intrude on his quixotic crusade. 'You really think someone would try to take a swing at him.'

'It's amazing what offends the brutish mentality, but the media will be an even greater problem so we had better get our act together. Once this barrel starts rolling no one will have the chance to jump out.'

Clarey was thoughtful. 'If only I could truly comprehend the mind of the beast we're up against.'

'It may applaud.'

'You really think so?'

'It'll have to evolve out of its hang-ups one day.'

'I hope it's before this performance.'

'How about setting a date for next month?'

'Sooner if you like.'

'Private performance in town hall?' Kitty suggested.

'Fine - but one proviso.'

'What's that?'

'No one must know of his identity before the performance, and not even you see him sing before then.' Kitty was about to protest. 'I will let you have a complete recording of the programme we choose and list of the instrumentalists.'

Kitty was unable to refuse. 'All right.' She trusted his judgement better than Bernard's to whom she had conceded much more than that in the past.

The bass baritone was looking self-satisfied, like a drake that had just laid an egg. At that moment he probably wouldn't have minded if a damp squib hatched out.

CHAPTER 55

The Hurglabat stretched its tentacles into the tunnels under Rara Avis Ridge burrowed by Flunkin's miners. They were filled with sweet aromas wafted from Lustreland. The invitation was too tempting. The monster's gelatinous body flowed from its home under Darkle Deeps and through the subterranean caverns deep beneath Rara Avis Ridge to position itself under the heart of Lustreland. There was little chance of the Hurglabat being shrivelled by a random shaft of the Ligh Tofrea Sun now that had virtually faded. Soon it would be able to crash into that benighted domain and devour. No creature, however magical, would be able to escape its voracious appetite.

Silently the monster oozed closer and closer to the Halls of Government, its long tentacles still anchored to the underside of Darkle Deeps. From there it listened to everything, from the panicking machinations of Lustreland's elite and the Machiavellian manoeuvring of the Mystic Trine, to the blundering about of the guard trolls still trying to work out what had happened to the crystal lattice.

The land surged a little as it moved. Residents didn't notice. They had other things on their minds. The Ligh Tofrea Sun was about to do the impossible - and set. Neither were Lustrelanders aware of trees shrivelling as pure evil brushed past their roots. Only circling rocs could see the ground slowly rippling like a ponderous, malevolent wave. The basalt trolls guarding the Halls of Government, who could survive any eventuality that didn't involve continental drift, had attributed the tremors to giant relatives turning in their sleep. After the destruction of the crystal lattice, they were more focused on the possibility of an army of goblins erupting from the ground to raid Lustreland's treasury.

But Flunkin and his crew had long since fled back to the woods. Most of his subjects were now revisiting their original idea about dropping the tyrant down a flooded mine shaft and, if the darkness had not been rapidly descending, Flunkin would have certainly met a prompt watery end. The more sensible were busy hoarding provisions in communal caves where they could sit and wait, well aware that Flunkin had been the cause of it all, but knowing it would be impossible to find him in the descending darkness.

CHAPTER 56

Whatever was seeping through the walls of Qulio's dungeon gave off such a pungent smell there could be no mistaking that it came from the moat. As the water was so polluted and congealed into a semi solid morass, some of its inhabitants had evolved lungs and webbed feet so they could skim over it. They needed to be quick; the swamp creatures that had the stamina to live below its surface possessed teeth like meat skewers. Even ogres crossed the drawbridge with lances at the ready. They used to carry torches, but the gas from the quagmire frequently ignited and burnt the planking.

Qulio had no way of telling whether his way with other life forms would have been effective on the swamp creatures, even if he had been able to slip out of his chains and escape. As long as nothing terrible was happening to him, he was content enough not to find out.

However, even Jobaloba did not spend forever on a meal. Once his appetite was satiated on gofferhog trotters and rat bane ale he wanted a little entertainment.

Through its insidious tentacles, the Hurglabat detected that this would be its last chance to influence the ogres before Bludon started to wonder about the missing warriors that had been devoured. He only had to make Qulio reveal how the Ligh Tofrea Sun could be extinguished, and then no power in any domain could stop the Hurglabat from feeding on dimensions like a parasitic worm hole. From the ogres pitiful essences to stars!

The more Jobaloba deluded himself about acquiring the Ligh Tofrea Sun for his own bleak land, the less likely it was to occur to his minds that ogres were allergic to strong light.

Qulio was hauled into the hall filled with the satiated ogre throng, bludgeoned, jabbed, and dragged by his hair to their chief.

However anxious the Hurglabat was to discover the secret of the Ligh Tofrea Sun, there was no remedy for the obdurate nature of an ogre and there was nothing it could do about Jobaloba wanting to have a little fun with Qulio first. To ogres, Lustrelanders were such delicate, pretty creatures they deserved to suffer. Fortunately, ogres had even less imagination than intelligence. Then Bludon remembered the ghoul who had taken up residence in the dungeons where it lived to gawp at people suffering. Its greatest pleasure in life was dashing off to goggle at horrible accidents, like mid air collisions between rocs and griffins, or a clumsy giant treading on a village. The ghoul always managed to get in the way of rescuers and was invariable able to collect a memento of the carnage. The loathsome entity regarded suffering as legitimate entertainment and, with a promise that it could watch if it came up with a good idea, the ghoul was brought in to view the victim.

It seemed to consist of nothing but saucer-shaped, lidless eyes and twisted slavering grin, unlike the ogres who were all body and bristles.

'Hmm,' the ghoul mused slimily. 'Set fire to his beard perhaps ... Hang him over the moat ...'

Bludon explained that Qulio had to be kept alive until he had told them how to find and extinguish the Ligh Tofrea Sun for good.

The ghoul thought a little harder. It soon came up with the solution from its larder of the unspeakable. 'Yupta Gum's chair!'

The ogres howled in enthusiasm.

As they dragged a massive stone throne to the centre of the floor, Qulio was puzzled as to why the ogres should get so excited over a huge lump of roughly hewn rock and could see no harm in being made to sit in it - he was grateful enough for the rest.

High in one of the harpy built turrets, Crystabel looked down into the roofless hall. She had swung across the moat on the creeper from a vine ambitiously trying to conceal what it could of the ogres' unsightly fortress. It was obvious that Qulio had to be rescued, but she had no intention of attempting it by herself. Fortunately the slow reflexes of the ogres' that did notice her allowed the nimble minstrel to escape from of Darkle Deeps as easily as she had made her way in.

Running through the goblins' secret tunnel, the minstrel soon reached the woods that bordered the realm. She whistled a sprite down from its tree and gave her a message for Juniper, after carefully writing it on the back of one of her song sheets because their frivolous minds were unable to retain complex messages: like their best intentions, sprites' bodies, and consequently their memories, were quite nebulous.

Realising that the only hope of saving Qulio was in her trembling grasp, the messenger tore through the trees like a tornado and, by the time she reached Juniper, a ribbon of excited sprites was following after.

Juniper was still wondering why Qulio hadn't returned and assumed that he was attempting to persuade some creature, be it slug or councillor, to see the rewards sweet reason could bring. As this was a task fraught with varying degrees of impossibility, these endeavours always took him some while.

The arrival of so many frantic sprites perplexed Juniper. Then she read Crystabel's crumpled message telling her she would never see Qulio again if she did not do as it instructed.

She dare not trust the tree sprites with the last part of the note's journey; the minutes in Lustreland ran at different speeds for different creatures. With no sense of time they could easily be enticed by the fragrance of a flower or take a detour to glide on the back of some breeze.

Although she was somewhat plump, enough sprites were mustered to lift Juniper aloft on one of the changeling's sledges. With the help of the modest magic at their command, they propelled her through the air at a speed that left a wake in the leaves and parted her curly hair. By the time she reached Rimonay's residence in the Halls of Government her bonnet and apron had been swept off, and yards of petticoat blown over her head, revealing bloomers embroidered with her favourite recipes.

Rimonay's tree sprite came out to see why so many of its relatives were making such a commotion. As their magic wore off, Juniper tumbled to the ground in a flurry of well laundered linen. There was no time for any explanation, other than Lustreland was on the verge of total destruction. Given its fairy nature, Rimonay's sprite would have preferred to read the recipes on her bloomers than deal with the end of existence - it knew that Rimonay had made a mistake in delegating the Second Minister to deal with it. The sprite daren't rouse the First Minister while she was communing with the mystic dimensions in her enchanted alcove, so sent the breathless Juniper to find Bruno.

The sprites manage to muster up just enough magic to take Juniper through the descending dusk and drop her onto the turret where Bruno sat trying to sort out the problem of the rapidly fading light and why dragons never married. This time she at least managed to keep her underwear under control.

Juniper's sudden arrival gathered the Second Minister's thoughts. He had given up wondering where Qulio was, the one person who might have been able to do something about his marigold sprite lying on the cushions in the chamber below and resembling a wisp of her former self.

Too out of breath to speak, Juniper thrust Crystabel's crumpled sheet of music into his hand.

Bruno read the note with growing horror. Now he was not only faced with restoring the Ligh Tofrea Sun, but having to rescue the only person who knew anything about it.

And where had that Dragon got to? The useless creature was probably still trying to gather up the precious pieces of its nest. Hardly had the ungracious thought crossed the Second Minister's mind when a distant red speck glittered against the darkening sky.

With Bruno, Juniper and the sprites swarming excitedly over it, the turret was already in danger of collapse; Sesame trying to perch on its crenels did not help matters. Bruno's head reeled at the din created by so many unrelated creatures too busy telling each other what was going on to listen to him.

In exasperation, he bellowed, 'Shut-up all of you!!' with a volume which Bernard would have been proud of. 'We have no time to chatter! Qulio must be rescued! Now who's coming to Darkle Deeps with Sesame and me?'

All the sprites, including the assistant Rimonay had provided him, vanished into thin air as only sprites could. Though the dragon would have liked nothing better than to singe a few ogres, it was disconcerted to be volunteered without prior consultation.

'I will,' Juniper declared.

Bruno told her high-handedly, 'You can't. Only one can ride on Sesame's back and it will need all claws to lift Qulio and the Minstrel out.'

She sniffed indignantly. 'Oh.'

'And I've got a sword proof robe and you haven't.'

He hadn't counted on a tiger lurking beneath the skin of this homely pussycat. 'You just be sure you rescue my Qulio, that's all! If you don't, I'll start a revolution in Lustreland, mark my words!'

'If we don't rescue Qulio, they'll be no light for anyone to write a placard let alone take aim at the ruling elite.'

That prospect quickly quelled Juniper's rebelliousness.

Once Bruno and Sesame had taken to the sky, the sprites returned and mustered their resources to carry Juniper after them at a safe distance.

When the Dragon and its rider reached the pass into Darkle Deeps the sprites and Juniper stopped, they could only wait to see if they returned.

CHAPTER 57

Qulio's stone seat was showing signs of not being quite what it seemed.

At the first twinge of movement the throne made he would have leapt clear in terror if the ogres had not taken the precaution of fastening his chains to it. Then the arms twitched and the roughly hewn patterns on the ends of them started to grow claws. Something behind the wizard's head gave a gurgle that could have only resonated from the bowels of Darkle Deeps. Then the stone came pliable and a tail lashed out to wind itself about Qulio's body.

The yellow-eyed ghoul was transfixed with delight at the spectacle, and even Jobaloba began to show signs of enjoyment.

Without the powers of an accomplished wizard, escape was impossible and there was only one thing Qulio could do under the circumstances.

He fainted.

With no terror to feed on, the stone throne resumed its original shape.

Disappointed, Jobaloba's minds decided that this was no fun after all and it was more important to make Qulio tell him how to find the Ligh Tofrea Sun. His ogres could have what was left of the wizard for entertainment afterwards.

Inexplicably, while Qulio was unconscious, the Hurglabat no longer felt threatened. But could this incompetent wizard harm it? After all, it was only the secret tucked away in Qulio's fearful thoughts that were a threat. As soon as the monster possessed that secret, dimension after dimension would fall into its vile clutches.

Qulio had expected to wake up to some new horror and his worst fears were realised.

As he lay sprawled on his back, ogre hands pulled the wizard's beard aside so Jobaloba could hold a rusty sword to his throat and place a studded boot on his chest.

'Where is Ligh Tofrea Sun?' the ogre chief demanded.

Despite the fact that something even less pleasant would happen to him if he refused to answer, Qulio was amazed to hear himself reply, 'I'm not telling you.'

Jobaloba was as astonished at this response as the wizard.

He stamped in rage. 'You will tell!'

'I will not,' Qulio persisted, even though it looked as though the next bout of stamping would take place on him. 'You have no right to any more light than you have now.'

'What is 'right'?'

'You would never understand.'

This slight on his minute intellects provoked the ogre chief to take a decision.

'Fetch crushing stones,' he ordered.

CHAPTER 58

Isolda sat motionless, grasping Peter's marble cold hand as he lay silently in his armchair as though quietly dozing. Some hours previously, for reasons which may never be known, the life parted from the gentle giant, leaving the husk it had worn for over sixty years.

Isolda knew that the heart of a man his size, age and indulgent habits must have found it hard to cope, yet that did nothing to cushion the shock.

After the doctor had left and private ambulance arrived to remove the body, Isolda went to Peter's antique bakelite phone to contact Indrina and Bernard. Aurora replied. She only knew that her parents had gone to an important concert somewhere and probably had their mobiles switched off. It didn't occur to Isolda that it was the one that had been widely publicised as Farinelli's second coming in the more wordy rags, and as the fellow with a girl's voice in the tabloids. In fact, there had been very little to suggest that the event was anything more serious than an end-of-the-pier talent night. Why should Isolda have suspected that Bernard, an operatic bass baritone, and Indrina, whose tastes in music were reasonably refined, would be there?

Indrina was bound to be upset about Peter's death as she had paid a call on him only yesterday and was probably the last person to see him alive.

Isolda had always been able to tell when he was expecting someone by the haste with which he returned to his cellar hideaway, barely allowing her enough time to get up to the hotel's roof garden to see who it was. It was impossible to fathom the reason for all those secret visits by his accountant - Isolda only knew they weren't romantic - and Peter did not have any financial problems that needed Indrina in her professional capacity. So, if they had been social calls, why all the secrecy? The wine waitress would have probably been little wiser if she had been able to eavesdrop on their last conversation.

That evening Indrina had not been carrying a briefcase and her stroll through the orchard was leisurely, as though she was floating on a cloud of contentment.

As usual, Peter quickly ushered her inside.

Indrina tossed the jacket she was carrying onto an armchair. 'It's all over. Your wives' people have been avenged.'

Although aware of the accountant's efficiency, Peter hadn't been expecting a result so soon. 'How did you manage it? How can you be sure it worked?'

'When several hundred billions in pounds, euros, dollars, and bullion suddenly land in the accounts of international charities and agricultural aid schemes, it tends to attract attention. A worldwide network of "generous benefactors" is now scurrying for their boltholes.'

To Peter, measuring distance in parsecs made more sense than the figures involved. 'How much?'

'Everything.'

He had to sit down. 'A dragon! A veritable dragon!'

'Oh, I'd rather be a unicorn or pussycat. Bernard would never allow smoking in bed.'

Peter's large, brown face glowed with delight and incredulity. 'How did you do it?'

'You supplied all the information required. This syndicate used multiple passwords in their transactions and only online. That way they had no need to produce identification at some counter and avoided the risk of being visible to some hacker or whistleblower. Their dependence on electronic transactions was also their Achilles heel; that and the arrogance to believe their setup was impenetrable. It was easy as simultaneously unlocking half a dozen safes.' Indrina laughed at Peter's amazed expression. 'Don't worry about it. They've been well and truly dealt with and several deserving causes have received something towards rectifying the damage they caused.'

'I'm flabbergasted.' Peter flopped back into his armchair. 'You and my informant both astonish me.'

'Congratulate them for me when you next meet.'

'I'll speak to her tonight and she'll be paid in full by tomorrow morning.'

It was an odd thing for Peter to say but, as it was obvious that nothing else was going to be forthcoming, Indrina inquired tentatively, 'Now it's all over, how about telling me who she is?'

'Just some useful fairy.'

'I asked for that. What sort of fairy? Fell off the Christmas tree?'

'No.' Peter smiled secretively. 'In her condition, she would never have managed to get up there in the first place.'

'Hmm, an infirm fairy who's got a price.'

'That's about as close as you'll get.' Peter switched on the radio for a World Service news bulletin. 'How long does this sort of thing take to attract attention?'

'Shouldn't be long if Reuters and Twitter have picked it up and our present government genuinely doesn't already know anything about it.'

'Think they do?'

Peter was interrupted by the smooth voice of a political commentator declaring with all the assurance of ignorance, 'Of course, this conspiracy of faceless men may have had masters directing the campaign of destabilisation which facilitated these arms and trade deals. They will probably prove as difficult to track down as their minions. Most of those who could be traced have already been charged with illegal weapons deals and currency irregularities. It has been unofficially reported from several countries that some of them have chosen to co-operate instead of face heavy prison sentences. It seems that the nature of some disclosures is so controversial, it is essential to corroborate them before they can be made public. Whatever the outcome of this global scandal using trade deals to manipulate the world economy, this massive network funding the exploitation of developing countries by installing sympathetic regimes has been broken up. For this to come out so dramatically, someone pivotal in the scheme must have been responsible for transferring the organisation's assets into the accounts of international and Third World charities.

'The hunt for the criminals who ran his organisation continues around the world. One of them was probably a "Mr Paton ". A suicide note apparently by him had been stopped from blowing into the water of the Thames by a schoolgirl on a day trip to Tate Modern. Shortly afterwards, a body was discovered hanging beneath the Millennium Bridge.'

Peter switched off the radio. He and Indrina were silent for several minutes. The consequence of unlocking so many cybersafes was only just starting to sink in.

'It won't spark any wars, will it Peter?'

'The worst that could happen is that that they lose their easy access to the resources of the countries they exploited. Then the only unrest will be in the populations who no longer have access to cheap food and petrol.'

'Let's hope.'

At last Peter relaxed. 'I think this calls for a celebration.' He went to the cabinet where he kept the cigars, brandy, and preserves.

As night fell, when the hotel was quiet, Peter placed the documents tidying up his estate on his desk.

When he lifted the large crystal from its box for the last time, Rimonay was already waiting for him.

She was more irritable than usual. 'What kept you? You know the problems we have here.'

'The idea takes some getting used to,' apologised Peter. 'I had to make sure Isolda and the others weren't given any problems. After all, there will be no coming back to rectify mistakes.'

Rimonay mumbled something about being over sentimental, and then got down to business. 'Qulio could soon be lost. Things will happen rapidly now. If he dies, Lustreland will remain in darkness and the Hurglabat devour its population. Then the monster will use the power that generates to re-create itself in your dimension. Minor conflicts there will escalate into wars and minor viruses develop into major plagues, destroying the civilisations on Earth long before climate has the chance. That will give the Hurglabat enough malign energy to become cosmic - So you can put down that brandy glass and wipe away that self-satisfied expression!'

Peter believed that he had the right to be pleased with himself. 'But the international conspiracy here has been blown apart?'

'For every rogue you've caught, there are a thousand more willing to feed the beast, and a thousand gullible humans for every one who thinks for themselves. Evolution owes no one a living.'

CHAPTER 59

The Ligh Tofrea Sun had now virtually set on Lustreland. Crowds swarmed to the forbidden Crystal Mansion in the hope some miracle would save them from the descending darkness.

The Ruling Council had summoned the Mystic Trine and challenged them to do something about it. Realising that the descending gloom was the result of their small conspiracy, they had no solution and were having trouble enough recognising each other in the dark. It didn't help that their spell power was being pooled to design Lustreland's first battery powered torch. As the witches and wizards believed electricity to be the emanations of powerful, but badly phrased curses, all they could raise between them were a few sparks and several nasty shocks.

The First Minister arrived at the Crystal Mansion in an attempt to stop the panic from spreading, the invariable consequence when multitudes are faced with a crisis and no contingency plans. Despite Rimonay's efforts, Lustreland retreated into desperation. Sprites hid inside their flowers and closed their petals. Creatures that had well stocked burrows dug in and hoped the nuts wouldn't run out before things got back to normal and whole villages jumped into bed, pulling blankets, bolsters, and beards over their heads.

The descending gloom hardly mattered in Darkle Deeps. Sesame was adept at night flying and soon arrived at the jumble of stone which was the ogres' fortress.

Qulio had repeatedly refused to tell the ogres anything about the Ligh Tofrea Sun and the watching Crystabel could see that the weight of the stone on his chest was crushing the life out of the wizard's frail body.

The ogres, so annoyed at his intransigence, were on the verge of the rational thought the Lustrelanders should have been using - the verge was not quite close enough, however.

The Hurglabat knew that its only hope of discovering the Ligh Tofrea Sun would die with Qulio. Its tentacles rattled the walls of the fortress in frustration as it tried to infiltrate the minds of Jobaloba, only to find that his limited brain cells were too occupied by rage. The wizard would be killed long before it occurred to the ogre chief that dead people don't talk.

Then salvation for the Hurglabat arrived in the unlikely guise of the minstrel attempting to distract the ogres. The last thing they had expected to see in the light of their torches was Crystabel prancing acrobatically high on the fortress's crumbling walls and offering to entertain the irritated throng free of charge. Well aware that ogres detested beautiful music, she had untuned her lute to make it jarringly discordant. As an example of her talent, she screeched a few modern, atonal "tunes" even the Hurglabat had to recoil from.

Jobaloba found the minstrel a welcome relief from trying to extract information from Qulio. While he and his retinue paused to listen to noises that would have paralysed the hearing of any normal creature, he pondered on what to do with her once the concert was over. No ogre had kept a court minstrel before, mainly because no other minstrels had been reckless enough to stray into Darkle Deeps.

Crystabel was inexhaustible; skirling tune followed eardrum-denting ditty. The ogres were captivated by the discordant din which reminded them of the deliciously remorseless throb one of their drummers used to make day after day by smashing two rocks together. Someone able to resurrect such lullaby memories shouldn't be interrupted. At last the war weary, exhausted ogres started to doze off. One by one they fell into a deep slumber until cavernous snores vibrated the dank hall.

When the ogres' red eyes ceased flashing and none of them was liable to wake without a good bump on the head, Crystabel signalled to the waiting Sesame and Bruno above. Then she darted down to Qulio.

As the dragon descended into the hall she was attempting to remove some of the rocks pinning down the wizard. They were too heavy and it took the Sesame's strong claws to lift them.

Bruno gently raised the wizard.

His thin body crumpled untidily into his arms like a rag doll. Qulio's eyes were half closed and his lips parted as though life had escaped from them in mid protest. Strands of torn beard danced lightly on the clammy, rising heat of the chamber in cruel mockery of their owner's lifeless body and condensation covered the wizard's pallid skin in a glistening film.

Bruno clutched the limp Qulio in a desperate attempt to reassure him back into life.

Not so much as a reflex twitched.

The urgent flapping of Sesame's wings told him it was time to leave. Bruno lifted Qulio onto the dragon's back. They would have departed gently through the chasm where the roof had once been if it had not been for the ghoul. The thrill of seeing someone suffer had kept the creature awake; now that entertainment was being rescued it was more than it could stand and its banshee like wail assailed the ears of the sleeping ogres.

Sesame had hardly left the ground when there was an eruption of lances, swords, knives, and rocks.

With a desperate snatch, the dragon caught hold of Crystabel, crushing her lute. This the minstrel dropped on Jobaloba as she twisted and turned to avoid the missiles. Although his robe saved Bruno from injury and they were soon airborne, it was obvious that his mission had been futile.

All the way back to Lustreland the Second Minister held Qulio's long, limp body, hoping it would show some flicker of life. Despite the catastrophe overwhelming the region, uppermost in his thoughts was how he could tell Juniper that he was dead.

On the border with Lustreland swarms of sprites who had not hidden from the darkness were waiting to see their favourite wizard once more. They took him from Bruno and laid him on the mossy ground, touching his hair and clothes, unable to understand why he was motionless.

The only one resourceful enough not to be overwhelmed was Crystabel. 'I've an idea.'

The others looked at her dolefully.

'Take him into the Crystal Mansion.'

'What for?' asked Bruno. 'What good would that do?'

'That's where Juniper is. Take my word for it. I never let you down before, did I?'

There was no point in staying where they were, so the Second Minister gathered up Qulio and Sesame carried them to the heart of Lustreland.

Even the light of the Crystal Mansion had become dim.

In its entrance stood Rimonay and Juniper, and before it Lustreland's Ruling Council and Mystic Trine. A crowd of the domain's most stalwart citizens surrounding them parted to allow Bruno to approach with Qulio's limp body.

He stood before the First Minister.

She wore a strange expression. Her eyes glittered eerily as though a sliver of the Ligh Tofrea Sun had lodged in her mind. Previously, Bruno had only been in awe of her, now he was afraid. The First Minister's crumpled cocoon of a body appeared to be on the verge of a terrible transformation, and not into something that would spread lace wings and flutter off into the domain's last sunset.

Rimonay sensed his fear and jabbed her stick at him. 'Well?'

'I've failed. Qulio is dead.'

'Take him inside,' she ordered.

Bruno obeyed. He was doomed, the same as everyone, and there wasn't much else he could do.

Everyone recoiled at the sight of Qulio's limp body being borne through the entrance and carried into the hallowed hall of the Crystal Mansion. The law forbidding ordinary people to enter now seemed ludicrous, and who was going to prevent the dragon from peering in through one of the mansion's upper windows?

Inside the ancient hall residual light flickered in the crystal foliage of its walls like the last drops of silver blood leaving a network of veins; miniature lightning threading its way out of grey satin.

Stick clicking on the floor of lifeless leaves, the First Minister entered.

Bruno laid Qulio on his robe.

Silently, Juniper took a comb from her pocket to tease the tangles from his torn beard.

CHAPTER 60

The Hurglabat gurgled in delight.

It no longer needed to destroy the Ligh Tofrea Sun. Some mysterious force had apparently beaten the parasitic monster to it. Whatever had happened to Lustreland's light, the domain was now doomed and within the reach of its voracious clutches.

The Hurglabat repositioned itself under Lustreland, ready to consume until its bloated body overlapped other dimensions. When it was powerful enough, it would no longer need to insinuate itself, but just spread like a suffocating blot over any realm it chose to devour.

Then the voracious entity erupted from the Halls of Government's lawn, carefully repaired after Flunkin's goblins had undermined it. Clods of turf rained down on several surprised trolls. Undaunted by the lack of light, they lowered their pikes and charged the huge, gelatinous monster rising from the ground. Then they detected its size by echolocation and realised that it would take more than them, mere pebbles with matchstick weapons by comparison, to stop it.

The Halls of Government shook as the foundations crumbled. Several gargoyles took leadenly to the air. Those without wings, or ones too weathered to be any use, clambered down from their perches and scrambled away, tripping up the ogres. Several sank their fangs into any part of the Hurglabat that presented itself, only to find that there were some things even stone had to spit out. Unable to absorb the irritating bits of grit under its belly, the Hurglabat's tentacles brushed the gargoyles aside and flattened any troll vainly trying to stick a pike into it.

Once above ground, the monstrosity ballooned out malevolently, enveloping the sprawling Halls of Government and surrounding streets.

Any Lustrelanders who had remained in what they believed would be the safety of home, dashed out with torches. They were just able to make out an infernal creature from the realms of nightmare that the darkness had invited in. They fled after the clicking footsteps of the gargoyles and trolls, who perhaps weren't so stupid after all - at that moment they should have been presented with a doctorate for having a sense of direction.

The Hurglabat's slime preceded it, sweeping away orchards, crops, and homes. Streets became rivers of mucus along which floated masonry, flower tubs, and tiled roofs.

The rara avis came down from their Ridge to find out what had happened to its permanent twilight. Having good night sights, they soon made out the mountainous creature oozing across at the land and dive-bombed it. Rocs dropped anything they could get airborne and griffins, wishing they had a furnace the size of a dragon's, puffed down ineffectual balls of flame - the harpies screeched insults.

Nothing could stop the Hurglabat. It continued to envelop Lustreland, meadow by meadow, orchard by orchard, street by street.

CHAPTER 61

From the vantage point of the Crystal Mansion, isolated in its island of dim light, Rimonay stood listening to the mayhem with smouldering rage.

Then she turned angrily to the jaunty figure of Crystabel who was standing a little way off as though enjoying a picnic. The ancient woman jabbed her stick at the minstrel.

'Well, you've come so far, why stop now?'

Crystabel smiled puckishly. 'Why not? Lustreland never appreciated its light. Hardly anyone here realised it was fading.'

'Lustreland cannot survive without it.'

'Why should that concern us?'

Rimonay's diamond eyes narrowed. 'Because your kindred will lose a comfortable home. Other realms will not tolerate your pranks as we have done... and because the cave deities were responsible for raising the Hurglabat in the first place.'

There was a gasp from the desperate throng surrounding them.

'What do you want me to do? Sing to it?'

'Don't play the minstrel with me. I'm well aware the oracle sent you.'

Crystabel's jauntiness was quickly quelled. 'How do you know that?'

The First Minister gave a cruel smile. 'You really believe that you created the monster, don't you?' The lack of response confirmed her accusation. 'But that was one prank even a cave deity isn't capable of. The Hurglabat had been lying dormant long before Lustreland existed. You merely seeded it with evil.'

'How can you know that?' Crystabel demanded.

'Some entities are even more ancient than you,' Rimonay cackled. 'Now keep to your side of the bargain.'

'You want the Light Tofrea Sun back?'

'And restore the Crystal Mansion while you're at it.'

The light voice of the minstrel gave way to a cavernous, indignant tone that ensured everyone in the vicinity heard the tirade. 'We sent this tree to save Lustreland from its own folly once before, only to have it forbidden to but a few! Your councillors are sycophants and cowards, your Mystic Trine scoundrels, and your people greedy and complacent! Why should we let you have Qulio back? Why should his Light of Reason continue to be your Ligh Tofrea Sun?'

'You've used that wretched man for long enough!'

The minstrel's outline became hazy and her gaudy costume merged with the darkness. 'He was wretched because he was afraid.'

'So are most people.' Rimonay raised her stick threateningly. 'You cannot deny me! These are the terms the cave deities agreed to.'

The minstrel laughed, and then dissipated in the dim light.

The small gathering clustered around Qulio stopped mourning to watch the wisps that they had believed to be a resourceful minstrel filter mockingly about their heads and through the many windows. After they had threaded their way into the pitch blackness beyond, the shadows began to lift.

The Crystal Mansion started to glow.

Stranger still, so did Qulio's body.

The light increased.

The realm of Lustreland was once again illuminated by the Light of Reason. In its radiance, the shape of Rimonay shimmered, her stick still raised to strike the minstrel.

She had turned to ice.

Bruno let out a sharp cry.

Qulio's hand, which he was clutching, suddenly twitched. As Juniper cradled the wizard's head his pale, liquid eyes flickered open and he became infused with the magical glow of the Crystal Mansion.

The wizard slowly sat up.

Rimonay's stick took on a life of its own and wriggled free of her frozen hand. After describing a gleaming spiral in the air, it became a diamond-scaled serpent. And then, shimmering with golden tracery, the staff of the Ligh Tofrea Sun recognised its owner and threaded its way through the crystal leaves and into Qulio's grasp.

The tranquil expression in those half-closed eyes indicated that he was aware of his transformation and at last accepted his true identity.

Bruno's knees buckled in amazement and he toppled over before the wizard. Qulio placed a hand on his head and invigorating warmth filled every fibre of his friend's body.

The radiance that had once cloaked Lustreland returned so suddenly the Hurglabat had no time to retreat to its subterranean refuge. The glutinous entity coating the land like a huge tick shuddered, and then began to wrinkle. The mucus rapidly boiled away as the monster shrank like syrup on a hot stove and the tentacles that riddled Lustreland shrivelled. A long-held, resonating scream shook the whole region, causing rock falls in Rara Avis Ridge and demolishing the ogres' fortress.

The vile substance seeped back down into the primeval chasm beneath Darkle Deeps that had spawned it. The rocks, no longer with living evil to support them caved in and the tar encrusted ground of Darkle Deeps began to slip. As the Hurglabat boiled away in an acidic soup, Jobaloba led the fastest retreat ever known to ogre. His great unwashed hoards clung to the cliffs of Rara Avis Ridge until the remains of the

Hurglabat eventually seeped away, regardless of the missiles its residents hurled at them.

When the ogres returned to Darkle Deeps the air seemed a little sweeter and its waters no longer had that rank smell. Not to worry, it would all come back given time.

The centre of Lustreland was like a building site some clumsy giant had blundered through. The residents returned to find out if they still had homes, trolls dug themselves out of the ground and gargoyles searched for what remained of their perches.

In the Crystal Mansion Qulio raised himself to his true height, his gown now surrounded by a corona of gleaming colours visible through its walls to the Lustrelanders outside.

His long fingers reached out to fondly touch Juniper's plump cheek and a tiara of stars spangled her floppy cap. She flung her short arms round his waist, half expecting to be consumed by the energy.

Even Sesame was awed by the transformation and dismantled part of a window to get a closer look. Unfortunately the sensitive scales on the dragon's neck would not allow it to pull its head back. Bruno had to leave Qulio to go and release them. Scolding as he did so, Bruno's tirade was cut short by a mildly disapproving look from Qulio: now one glance could achieve what a million remonstrations could not do before.

It was not benevolence that made Lustreland a better place, but the inhabitants learning the consequences of indifference.

And, of course, a certain cave deity was relieved that the Hurglabat hadn't consumed Lustreland and all the dimensions beyond after all. Though, like the returning stench of the ogres' swamps, Tov would undoubtedly come up with another joke which rivalled mass extinction given time.

CHAPTER 62

Most of the audience gathering in Down Clutton town hall looked distinguished enough to be local gentry, serious music lovers or musicologists. Many chose their seats in the concert chamber in a way that suggested they had firm ideas about acoustics.

As compère, Bernard took his position at the side of the stage. Indrina sat just below him in the first row as though ready to catch her husband if he were felled by some well-aimed missile.

Although the venue was remote and with limited seating capacity, the toupees, pates, hairdos, and hats that came through the entrance told Kitty, who was looking down from the gallery, that the tapes she sent out had lured in the right people. Fortunately they all managed to find seats before the media were allowed in.

By the sudden influx of squabbling paparazzi, reporters and cameras, Down Clutton residents must have thought their corner of the world had achieved notoriety at last. In his wisdom, and desire to have his picture on the national news, the local constable had insisted on thinning the rabble into single file before admitting them into the town hall. As the name of the performer had not been mentioned in the publicity for the concert, only the nature of the voice delivering it, demands to know the whereabouts of Mr Ditton-Davis were met with bland restraint.

Mrs Porter, no longer able to sell the story of the male soprano Clarey Ditton-Davis kept in his cellar, had told a Sunday rag of the torrid nights of passion with her employer. The gamble was worth it because so many women had done the same thing in the past without Clarey suing them.

During the preceding days Bernard had started to experience misgivings; it now seemed that these were justified as the din started to turn the occasion into a media circus. Perhaps the world was not as benign as he had persuaded himself, and he wondered how Kitty Callahan managed to keep her professional, unruffled poise.

With a sinking soul Bernard watched the agents of the free press tumble into the chamber to exercise the only sort of freedom that sells newspapers and sound bites. Some stood on chairs at the back with zoom lenses, others, displaced by the battalion of Steadicams that crammed every available corner blocked the gangways. Bernard wondered how any voice was going to be heard over the hubbub before it dawned on him that he was responsible as compère for controlling the commotion. The singer may not have been on trial, but his past life flashed before him in gigabytes of its worst moments.

A flat from the town hall's most recent amateur play toppled onto an upright piano with a discordant clatter. The resulting exchange between the sound engineer and stagehand responsible distracted the media, and the odd directional mic attempted to pick up what they were saying.

When the contretemps was over, an eerie hush descended.

Bernard knew that the moment of truth had arrived as the four accompanists came onto the small stage behind him to set up their instruments. Indrina recognised them as the women Mrs Porter had hustled from her sight one day. Kitty had approved them, so they were bound to be excellent musicians.

While they tuned their instruments; lute, violin, flute and played a few notes on the piano (not the upright), cameras flashed. The media were restless and sections of the audience growing impatient. Bernard glanced urgently to the wings for a sign from

Clarey to start his introduction. They were playing safe by beginning with the music originally written for the castrato, Gaetano Guadagni, "Che faro" from Gluck's "Orfeo", as it must have been familiar to everyone there, even the press.

At last a wave from Clarey's long hand gave Bernard the signal to rise and start the preamble. He doubted many would listen to it as he walked to centre stage and bowed to the quartet waiting their turn for notoriety.

Bernard did his party piece professionally, without so much as a quaver in his voice and received a few derisive handclaps from some of the experts who had already heard of Gluck. He wanted to scowl at them, but remained dignified, returning to his seat without looking back at the stage. Bernard would have continued to keep his head up, gazing beyond the audience, if it had not been for the startled expressions and gasps of amazement as the first bars of the aria magically filled the civic space like acoustic sunlight. It filled every dusty nook and cranny that had faded from view over the centuries. Small, carved grotesques added by ancient, anonymous carpenters seemed to smile as though, at last, given a reason to exist and grimy, rough hewn garlands of flowers in the timber beams danced in suddenly sympathetic shafts of sunlight.

Unable to bear it any longer, Bernard slowly turned to see who was making that exquisite sound.

He froze.

Photographers who had travelled from far and wide for this scoop somehow forgot where the shutter release was. Other reporters were actually putting away their notebooks and tablets while the music lovers lived up to their name by allowing that pure voice to tie knots in any lingering prejudice.

Bernard became aware of Mouse crouching in the wings beside him, grasping his hand to prevent him from running off. The compère remained transfixed and unable to collect his wits.

Clarey was obliged to introduce the next song he intended to sing.

The realisation he had never really known Clarey Ditton-Davis descended on Bernard in a spasm of contrition for being so self opinionated. He looked up at the gallery in a silent appeal to Kitty. If he wanted her to share his bewilderment he was unlucky. By her smug expression, it was apparent that Kitty Callahan had been aware of the singer's identity from the beginning. Bernard had been foundering around out of his depth once again and indignant glances in her direction were not going to make her feel guilty about anything.

He somehow recovered enough composure to announce the rest of the programme.

By the time the concert was over, Clarey had demonstrated the full range of his astounding voice, ranging from tenor to soprano.

Much of the media left in shame-faced retreat, well aware that their editors wouldn't accept copy about a castrato singer they had spent years vilifying as the country's greatest lecher. They might as well have published pictures with egg on their own faces. The popular press left the genuine music lovers and musicologists to lay siege to the anti-room where Clarey and Bernard had taken refuge. Kitty managed to usher most of them away with the promise that they could see him all in good time.

Bernard had overcome his amazement and indignation to be consumed by curiosity. 'Why did you never do this before, for pity's sake?'

Clarey thoughtfully wiped away his discreet makeup. 'I was afraid. From my early teens I've had to live with the guilt of something which wasn't my fault. I was brought up to believe that I should be in permanent apology for my unspeakable condition, which meant the termination of the family line. I only managed to cope because of Mouse's support. Making it public was quite another matter.'

'You looked as though you enjoyed the concert?'

Clarey scratched his chin. 'I know. At least what they say about me now is liable to be nearer the truth.' He laughed. 'And I don't care. Now Mouse will have to own up to being the father of his own children. He always was a randy little scoundrel. You wouldn't think so under all that vulnerable inoffensiveness, would you?'

Bernard was taken aback. 'You adopted his children?'

'Yes. I owed him that at least.'

'And none of his girlfriends sold their story to the press?'

'Why should they? They chose to let us raise the children, knowing they would be well cared for, and they have access to them whenever they want without the rest of the world sitting in judgement over their indiscretions. We are all very good at keeping secrets here, you know.'

The colour suddenly drained from Bernard's face and he sank into a chair.

Mouse was alarmed. 'What's the matter?'

Bernard gasped. 'I'm not sure. I don't know why - but I just thought about Peter.'

Clarey put a hand on the singer's shoulder to reassure him.

'I'm all right now,' Bernard told them, even though it felt as though he was under an emotional landslip.

'Good, you had our romantic rodent worried for a moment.'

'Stop scratching your chin like that,' Mouse scolded Clarey. 'You were doing it all through the concert. What is the matter with you?'

Clarey laughed. 'I don't know. For some reason I kept imagining I had this beard, a long, white beard which reached all the way down to my knees.'

THE END

www.ingramcontent.com/pod-product-compliance
Lightning Source LLC
Chambersburg PA
CBHW071258170626
46809CB00001B/264